Incident in Alaska Prefecture

Stoney Compton

The Prefecture Series
Book 1

NAZCA PRESS

In the years after the stars fell, young Noah Manaluk, an Inupiat Eskimo living at Point Hope, Alaska, eats a piece of possessed seal liver that changes his life. By the time he is 17 he is a shaman who can call game to the hunter's spears and fish into nets cast by the People.

Thinker, a Humpback whale, is the only one of his pod who perceives anything beyond his   immediate surroundings. He is aware of the longteeth waiting at the top of the world and cautiously moves to the middle of the pod.

He hears the summons and realizes another exists who can completely communicate with him - something that has never before happened in his life - and it wants to kill him.

Whalesong is the story of two disparate beings, enemies by the nature of their world yet closer in understanding than with any member of their own species. Two creatures that have as much to learn about themselves as they do the other, and come to rely on one another as they begin a journey which will not only change the world, but save it.

Paperback ISBN: **9781963479553** Hardback ISBN: **9781963479584**
eBook ISBN: **9781963479546**

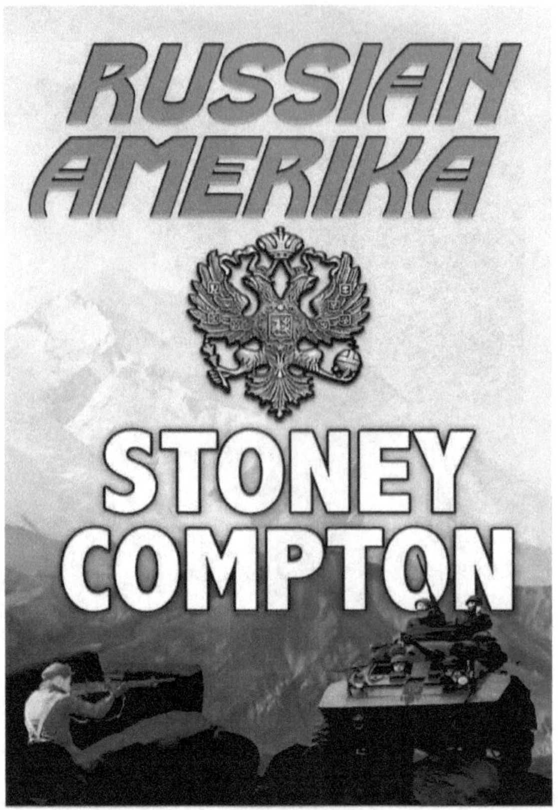

Alaska, 1987

In a world where Alaska is still a Russian possession, charter captain Grigoriy Grigorievich has a stained past—as a major in the Czar's Troika Guard he was cashiered for disobeying a direct order.

Now, ten years later, Grisha charters out to a Cossack and discovers his past has not only caught up with him, but is about to violently change his future, and the future of all nine of the nations of North America as well.

Revolution against an oppressor, continent-wide alliances, and an epic struggle of a people to be free–spanning Alaska from the Southeastern Inside Passage to the frozen Yukon river, this is an epic tale of one man's journey of redemption and courage to face old fears, new challenges, and help birth a new nation.

Paperback ISBN: 9781963479379
eBook ISBN: 9781963479249

Incident in Alaska Prefecture

Stoney Compton

This edition published by Nazca Press
A division of Misti Media LLC
Available in both Paperback and eBook Editions
1 2 3 4 5 6 7 8 9 10

Paperback ISBN: 9781963479942
eBook ISBN: 9781963479959

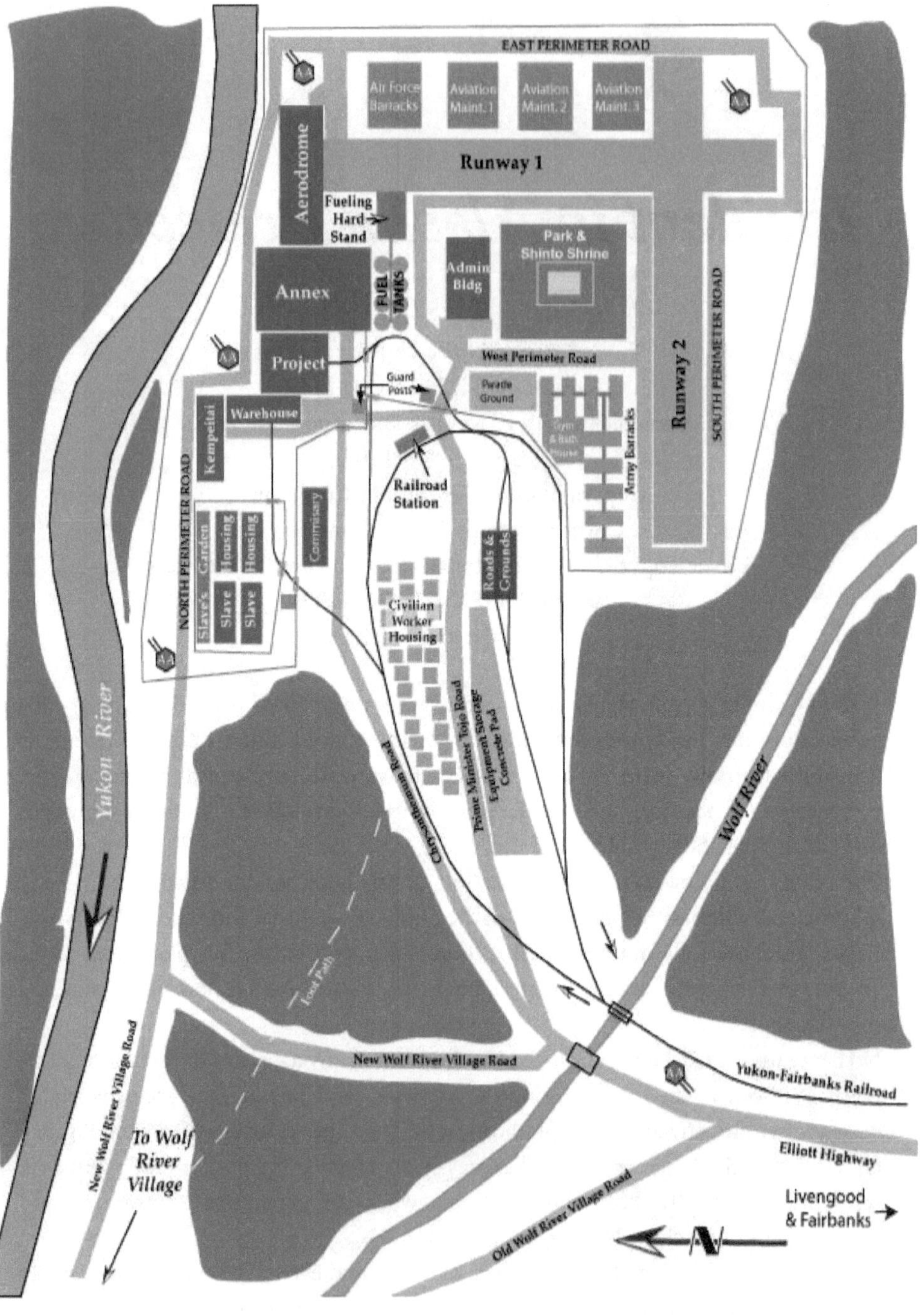

EAST PERIMETER ROAD
Air Force Barracks
Aviation Maint. 1
Aviation Maint. 2
Aviation Maint. 3
Runway 1
Aerodrome
Fueling Hard Stand
Park & Shinto Shrine
Admin Bldg
FUEL TANKS
Annex
Project
West Perimeter Road
Runway 2
SOUTH PERIMETER ROAD
NORTH PERIMETER ROAD
Kempeitai
Warehouse
Guard Posts
Parade Ground
Gym & Bath House
Army Barracks
Slave's Garden
Slave Housing
Slave Housing
Commissary
Railroad Station
Roads & Grounds
Civilian Worker Housing
Yukon River
Fox Path
Churchumann Road
Prime Minister Tojo Road
Equipment Storage Concrete Pad
Wolf River
New Wolf River Village Road
New Wolf River Village Road
To Wolf River Village
Old Wolf River Village Road
Yukon-Fairbanks Railroad
Elliott Highway
Livengood & Fairbanks
N

Dedicated with love and admiration to
Keith and Kim Busch
Supportive friends from the beginning

Author's Note

While researching this series of novels
I consulted the following works.

The Chrysanthemum and the Sword, Patterns of Japanese Culture, Ruth Benedict. Houghton Mifflin, 1946

The Horizon Concise History of Japan, Noel Busch. American Heritage Publishing, 1972

The Knights of Bushido, Lord Russell of Liverpool. Skyhorse Publishing, Inc., 2008

Japan: The Years of Triumph, From Feudal Isolation to Pacific Empire, Louis Allen. American Heritage Press, 1971

Japan: A Modern History, James L. McClain. W.W. Norton, 2002

SNAFU, Sailor, Airman, and Soldier Slang of World War II, Gordon L. Rottman. Osprey Publishing, 2013

War Slang, American Fighting Words & Phrases Since the Civil War, Paul Dickson. Dover Publications, 1994

Thanks to Wikipedia for leads to articles on German and Japanese commanders, ranks, uniforms, weapons, aircraft, Shinto, and a plethora of related subjects.

PROLOGUE

BERLIN, GERMANY
January 6th, 1945

ADOLPH HITLER CLOSELY WATCHED DR. THEODOR MORELL administer his morning injection. Within moments the Führer's spirits lifted, a feeling of well-being washed through him, and his palsied hands steadied. Nonetheless, he turned his head away from the corpulent doctor as soon as he could.

The man's body odor repelled most people, but when combined with his severe halitosis his presence repulsed one and all.

"Thank you, Herr Doktor Morell. As usual you have immensely improved my mood."

"Mein Führer, it is an honor to serve you." The man immediately collected his instruments and departed through the private door.

Once the door was shut Hitler waved his good arm around to dispel the doctor's odor. Since the July attempt on his life, his right arm did most of the work. A light knock sounded on the door leading to his outer office.

"Enter!" His voice had become vibrant again, which added to his elevated mood.

Reichsmarschall Herman Göring, resplendent in full dress uniform, strutted into the room followed by two men in brown business suits preserved from the late 1930s.

Two sparrows following a peacock, Hitler thought. He braced himself for bad news. Since the success of Operation Watch on the Rhine, or as his troops termed it, *Ardennenoffensive*, and splitting the

Allied armies, the tables were slowly turning against the Third Reich again.

He wondered why the Reichsmarschall wore a smirk rather than his normal pressed lips. Perhaps the news *wasn't* bad.

"Mein Führer, I bring you astounding news! *Uranverein* has produced results to a degree that will win the war."

"Do remind me which project we are discussing."

"Our project to smash atoms, to make weapons capable of unleashing unimagined force, using uranium. Some of our Jews originally came up with the idea in the 1930s."

"Have those Jews been exterminated?" Adolph could feel his heartbeat increase, reminding him of old times, which made him feel even more animated.

"Of course, mein Führer." Göring's right eye squinted ever so slightly, and Hitler knew the man was lying. As his interest had been piqued, he dismissed all thoughts of Jews.

"Tell me of this weapon."

Göring stepped to one side and with a flourish, waved his left arm at the men behind him. "I present Doktor Erich Schumann, and Doktor Kurt Diebner. They have persevered and accomplished a miracle."

Hitler waved dismissively at Göring. "Then allow them to speak!"

Göring's mouth closed with an audible snap.

"Mein Führer," the first man said, "I am Erich Schumann and this is my colleague, Kurt Diebner. We have successfully created a bomb that will destroy, at the least, an entire city, and perhaps a small country."

"A bomb? How can *one* bomb destroy a city the size of London?"

"It is a very complicated weapon that requires incredible amounts of fissionable elements. Suffice it to say that we have created two such bombs, but have yet to test them in the field."

"Do you believe they will work on that grand of a scale?"

"Yes, Führer. I would stake my life on it."

"You already have. How large are the weapons?"

"Many tons. They would each require our largest bombers for

delivery."

Hitler's gaze swung to Göring. "Do we have such aircraft?"

"Of course, mein Führer. Two Heinkel He-390s are being loaded with the weapons as we speak. Our question for you is; where do we drop each of them?"

"How far can the aircraft travel?"

"To the east coast of the United States in one direction or to Moscow in the other."

"All of you come with me." Hitler stood and slowly walked over and opened a third door revealing his private war room. Maps festooned the walls where six officers moved markers, spoke urgently into telephones, or conversed between themselves.

As soon as Hitler entered the room all motion ceased and the six men snapped to attention and rendered a perfect salute.

"Heil Hitler!" the SS colonel snapped. The other five echoed his words.

"What are the dispositions of our armies on the Eastern Front? Don't give me platitudes–I need the truth!"

The colonel stood tall. "We are outnumbered five to one, mein Führer. Our forces are falling back and our non-German troops are deserting in droves. The situation grows darker by the hour."

"If you could drop *one* bomb that could devastate a radius of–" Hitler turned to Doktor Erich Schumann and cocked his head.

"If you time it for an air blast," Schumann spoke quickly, "you could wipe out five square kilometers."

"Is that all?" Hitler felt the old throb in his temple that warned him against further agitation if he valued coherency. He stopped and took a deep breath, willed his heart to slow. "How can five square kilometers win the war?"

"That would cause instantaneous annihilation of everything in that area, mein Führer!" Schumann didn't seem as sure of himself as before. "The damage would be incredibly wide spread beyond the detonation point, it would just take them longer to die."

"*How* wide spread?"

"We estimate at least a one hundred kilometer radius, Führer. All we have are conjectures as how debilitating the weapon will be in the long run. We need to test it."

Hitler turned back to the colonel. "Where?"

The colonel tapped a wall map with a long pointer. Where the tip touched, the map bristled with miniature flags denoting Soviet Army divisions.

"If the choice were mine, Warsaw is the place I would use it to achieve fullest potential. If what this man says is true, we could cripple the Russian advance, perhaps fatally."

Adolph turned back to Göring. "Make it happen."

"That's one of the weapons, Führer. Where do you want the other one dropped?"

"Washington, D.C., you said your bomber could fly that far."

"It can get there and deliver the device, but it will be a one-way mission."

"Make the crew all members of the Knights of the Iron Cross with Golden Oakleaves, Swords, and Diamonds. Award them yourself in my name with the gratitude of the German people."

Reichsmarschall Hermann Göring stretched to his full height and attempted to pull his gut up to his chest as he saluted. "I will order both missions immediately, Führer!"

Hitler nodded his understanding and walked back into his office. The two scientists glanced at Göring before following the Führer. Schumann gestured for Diebner to precede him out of the office and then hesitated in front of his leader.

"If you don't mind me asking, Führer, why did you target Soviet armies and the American capitol?"

"If we kill the body of the Russian snake the head will wither and die in Moscow. With the Western serpent we must kill the head."

CHAPTER 1

LIVENGOOD,
ALASKA PREFECURE
February, 1967

Levi's phone rang and he answered while continuing to read the railroad maintenance report.

"Mr. Fischer," the instantly recognizable voice said, "this is Major Miamatsu. Please board the next bus into Fairbanks and report to my office."

"Yes, Major. I'm not sure what the bus sched—"

"The southbound bus from Yukon Station will be in Livengood in seventeen minutes."

"Thank you for the information. I will be on it."

Miamatsu hung up.

Jim Spreter looked up from his work.

"Major Miamatsu?"

"Yeah. I've got sixteen minutes to catch the bus."

"It's been three days since Suzuki died, I thought maybe they had it all figured out."

"He didn't mention Suzuki. He didn't say why he wants me there."

"Good luck, Fish."

He hurried to his cabin and grabbed his travel kit. The waterproof packet contained matches, flint and steel, a small can of sterno, and a chocolate bar. The packet fit easily into his parka pocket, didn't weigh much, and could literally save his life.

The bus officially seated 44 people but only six passengers sat scattered about when he boarded. He showed the driver his transport pass and his identification even though he had personally hired the man three years earlier. This was no time to skip protocol. Besides, any one of the other passengers could be a government agent seeking laxity in basic operations and hungering for an opportunity to report someone for ignoring standard security on the bus.

Four of the other passengers were definitely Japanese, another was probably Korean rather than Chinese as he was well dressed, and the sixth man was a Negro. As the driver was an Athabascan, Levi felt conspicuous.

At least they don't know I am Jewish.

He quickly glanced around to see if anyone registered his thought. He felt appalled that he allowed it to cross his mind. Levi did not personally know any other Jew than himself. At times he was not sure he knew himself; it didn't seem safe.

The bus made good time on the frozen gravel road and its interior was toasty. In an hour and a half they reached Fox where two people got off the vehicle and three more boarded. He read the bright posters above the bus windows so many times he had them memorized.

All extolled the virtue of labor and the prosperous glory of the Japanese Empire and the Greater Pacific Co-Prosperity Sphere. Half an hour after leaving Fox they pulled into Fairbanks just as the sun dipped below the horizon. Throughout the trip the bus had passed only two private autos and three Japanese armored patrol cars.

The bus station sat a block from the Kempeitai Headquarters. Levi rucked his parka hood out to maximum length and walked steadily toward the building. A haze of ice fog hung over the town, diffusing the garish, blinking neon signs in Japanese and English advertising alcohol, women, baths, and various other sanctioned vices. Music leaked from some of the establishments giving the scene a surrealistic harmonic background by mixing cowboy music with a lone samishen.

At these temperatures if one breathed too deeply the lining of the lungs would frost and freeze; that promised a painful death.

Haste did not pay positive dividends in this climate.

Walk fast enough to stay warm and slow enough not to sweat.

That had been one of the most repeated pieces of advice given him when he approached his first winter in Alaska Prefecture. He used it as a mantra to pace himself when agitated, which accurately described his current mental state.

The first person he saw when he entered Kempeitai headquarters was an armed guard in dress uniform holding a new Type 100 machine-gun. Levi showed his identity card and moved past when the guard nodded.

A slender Japanese man moved forward.

"Mr. Fischer? I am Juro Sendai, Major Miamatsu's assistant. Would you follow me please?"

Levi followed, wondered why he was being treated so deferentially. The last time he had been here as a witness in the traffic death of a Japanese child, he had been treated rudely, like a criminal. His former memories of this building had hardened into a shell of fear around the experience.

Miamatsu stood inside his office as Sendai motioned Levi forward.

"Have a seat, Mr. Fischer."

Levi glanced behind him to discover Sendai had vanished. He sat.

Miamatsu carefully sat in the chair on the other side of the desk, leaned back, and regarded Levi.

"Your work has been exemplary, Mr. Fischer. You have served the Emperor well."

Even though confused, Levi snapped his head forward in a bow he timed at ten seconds. When he looked up again, he thought he detected a thin smile on Miamatsu's face.

"Therefore you are to be rewarded."

Levi's agitation ratcheted up to a higher degree. The Japanese predilection for advancing people past the point of their competence and then destroying them for failure was well known to him. He realized that never before in his life had he been in more danger than at this moment.

"Rewarded for what? I don't understand."

Miamatsu's face betrayed no emotion as his eyes held Levi's.

"You are now Director of Labor for the Yukon-Fairbanks Railway Project."

"Why?" he said through a gasp, "I, I mean, thank you. I am greatly honored, but how is it that I warrant such a boon?"

"You have shown diligence in every position you have held. This has been noticed. Furthermore, you have effortlessly picked up the burdens of your late supervisor, Mr. Mathieson, in addition to your own tasks."

Whitey Matheson had been dead for six weeks. After years of working with the man, handling Whitey's responsibilities had been as effortless as an afterthought. For this they were promoting him yet again? The decision made no sense to him.

"We realized that you were the perfect person to fill the void left by Mr. Suzuki. Being single and without family, the only hold we have over you is your very life for a perceived failure. On Monday you will present yourself at the headquarters building at Yukon Station for orientation.

"As of this moment you are awarded Lotus clearance, a thirty percent raise in wages, and privileges to be defined at a later date. Here are your official orders." He handed Levi a thick sheaf of paper, folded but not sealed.

"Congratulations, Mr. Fischer." Miamatsu stood and Levi scrambled to his feet, immediately giving the man a first-degree bow, frantically searching for a reason to refuse.

"You will now be driven to the station to catch the afternoon train to Livengood. Your furniture and baggage will be moved for you. You will be met at Yukon Station when you exit the morning train on Monday." Miamatsu motioned him toward the now open office door.

Juro Sendai stood at attention as Levi walked past him and down the long corridor, mind racing, clutching his orders, and trying not to tremble or weep in his defeat.

He reflected that all this had started three days ago with the door to his office bursting open.

✪

Levi Fischer had just laughed at Jim Spreter's joke when the front office door crashed open and someone stumbled in and fell full length on the floor. Bone numbing cold rushed through the opening; its bitter breath fogged the warm room.

"What the hell?" Jim yelled as he jumped up and slammed the

door. The temperature in the office had already dropped over twenty degrees.

Levi hurried around his desk and rolled the person over. The frost bitten face took a moment to identify. The man's eyes darted aimlessly and his lips moved without sound.

"Mister Suzuki? Can you hear me?" Levi looked up at Jim. "Get a blanket, he's nearly frozen solid."

With obvious effort Suzuki focused on Levi's face and tried to speak.

Levi bent down and put his ear next to the man's lips.

"...warn them..." came the breathless whisper.

"Warn who, about what?"

"...project...must stop..."

"I'm sorry, sir. I don't understand. Wait until we get you some medical help."

"No time!" the man gasped and then went slack. All animation ceased.

"Mr. Suzuki? Sir, can you hear me?" Levi looked up as Jim returned with a blanket. "I think he's dead."

"Let me see." Jim knelt down and put two fingers on the man's throat. "He's not supposed to be *here,* dammit!" He shifted his fingers for a moment before rocking back on his heels.

"Yeah, he's gone. We better call the police."

Levi dialed the local number for civilian police.

"Prefecture Police Department, Scanlon speaking, sir."

Despite himself and the situation, Levi had smirked. Corporal Scanlon's entire department was a small, two-room building on the other side of the train station and he was the only officer.

"Charlie, this is Levi over in personnel. Mr. Suzuki just busted into the office and died."

"What? Just died?"

"Yeah, can you come over?"

"I'll be right there."

Levi hung up the phone and squinted his eyes at Jim. "What did you mean, 'He's not supposed to be here!'"

Jim hesitated, then said, "Well hell no! He's supposed to be up at Yukon Station. What kind of a question is that?"

"Sorry, it just sounded like you knew where he—oh, to hell with it, never mind."

Three minutes later Corporal Charles Scanlon walked through the door and nearly stepped on Mr. Suzuki's corpse.

"Shit, you weren't kidding," he said staring down. He pushed the door shut behind him and opened his parka. "Tell me what happened."

They did.

"What did he say?" He scratched away at his little notebook. "Tell me that again."

"He said, 'warn them, project must stop,' and 'no time.' Then he died. I called you. All of this happened in the last ten minutes."

Scanlon wrote furiously for nearly another minute. "I don't dare disturb the body. He's Japanese and we ain't. They got some pretty strange laws y'know." Scanlon looked worried.

"We can't just leave him here!" Jim said.

Scanlon swept them with his gaze.

"The hell you can't. I'm securing this as a possible crime scene. You both have to leave until the place has been cleared by the Kempeitai."

"Crime scene!" Jim shouted. "There was no crime committed here! The man pushed through the door, fell down, and fuckin' died! How is *that* a crime?"

"Sorry guys, the Japs will sort it all out. There's nothing more I can do."

"Jim," Levi said in a low tone, "Let it go. He's right, there's nothing we can do about this. Take the rest of the day off."

"Okay, Levi. Thanks."

"Don't talk to anyone about this. Where you gonna be? The Kempeitai will want to talk to you" Scanlon said.

"For Christ's sake, Charlie, we're in *Livengood*. I'll either be at the Roadhouse or in my cabin."

Jim Spreter stomped out of the door pulling on his parka as he went.

"Call the Kempeitai, Charlie," Levi said. "Let's get this show on the road."

"You'll have to leave, too," Charlie said as he stood up.

"That's not going to happen unless you leave with me and we lock the door."

"What? I'm a corporal in the Prefecture Police, so you gotta do what I tell you."

"You are the one who said 'crime,' not me. I know I didn't commit one, and I know Jim didn't commit one. I'm not leaving you here alone to alter the *crime* scene."

A look of shock went over the beefy man's face.

"You accusing me of something, Fischer?

"Just call the damn Japs, okay? We're wasting time."

Glaring, Charlie pushed past him, picked up the receiver and didn't look down until he started dialing.

"Good afternoon to you, too. This is Corporal Charles Scanlon at the Livengood station. I want to report a dead man." He stared hard at Levi while he listened. "Yes, I know the man, his name is, uh, was Hiraku Suzuki, works for the railroad out of Yukon Station."

Levi kept his face blank and his emotions bottled up. If there had been anyone else he could have called, he would have. He suspected the only way Charlie ever made corporal was by volunteering for this one-man station in the middle of a boreal forest.

"Hello, I— yes, Suzuki. Livengood, on the Elliot Hi— uh, yes. Yes, Major, I will do that. Very go—" Charlie slammed the receiver onto the cradle. "Son-of-a-bitch hung up on me!"

"What did he say?"

"We gotta write a report, every detail of what happened. They'll be here within two hours."

"*We* have to write a report?" Levi said with a thin smile. "As you so loudly pointed out, you are the police here. I'm just a witness."

"You type better than I do!"

"If the report doesn't have at least one misspelled word in every sentence they'll know you didn't write it."

"Why you being such an asshole, Levi?" he said with a pained look.

"It's an affliction I Just caught. I think there's something contagious going around. Let's lock the door and go to your office; you didn't give them the location of the body anyway."

"Damn, you're right! C'mon."

Charlie was still laboriously pecking at the typewriter with two fingers when the door opened admitting four men and another massive volume of frigid air and attendant fog. They slammed the door behind them. Two of them wore army uniforms and one of the men in civilian clothes looked around the room and then stared down at Charlie.

"Where is the body of Mr. Suzuki?"

"Over at the railroad office, where he died," Charlie said.

The man looked at Levi with hard eyes. "Who are you?"

"Levi Fischer, Mr., ah—"

"I am Major Miamatsu, Imperial Army Kempeitai. You are head of personnel for this section of the Yukon-Fairbanks Railroad, no?"

"Yes," Levi said trying to hide the surprise in his voice.

"Were you in the office when Mr. Suzuki died?"

"Yes."

"Show me." Miamatsu nodded toward the door.

The other man in civilian clothes opened the door while carefully observing Levi's every action.

Levi pulled on his parka.

Charlie said, "Shouldn't I com—"

"Finish your report," the major snapped and motioned Levi out the door.

The cold bit at his face and he wanted to pull his hood forward to create a safe dead-air space. However, Miamatsu wore only an overcoat and fur hat with the earflaps snapped up. If the major wanted to show how tough he was Levi would at least match him.

A black Mitsubishi sedan sat in front of the police station, engine running. Behind it a gray Mazda van idled. Red Japanese characters for "law soldier," what everyone referred to as the Kempeitai or secret police, adorned the side.

At the office Levi stepped to one said and said, "He's on the floor, just inside the door."

Miamatsu nodded and said, "Wait here. Hamada, you're with me."

The other man in civilian clothes followed the major.

The cold bit at Levi's face and ears, and his nostrils stuck together when he breathed through his nose. It was far too cold to breathe through his mouth so he pulled his parka hood to full extension. Both of the soldiers flanked him with their parka hoods completely hiding their heads. He wondered how long he was going to have to be out here before this thing was finished.

The door opened and Miamatsu snapped, "In, all of you. Be careful not to step on the body."

The soldiers waited for Levi to enter before eagerly crowding in behind him. Hamada was busily taking photos of the body and using one of the new electronic flash units for illumination.

Suzuki was still on the floor. However, his parka had been pulled open to better display his conservative suit coat, once-white shirt, and tie. All were saturated with frosted blood.

"Oh my god," Levi blurted. "We didn't know he had been injured."

"Tell me everything," Miamatsu said.

"Well, Jim Spreter and I were here—"

"There was another person present when this happened?"

"Yes, Major. James Spreter, he's my assistant."

"Where is Mr. Spreter at this moment?"

"Either at home, or the Roadhouse Bar. I'd wager he's at the Roadhouse if I were a betting man."

Major Miamatsu looked up at one of the soldiers in uniform and snapped in Japanese, "Find Spreter; search the bar first."

The soldier nodded and hurried out the door.

Over the years Levi had picked up enough Japanese to understand the kernel of their conversations. He never tried to speak the language or show any sign of understanding when being spoken to by a Japanese. Since a lot of Americans never bothered to learn more than a few phrases Levi felt it was his secret weapon; if you didn't offer the information they always assumed you didn't understand.

Levi had just finished repeating Suzuki's final words for the second time when Jim walked through the door trailed by the soldier.

"Name?" Miamatsu said, staring up at Jim, who towered over everyone else in the room.

"James Spreter, chief personnel clerk for the Yukon-Fairbanks Railroad, sir."

Miamatsu wrinkled his nose. "Have you been drinking, Mr. Spreter?"

"Sure," he said with a shrug. "Levi gave me the rest of the day off so I was enjoying myself."

"Tell me what happened here today."

"Didn't Levi tell—"

"I want to hear *your* version."

His story didn't deviate from Levi's until the end.

"I didn't hear what he whispered to Levi, I was too far away. I checked for his pulse and couldn't find one." Jim unbuttoned his parka and pulled it off, dropped it on his chair.

"Neither of you thought to open his coat?"

"We thought it best to call the local police," Levi said. "So we did."

Miamatsu rolled his eyes and Levi decided the guy had some promise as a human being after all. Hamada's cheek muscles twitched before they got the order not to smile.

"I understand. Mr. Suzuki has been murdered. Did he have any enemies here?"

"Suzuki?" Jim said with a laugh. "I mean, none I knew of. He was always quiet, straight forward, and all business when he was down here."

"We didn't even know he was in the area," Levi said. "He only comes down here for inspections once a month. We thought he was at the Yukon Station headquarters."

Miamatsu gave Levi a level look. "Your dossier showed that this is a relatively new position for you, no?"

"I have been acting head of personnel for five weeks."

"Your predecessor was promoted?"

"No. Mr. Mathieson died. They said it was a heart attack."

Surprise flashed across Miamatsu's face for the first time since he arrived.

"There was no mention..." he gave Hamada a beseeching look before turning back to Levi. "Was he perhaps a corpulent man with poor eating habits?"

"Hah," Jim said. "He and I worked out at the little gym we built. He was in as good of shape as I am."

Miamatsu glanced over Jim's muscular physique and frowned. Hamada put a lens cap on the camera hanging around his neck and pulled his parka around it.

"Was an autopsy performed?"

"We don't know, Major," Levi said. "The army took him away and we never heard any more about it."

"Did you also witness his demise?"

"No. We found him in his cabin, dead."

"Why were you at his cabin?"

"We came to work and the door was still locked. He was usually here at least an hour before we would arrive. That morning he wasn't, so we went to check on him."

Miamatsu pulled out a small notebook and rapidly wrote

Japanese characters in neat, tight lines. He turned to Levi's desk, picked up the telephone receiver and dialed. He spoke only Japanese and instructed the person on the other end to obtain a copy of Mathieson's autopsy report by the time he returned to Fairbanks.

Hamada leaned against the wall, one hand loosely holding the other while he watched Levi and Jim with weary eyes.

What is this about? Levi wondered. *Whitey's been dead for over a month. Does this guy think there's a connection?*

Miamatsu hung up the phone and snapped orders to the soldiers to get the litter. They left the office.

"Mr. Fischer, there will be additional questions for you about this matter. It is interesting that the two of you are at the focal point of two deaths. Neither of you are to leave this area until further notice."

Jim lost his half smile and stood straighter. "Major Miamatsu, my wife and daughters live in Fairbanks. I go home every weekend–"

"That is acceptable, Mr. Spreter. However, do not travel farther than Fairbanks or you will be placed in custody. Do you understand?"

"I understand."

The soldiers returned with a stretcher, placed Suzuki's corpse on it, covered him with the blanket and carried him out. Corporal Charles Scanlon marched into the office and held out three sheets of paper to Miamatsu.

"Here you are, Major Miamatsu. My report; all typed and correct." He started to grin but the effort died as soon as he looked into the officer's face.

Miamatsu looked down at the report and slowly pulled it out of Charlie's hand. Without reading any of it he handed it to Hamada, and said in Japanese, "This will not be a good example of written English, but search for anything relevant when we get back to the office."

Hamada accepted the pages and closed his eyes in a long blink.

Miamatsu turned to Levi. "If you think of anything you may have inadvertently omitted, call me immediately." He gave him a business card.

The two Japanese detectives pushed past Charlie and left the office.

When the door shut Charlie turned to Levi.

"What did you tell them?"

"We told them what happened. What did you think we would say?"

"What about my report? They were supposed to read it here!"

"You might catch them if you hurry," Spreter said. "You could explain it to them."

"One of these days I'm going to catch you assholes—"

"Charlie, shut up and go away," Spreter said, rolling his shoulders.

As soon as the door shut, Levi looked at his friend. "Jim, what is going on?"

Jim Spreter looked back and said, "Anything worth knowing that I know, you already know about, Fish."

"Why doesn't that get rid of the doubt in my gut?"

"Because, deep down, you're a cynic, Fish."

Levi couldn't argue with that.

CHAPTER 2

*"Winter solitude—
in a world of one color
the sound of the wind."*
— Matsuo Basho

ELLIOT HIGHWAY,
ALASKA PREFECTURE

MAJOR KATSU MIAMATSU HAD NOTED FISCHER'S TURMOIL AND wondered at the man's agitation. He thought back to the night of the murder.

If Fischer is as clean as his record reflects, he might be useful as the replacement, Miamatsu had thought as he stared out the car window, *but that is not my giri to decide.* The snow-covered forest moved steadily past, opening now and then to reveal a quick glimpse of a moonlit meadow or the mirrored cleft of a frozen creek.

He appreciated the harsh extremes of interior Alaska Prefecture. If one could not embrace and bend with the seasons like the willow, then one should seek the heat of more populous places like the slums of San Francisco. Unbidden, Miriam came to mind and he shook his head and forced his thoughts elsewhere.

Still staring out the window, he spoke to Sergeant Hamada.

"Who killed Suzuki, and why?"

"Those are the two questions I have been mulling since we discovered there had been a crime, Major."

"The killing has to be political," Miamatsu said. "Suzuki still had his purse and identity badge. Of course that may not have been what the assassin sought. What else could it be?"

Sergeant Hamada shrugged. "To silence him, perhaps? Suzuki

knew his proper station in life and worked tirelessly for the *on* he owed the Emperor. Perhaps he had defected to a different *han*?"

A dimly lit cabin over a hundred meters away from the road surrounded by a large, snow-covered meadow, captured Miamatsu's attention for a moment. He wondered if it was a farm.

"That is even more troubling," he said. "We both know Suzuki was a Kempeitai agent and part of our *han*. Mathieson was not a member of anything. I called Sendai and told him to obtain a copy of Mathieson's autopsy. His death obviously did not raise the flags it should have."

"Does that mean someone in the Kempeitai suppressed the potential importance of his death?" Hamada asked.

Miamatsu set the question aside while he contemplated the full meaning of the possibility. In an organization where secrets were common currency it might be easy to hide one for a time, but to what end? The silent tiger in the center of this discussion began to move so close it could no longer be ignored.

"Both murders had something to do with the Project," he said softly.

"Then we must solve this quickly, Major," Hamada said.

"The copy of Mathieson's autopsy will be on my desk by the time we return to the office tonight. There may be something there that others missed and once found we can safely push aside fears of a conspiracy."

"What if we find a conspiracy?" Hamada asked.

"If we do, we have a much larger problem than the death of a functionary. We would be seeking people committing sedition."

Light flashed past in the dark night. Miamatsu realized they had turned onto the Steese Highway and had just passed through the small mining town of Fox. In fifteen to twenty minutes they would arrive in Fairbanks.

"I need to clear my mind, Norio."

Katsu Miamatsu relaxed into the soft seat cushions and sought the clarity of nothingness.

"Major Miamatsu, we have arrived," the driver said, holding the door open.

"Thank you, Yori. You made excellent time."

The driver made a second degree bow as Miamatsu and Hamada exited.

Miamatsu's assistant stood at attention in the hallway to his office. When he was within five feet of him, the assistant bent from the waist.

This isn't good, Miamatsu thought, *he thinks he has failed me.*

"Juro, is there a problem?"

Juro stood upright. "I could not fulfill your request, Major Miamatsu."

"Which request?"

"For a copy of the Mathieson autopsy report, Major."

"Who refused you a copy?" he said with heat in his tone.

"I was told there is no report, that Mr. Mathieson was not autopsied."

Miamatsu motioned toward the door with his chin and Juro opened the door and followed him and Hamada into his office.

"Shut the door."

Miamatsu pulled off his parka and hung it on a peg. Hamada opened his parka and dropped into a chair.

"Did the clerk you spoke with say why procedure had not been followed?"

"No, Major. He was as mystified as I was when he discovered the omission."

"Is Mathieson's body still in the morgue?" He knew what the answer would be but he still needed to hear it.

"No, Major. Mr. Mathieson was cremated two days after his death."

Despite the outrage he felt, Miamatsu betrayed no emotion. He glanced at the sergeant for a moment.

"Well, it was a thought. I will have to find a different approach to my theory."

"Is there any other task I may undertake for you, sir?"

"No. It's after office hours. Go home to your wife and children."

"Thank you, sir." Juro gave him a quick bow and left.

He sat at his desk and thought about the ramifications of the lack of an autopsy.

"Either there was an autopsy and the results are secret," he said to Hamada, "...or no autopsy was performed as they already knew how he died because they had him killed. We'll work on this tomorrow, Norio. You go get some sleep; I have a report to write. Leave the report the incompetent wrote."

Sergeant Norio Hamada stood, dropped the report on Miamatsu's desk, and nodded.

"Thank you, Major. I'll see you in the morning."

Miamatsu picked up the report and quickly scanned the assembly of deleted words and laborious circular explanation before dropping it on the desk. He moved his chair over to the typing table and rolled a blank official report form into the machine. Avoiding any speculation, he put down the facts as related by the witnesses and his own direct observations of Suzuki's death. In the space reserved for cause of death he typed, "Unknown. To be determined by autopsy."

He pulled the report out of the typewriter, dated, and signed it. Before walking out the door he checked his reflection in the mirror and used his comb to tidy his appearance. He had to look his best even at this late hour.

Anticipating he would have to leave the report in his supervisor's attention box he was surprised to see the office door open. He stopped at the door and knocked.

Lieutenant Colonel Akio Toragawa looked up from the report in his hand and acknowledged Miamatsu's second-degree bow.

"Come in, Major, I have been expecting you. Pull the door shut behind you."

Miamatsu complied and, standing at attention, handed the report to his superior.

"Please, sit. Would you like tea?"

"Thank you, yes." The light lunch no longer lingered after six hours and his physical hunger nearly matched his mental appetite for information.

The colonel poured tea and sat the pot back on the warming flame. He read the report, laid it on his desk, and stared at Miamatsu.

"Any guesses as to cause of death?"

"He was either shot or stabbed. All of the clothes on the upper body are saturated with blood."

Toragawa nodded and his eyes hooded further.

"How did this murder compel you to request the autopsy report of a different person?"

"Until apprised by the men in the railroad office, I did not know of the recent death of Mr. Mathieson. Two unnatural deaths within five weeks in a place as small as Livengood seemed unusual to me and I wondered if they were somehow linked."

"Why do you believe Mr. Mathieson's death was unusual?"

"I am led to believe the man died of a heart attack."

"Why do think that is unusual?"

"He was in excellent health, extremely fit, and thirty years old."

"And your conclusion?"

"I do not yet have one, Colonel. I first need to see Mr. Suzuki's autopsy report and gather what information I can about Mr. Mathieson."

"Allow me to save you some time and effort, Major. There is no link. Mr. Mathieson died of natural causes."

Miamatsu waited a few breaths for more information.

"Ah, that is good to know. I am grateful to you for the assistance."

"We all serve the Emperor."

Miamatsu stood and bowed.

"Thank you for your time and instruction, Colonel."

When he shut the door behind him Katsu Miamatsu allowed himself a small shudder. His earlier casual consideration of a conspiracy had solidified into a certainty, and he had thrown out a hook baited with his career, as well as his life.

CHAPTER 3

"Wintery day,
On my horse
A frozen shadow."
— *Matsuo Basho*

YUKON STATION, ALASKA PREFECTURE

Captain Hirako Atsumi sat in the train station watching wind driven snow stream sideways past the windows in the gray morning. The flying flakes mesmerized her, pulling her back to her days at *Rikugun Yonen Gakko*, the military preparatory school in Tokyo. As one of the first ten women admitted to the school, the severe discipline had been even more pronounced due to the misogynistic attitude of the Imperial Army and the Japanese culture as a whole. All ten women were expected to fail.

Hirako not only persevered, she excelled. Two of the women in her class quit during the first month. Before the rest graduated three had taken their own lives, and another three had been cut from the program. Only Moriko Satsumi and Hirako graduated and were permitted to attend the Nakano Intelligence School.

More women had followed their footsteps, of course. In the four years they spent at the academy their determination and industriousness earned the grudging admiration of their male classmates. Her mastery of *aikido* had saved her from rape and resulted in the attacker being expelled from the military after he mended in the hospital.

The attacker's resulting act of *seppuku* absolved him of a dishonorable life. She often wondered if his official punishment had been for the crime of assault on another cadet, or the crime of not being successful at raping a mere woman.

Thereafter Hirako did her best to disguise her feminity and obvious pulchritude. When in uniform she was strictly military and businesslike, only in private did she relax and allow herself to indulge in small vices and pleasures.

She blinked and thought about her current assignment. As honcho for civilian personnel it was her duty to vet top echelon employees. Many Americans had been hired by the military in Alaska for the same reason the military had admitted women into the ranks, the massive loss of young Japanese men during the war.

Last week Mr. Suzuki had died a violent death. In less than a half hour she would welcome his replacement. To her knowledge, Mr. Fischer would be the first Jew she had ever met. The Reich worked diligently at their extermination and had reduced their numbers to a tiny fraction of what they had been in the 1930s.

On one hand she didn't really care what the round eyes did to each other. On the other hand she understood that Jews were highly intelligent and therefore very useful. She had never understood the German mentality, but she certainly appreciated their technology.

I just wish they would share it with us.

A heavy gust of snow-laden wind howled past the window. The wind also carried the thin wail of the morning train. A quick glance around revealed the terminal filled with people waiting to board the train back to Fairbanks and points south.

The whistle sounded again, much closer this time. She also heard the engine bell announcing entry into the Yukon Station yards. When the massive engine rolled past the window she stood and watched the platform outside as the passenger cars ground to a stop.

The conductor lowered the steps and people streamed out of the coach and hurried through the heart-stopping cold to the station doors. Hirako pulled her parka together and buttoned it as the first gust of chilled air entered along with the arrivals through the second set of doors in the arctic entry. Most of the travelers knew where they were going and in classic Asian single-mindedness proceeded to the next point of their journey.

Finally three men wandered in, looking around and frowning with bewilderment.

"Mister Fischer!" she snapped, as if addressing an underclassman.

He jerked his head around and looked at her, shifting a suitcase from one hand to the other before giving her a third degree bow. She didn't return it.

"How did you know who I was?"

"I didn't until you looked at me when I said your name." She held out her hand in the American manner. "I am Captain Atsumi, your direct supervisor."

He hesitated, then shook her hand and said, "Pleased to meet you, Captain. Thank you for meeting me. I've never been north of Livengood before."

"You are welcome. However, I must point out that this is part of my duties. You are here to fill large shoes and it is in my official interest to help you familiarize yourself."

Fischer glanced around the room as people moved out to board the train. Even without her training she would have perceived that he was distinctly uncomfortable, even fearful.

"Do you have any luggage?"

"Just this. By the time I returned to my cabin in Livengood on Friday all of my possessions had been packed and moved up here. I figured food prices here would be higher than down there so I bought groceries."

"Good thrifty thinking. Are you ready to go?"

"Of course," he said in a dubious tone.

She stifled her smirk and led the way to her staff car. The driver stood by the back door and opened it for her. She slid across the seat and beckoned for Fischer to follow.

In moments the driver was maneuvering through the blowing snow and gusting wind.

"May I see your orders?"

He pulled the papers from an inside coat pocket and handed them to her. She glanced through them, and speculated if he read or spoke Japanese.

"I looked at them," he said, "but since I don't read or speak Japanese they didn't reveal very much."

I wonder if he just read my mind.

"You said you had never before visited the Project. Do you know what is being done here?"

"Not a clue. Until Friday I didn't have the necessary clearance and since then I've not had the means or opportunity to investigate. I spent the week end wondering what lay in store for me up here."

"If you are as diligent in your labors here as you have been in Livengood, you will be rewarded with enhanced status and pay. We will further discuss the goals and scope of the Project in my office."

As he listened to her he stared out the side window at the large buildings, the three-meter fencing, and military vehicles. The car stopped at a security point. Captain Atsumi rolled down her window and nodded at the guard. He snapped to attention and saluted as the gate opened and the car moved forward.

The driver pulled up in front of a three-story building. She opened her door and got out, motioning for Fischer to follow. They hurried up the steps and entered the structure. Once through the arctic entry the over-heated air in the building enveloped them.

"My god, but it's hot in here!" Fischer blurted.

Captain Atsumi didn't think it politic to point out that the most important person in this building was nearly eighty years old and he intensely disliked cold.

"This way, please." She nodded to the security guard at the desk inside the door and walked up the steps, carefully not swaying her hips too much. She wasn't sure why she clenched her jaw, other than it was a coin toss between military attitude and concentration.

Once on the second floor she unlocked her office door and entered.

Fischer followed her in and stopped, glancing around while exuding anxiety and sudden sweat. She noticed he still had the suitcase handle gripped tightly in his left hand.

"Please close the door and sit down, Mr. Fischer."

He sat the suitcase down next to the closest chair and pulled the door shut.

"Do you want me to lock it?"

"No. Please take off your parka and sit." Her coat already hung on its hook, and she settled into the chair behind her desk.

He removed his parka and laid it over the suitcase as he sat down.

"So what do they do here?"

"What do you think they do?"

"I really have no idea. My old job was to insure there were

adequate laborers and supplies to keep the railroad operational between here and the border of Yukon Station. Beyond that I never asked about, or was told of, the nature of Yukon Station. I didn't have the security clearance for that information"

She frowned and looked away for a moment.

Where to start?

"Actually it is a very long conversation and there are preparations that must take precedence. Suffice it to say that you will continue to handle personnel procurements and supervision of the entire railway from here to Fairbanks."

"Couldn't I have done that from Livengood, Captain?"

"Of course, but General Yamashita wished to have you here for his convenience."

"Oh, I see."

"Did Major Miamatsu reveal your secondary role?"

"*Secondary* role? No, he did not mention a secondary role." He crossed his arms in front of his chest and crossed his legs.

Hirako nearly laughed.

"Mr. Suzuki was also a Kempeitai operative."

"The *secret police*?" He actually moaned before he could contain himself.

"Why are you so agitated, Mr. Fischer?"

"I know nothing about police work or investigating!"

"All that is required of you is careful observation. Nothing more."

He uncrossed his legs but held his arms firm over his chest.

"Observation, of what?"

"Everyone with whom you come into contact. Workers, soldiers, civilians, everybody."

"What am I watching for with all this observation?"

"Aberration, unusual actions, suspicious behavior, that sort of thing."

His obvious reticence surprised her. All of the Americans she had previously met were more than eager to accept more power and prestige, no matter what the cost to them or others.

He glanced around the room and refocused on her.

"How would I know if something was unusual or anything? I just got here."

"I don't expect you to discover a nest of saboteurs immediately," she said with a smile. "We want you to be very aware of existing conditions at the beginning of your tour. That way if something odd transpires, you will notice it."

"Are *you* Kempeitai?"

Let him figure that out, she thought.

"Allow me to show you your new office." She stood and he shot to his feet, bent over, and grabbed his gear. Captain Atsumi straightened her uniform dress and led him through the door and down the steps.

She thumbed back over her shoulder.

"The third floor holds the offices of Lieutenant General Tomoyuki Yamashita and his deputy, Major General Tsuji. To step on that level without an invitation from one of them would mean your death."

"I understand," he said.

She stopped in front of a door. "This is your office." She opened the door and walked through.

A woman straightened to her feet behind the desk and snapped into a first-degree bow.

"This is your secretary, Tomiko Watanabe. She is your gatekeeper and you will find her most valuable."

Still in a bow, the secretary said, "Welcome, Mr. Fischer."

"Thank you," he said and motioned for her to straighten. He glanced around. "And where am I to sit?"

Both women laughed and Watanabe hurried over and opened another door.

"This is *your* office, sir, much more comfortable, neh?"

"I'll leave you to Tomiko's care, Mr. Fischer. Please report to my office at 0900 tomorrow."

Without waiting for a reply Captain Atsumi left the room.

CHAPTER 4

YUKON STATION,
ALASKA PREFECTURE

LEVI TURNED AND SAID, "YES, CAPTAIN," AS THE DOOR CLICKED SHUT behind her.

"May I take your coat, Mr. Fischer?"

He handed Tomiko his coat and sat his suitcase on the floor as he surveyed the room. The office contained a sturdy desk with a new chair behind it and two rather pedestrian chairs at angles in front of it. A thick rug covered the floor and, with the exception of the desk lamp, the lighting was subdued and recessed.

He turned to Tomiko. "Unless there is an officer present, please call me Levi. It bothers me to work with someone who addresses me by my last name all the time. Okay?"

"Of course, M—ah, Levi. I must say, this is very unusual."

"It's very American and I cling to informality," he said, grinning.

She relaxed and gave him a brief smile. "So what would you like to know about your duties, Levi?"

"What are they? What do we do here?" He waved at the wall and dropped into his new chair, gestured toward her. "Please, have a seat."

She automatically gave him a quick nod and carefully sat down. "We are the main personnel office for the rail—"

"I know *that*," he snapped. He hesitated and in a kinder tone said,

"Pardon me, I'm nervous and feel like I'm out of my depth. I know about the roads and grounds part of things, but what is the railroad for? What is the function of this station?"

"I am very sorry, Mr. Fischer, but I am not allowed to reveal classified information. You will have to ask Captain Atsumi."

Before he could point out his new Lotus clearance, the telephone on his desk rang, startling him. "This is Levi Fischer."

"Mr. Fischer, this is Major General Tsuji. Please bring your papers and orders up to my office."

The line went dead; he replaced the receiver, and frowned.

"Does Major General Tsuji greet all of the new people?"

Tomiko gave him a neutral stare. "Just ask the person at the top of the stairs to show you the way to his office, Mr. Fischer."

He had seen the stairs when first entering the building and it took but a moment to gain the second floor. Captain Atsumi waited a few feet from the steps.

She smiled and said, "We meet again. Follow me."

Without knocking, she opened an office door and entered. Three busily typing women in civilian dress and two men in uniform examining papers and making notations sat at desks. None of them looked up at their entrance.

Captain Atsumi opened another door. He expected to see yet another secretary or gate guard and was astounded to behold a Japanese major general in full uniform behind the striking cherry wood desk.

He immediately followed the lieutenant's example and snapped to attention before executing a first-degree bow. When they stood upright again the general nodded his head.

"Welcome to Yukon Station, Mr. Fischer. I am Major General Tsuji, the right hand of General Yamashita. When I speak it is his voice that you hear, do you understand?"

"Yes. General Tsuji, I understand."

"You have been carefully investigated and cleared by the Kempeitai to fulfill the role selected for you. From now until you are told otherwise, you will explicitly follow the directions given to you by Captain Atsumi. It would be in your best interest to become as Japanese in thought and deed as you possibly can. If you are successful in this role, you will be generously rewarded."

The few moments of ensuing silence spoke volumes.

"Excellent. You may leave."

Again Levi bowed deeply then pivoted and left the room following Captain Atsumi. His heart hammered so loudly he felt sure everyone in the next room heard it. Not one person gave them any obvious attention yet he knew they all carefully scrutinized him.

Captain Atsumi walked him to the stairwell and wordlessly nodded for him to continue down. He entered his office and waved Miss Watanabe down when she stood. He glanced up at the clock.

"It is after five and I have absolutely no idea where I live. Who should I ask about that?"

She smiled at him and he suddenly realized that Tomiko Watanabe was an attractive woman.

"I would be happy to drive you to your new quarters, Levi."

"I would appreciate that. Who arranged my office?"

"I did. They provided me with a diagram of your old office."

"I am impressed, everything is here except Jim Spreter."

She laughed. "Mr. Spreter now has your former position. I believe he is happy where he is."

"Jimbo's no dummy," he said holding down the sarcasm.

"Would you like to see your new quarters?"

"Yes, please." He pulled on his parka and grabbed the suitcase he was tired of carrying.

Her striking parka was Athabascan made, boasting rich furs and intricate floral beadwork around the hem. From each parka sleeve hung an ornately beaded mitten that matched the design on the parka itself.

They went outside where the wind created miniature icy tornadoes and stung where it touched bare skin. She pointed to a small, green Toyota coupe. He opened the door and fought the wind as he crawled in the passenger side while she unplugged the heating element from the post socket and wrapped the cord around a small metal cleat.

The car started immediately and the heater vented warm air into the cab.

"I appreciate this, Tomiko."

"You are most welcome. Have you met with Mr. Gunther Charles yet?"

The name was familiar but the past few hours had been full and confusing.

"Charles?" The name brought a dim memory of a heavily muscled man to mind, but at first he couldn't remember a face to go with it.

"He was Mr. Suzuki's assistant. Many of us thought he would inherit your position."

"Including him?"

"Yes, I believe so."

"How is it he was not in the office today?"

"He was this morning but he went into the field as he often does. Here are your quarters, Mr. Fischer, I mean, Levi." She smiled.

"Thank you, Tomiko, I appreciate the ride."

"You are most welcome. I will see you in the morning."

He briefly stood on the small porch and glanced around the collection of small houses in the darkness and drifting snow. He wondered if the wind always blew off the Yukon River. Farther south in Livengood and Fairbanks the wind rarely nudged the winter landscape.

Up here the weather reminded him of blizzards he remembered as a kid in Nebraska. Smoke from the chimneys shredded quickly into oblivion by the wind. He shivered and entered his new home.

Someone had done an excellent job of placing the furniture. His clothing had all been folded and neatly put away in a bureau obviously inherited from the late Suzuki. He harbored no doubt that at least one listening device lurked in an unobtrusive location, safely out of sight.

However, not out of mind.

A medium sized wood stove radiated heat and the cabin felt snug and welcoming. A wall clock bearing Japanese characters ticked away the dark afternoon. His radio, freshly dusted, squatted on a shelf, thoughtfully plugged into the nearest wall socket. He switched it on and it filled the house with one of Mozart's symphonies. He felt surprise; he had expected Japanese music.

For a few minutes the recorded orchestra created the illusion that musicians crowded the room to capacity. The music stopped and the phantom audience enthusiastically applauded. The house felt empty again and he switched off the radio when an official newscast began.

Why wasn't Gunther Charles introduced to me? I know we've met before but not under circumstances like this. Will he be antagonistic because I got the job? Can it matter?

Levi felt weary, tired of living in constant fear of those who ruled his life in small and large ways. Obviously there was much more going on here than just maintaining railroad tracks, runways, and the connecting streets. What was the huge building inside the barbed wire compound?

Over the years he had gained a great deal of engineering knowledge both mechanical and electrical. He yearned for a formal education but admission into advanced studies would necessitate close examination of his personal history.

Levi had seen power plants before, quite large ones, and none of them were even half the size of this structure. The only power lines emerging from the building followed the railroad south and were inadequate to carry large loads of electricity. For what purpose were they using all of that power?

Who could he safely ask? Being a total stranger in this place he felt alone and threatened. He would have to start all over again to blend into the background fabric of this small society, if that was even possible.

Deep inside him something stirred and it took him a moment to recognize it as anger. Anger he could ill afford, but felt unable to suppress.

CHAPTER 5

"Moonlit plum tree—

wait,

spring will come."

— Matsuo Basho

WOLF RIVER GENERAL STORE

Audry Anderson finished filling the cooler with beer, most of it was the Fairbanks brewed Borealis brand shipped up on the train. She always kept some imported Nippon Star on hand for the occasional Japanese or even more rare Chinese or Indian who might wander in with money and thirst in equal proportions. Her morning had been slow as expected.

When the temperature dropped below -40°F most people stayed home in front of their own stoves.

With a blast of cold air a figure came through the front door and shut it quickly, stomping feet, and unzipping their parka.

"How's my favorite storekeeper?" a voice boomed out of the heavily frosted hood.

"Glen Bassett! Good to see you. You have any meat you can sell me?"

"Don't I always fill your needs before I go near the Nips?"

"Only the ones that involve wild game," she said with a laugh.

"Okay, I won't push that any further." He pulled off his parka and went over to the huge, glowing woodstove to slowly rotate in front of it while slapping ice crystals out of his heavy beard.

"Damn but it's cold out there."

"What are you bringing in this trip?

I have two moose, a few lynx, mess of rabbits, and four caribou.

How much do you want?"

"Two moose hindquarters and six to eight rabbits, depending on size. I still wish you'd lay off the lynx; I'll never buy them. You going back out soon?"

"In a couple of days. I need a good drunk. How much beer do you have?"

"As much as you want until you start breaking furniture."

"You say the nicest things to me. Anything of interest happening?"

"Suzuki's dead."

Glen's smile faded beneath the now-dripping moustache on his bearded face as he stared at her.

"What? How?"

"He stumbled through the door at the Livengood office, fell down, and died."

"Heart attack?"

"Don't know. They're doing an autopsy. But the word is he was shot or stabbed."

He glanced around the room. "We *are* alone in here, right?"

"Glen," she shook her head, "I would have let you know as soon as you walked in if we weren't."

"Sorry, Audrey. Sometimes my paranoia gets the best of me."

She made a fleeting, tired smile. "Just because you're paranoid doesn't mean they aren't following you."

He lost his grin. "Thanks for the reminder." He shook his head to shake the moisture off his beard and moustache.

"You're welcome."

"So is Gunther the Director of Personnel now?"

"Nope. They pulled in someone from the Livengood section. Levi Fischer. Ever heard of him?"

"What the hell! Gunther was next in line, dammit."

"Well, I'm sure if you explain that to the Japanese they will make everything the way you think it should be."

"Has he been vetted?"

"Partially, security will let us know the full story."

Glen frowned at her but she knew he was tossing the situation around in his mind. She felt that he said too many things out loud that he shouldn't, but after spending so much time in the bush alone the idea that someone might be listening rarely occurred to him.

"Have you met this Fischer guy?"

"No. He just got here yesterday."

Glen opened his mouth and she knew he was going to ask something she wouldn't answer. He must have come to the same conclusion because he shut it again. He edged closer to the stove and regarded her.

"Is this going to change our command structure?"

"Not to my knowledge. Keep in mind how recent his addition to the project is and that he hasn't been completely vetted yet."

Glen nodded. "How about a Borealis?"

"I thought you'd never ask."

CHAPTER 6

YUKON STATION

"HERE IS THE LATEST WORKER REPORT," TOMIKO WATANABE SAID, laying a sheet of paper on Levi's desk. "If you find any discrepancies please tell me at once."

"Thank you, Tomiko."

He bent over the typed list filled with figures. The first thing he noticed was a column heading "Death by Occupation" with numerous entries beneath it.

"Forty-two deaths in one month?" he said aloud, looking up at his secretary. "That's more than one each day!"

"Please note where they worked," she said quietly.

"Plant construction? I thought the plant had been constructed over a year ago."

"Perhaps part of it, Levi, but not all of it."

"Are these people working outside in the cold?"

"No. However, also notice that all are Chinese workers."

"Really?" He scratched his head. "There are no Chinese workers between here and Fairbanks. Why are there so many up here?"

"I suggest you ask Captain Atsumi. She can answer all of your excellent questions."

"You can't?"

Spots of color rose in each of her cheeks and she stared down at the floor before whispering, "I dare not, it is not my place." She bowed deeply and left his office at a brisk pace.

The day had begun just as poorly. He had reported to Captain Atsumi's office at 0900 and was told she had been called away on an urgent matter. After all of the mental anguish he had endured preparing himself for the visit he felt, in equal parts, both elation and despair.

Trying to understand the reports stacked on his desk further irritated him. Everything seemed overly compartmentalized. The power plant was a category unto itself and there was no data of any sort about the annex out of casual sight behind it.

Roads and Grounds Department, logically, was also a separate entity. The compound supporting the other two was the final entry. Only one death had occurred outside the power plant. All of the others had occurred within the huge structure.

What the hell is killing so many people here?

His phone rang and he jumped at the shrill sound before he gathered his concentration and answered.

"This is Fischer."

"By now you have many questions for me, yes?"

"Very prescient, Captain Atsumi. Yes, I indeed have questions as well as needing a more complete overview of the operation here."

"Come up to my office and I will explain all." She hung up.

He sat for a few moments to gather his thoughts as well as calm his jumbled emotions. All of his adult life he had hidden behind numbers, personnel numbers, supply numbers, quotas, they had become friends he could literally count on. Therefore waste irritated him and the deaths of so many workers seemed extravagant to the point of criminal. However, he knew he must approach the situation with finesse; he must never lose sight of his professional and personal limits in this place.

She met him at the door of her office. "Please have a seat. May I offer you something to drink?"

"No, thank you." Her conciliatory manner immediately called for caution on his part. He didn't know her and wished to take no undo liberties with protocol or female Japanese temperament.

She sat down in the other guest chair rather than behind her desk, carefully crossed one leg over the other, and gave him a soft smile.

"I apologize for not being in the office this morning as planned."

"An apology is not necessary. I understand there must be many other tasks requiring your time."

"True, but you are my number one priority at the moment."

"I am honored, but in what way?"

"You have been thrust into a situation of which you know nothing. My task is to bring you up to optimum operational level as swiftly as possible."

"I see. Perhaps you could clear up a number of puzzlements I have already encountered."

"Such as?"

"What is the function of this place?"

Her soft smile withered and died.

"What do you think it is?"

"I really have no idea. As I mentioned yesterday, my previous position required me to insure adequate laborers and supplies to keep the railroad operational between Fairbanks and the border of Yukon Station. Beyond that I never inquired, nor was informed, as to the nature of Yukon Station."

Something flashed in her eyes and she looked away for a moment.

"You have been given Lotus clearance. That means you have been deemed worthy to understand and protect the true nature of this project. Your training begins now with the understanding that everything you hear in this room is classified and not be shared with *anyone* else."

"Excuse me, I have changed my mind."

She sucked in her breath and stared at him in shock. "What do you mean?"

"Could I have a glass of water, please?"

She relaxed and nodded to the pitcher and two glasses on her desk. "Help yourself."

He drained a full glass.

"Please continue, Captain."

"The government of Germany has not shared its impressive technical advances with the Empire of Japan. They developed atomic weapons with which they ended what your people called the Second World War. They have people living on the moon, and they have briefly visited Mars. If we had not developed jet engines at the same time they did, and had to depend on the Reich for them, we would still be flying only reciprocating engine aircraft.

"Japan has worked diligently to lift her client nations out of the shards of global conflict without any assistance from her allies in that conflict. It is an onerous and on-going process."

"Did they promise assistance during the war?" Levi asked.

"They promised many things that have since been conveniently forgotten. Technological assistance is merely one of the items not forthcoming."

"How does this information figure into our discussion?"

"The Empire has started programs of its own. Programs that, were the Germans to discover their true nature could cause a third world war."

"What kind of programs?"

"Atomic energy. Atomic weapons."

Astonishment hit him between the eyes as hard as if it had been a physical blow. Levi felt the blood drain from his face to the point he suddenly felt faint.

"Here?" he whispered, spreading his hands.

"What better place? We are deep inside Alaska Prefecture where, other than the small legation in Anchorage, the German government has no official status. We are also on a railway which takes cargo and passengers to one of the largest Imperial Army air bases in North America."

He immediately visualized himself in the middle of the biggest bullseye in the world. If the Germans learned of the project they would instantly atomize the whole Interior of Alaska. A wave of terrific pain welled up in his chest and he pressed on it with both hands and groaned.

Years of hiding, subterfuge, and evasiveness came to a violent, pulsating head that continued to swell. Since the age of ten he had tiptoed through life like a mouse sneaking past a huge, Nazi cat. Now the Japanese had thrown him into the world spotlight of what people referred to as the "Quiet War" between the Axis partners.

"Are you ill, Mr. Fischer?"

His vision dimmed and Captain Atsumi's voice swelled into a roar in his ears. The pain ripped further into his chest, bursting the essence of his fear, and he vomited pain through a howl.

"Arrrggghhhh!"

Captain Atsumi grabbed her phone and spat Japanese into it. Levi caught the words for "medic" and "immediately."

The pain abruptly receded and his head cleared with the

suddenness of a thunderclap. An even more intense shaft of reasoning had penetrated and enlightened his thinking.

"It's okay," he gasped. "Truly, I am fine."

She pulled the phone away from her ear while staring at him, said, "Cancel that request, it is nothing," in a low tone before hanging up.

"Would you mind explaining what I just witnessed, Mr. Fischer?"

"I don't know if I can. I'm not sure myself."

"Have you had seizures prior to this?"

The world had become crystalline and completely transparent. Years ago there had been an acquaintance that used morphine in excessive amounts, claiming it gave him release from the trials and tribulations of a mundane world. One day the man was found dead of an overdose and Levi's first thought was that his friend was now free of all fears.

Suddenly he understood that incredible, total lack of fear-chained inhibition. He further realized that his days probably numbered fewer than he previously thought, and he didn't care. He also knew that this might be something he should not share with the captain.

"It wasn't a seizure, Captain Atsumi. It was an epiphany." He smiled into her face and held her gaze with his own.

The surprise in her eyes slowly gave away to speculation and more personal interest in him than previously demonstrated.

She blinked first. "What is the crux of your epiphany?"

"That I am but the plaything of forces beyond my control and only perceived compliance on my part truly matters."

"Very Zen. However, that could be a very dangerous philosophy."

"This is true, but I no longer care. Tell me, what is the nature of my duties and how much must I honestly accomplish in order to create the illusion I am competent. Give me those answers and I will forever be in your debt."

"You frighten me, Mr. Fischer! I have no idea if this office is monitored or not. What you are espousing is at the very least sedition—"

"No. It is not sedition. It is brutal honesty and I understand why that is so difficult for you to recognize."

"I see. Go and put on your cold weather gear, we are going to tour the areas for which you are responsible while we talk."

Levi wondered if this new attitude had also given him the gift of knowing what others thought. She wanted them out of the building before continuing the conversation one further paragraph. He grinned and hurried back to his office.

Tomiko looked up when he hurried through her office into his own. "Is there a problem, Levi?"

"Yes, but there is nothing we can do about it at this point," he said in a cheerful tone. He grabbed his parka and went back through the outer office. "I will be touring the facility with Captain Atsumi. I don't know when we'll be back."

The thermometer next to the entrance sat frozen at -35°F but it didn't feel any warmer than it had the day before. Captain Atsumi pointed to a late model Toyota pickup and he slid into the passenger seat. It started immediately and she turned the heat and vent fan full blast.

"This posting is very important for me," she said without preamble. "I am the *first* female officer in the Imperial Japanese Army. Some of my superiors believe I impinge on the honor and tradition of the IJA.

"They all hope that I fail in my duties. There are now more women in the ranks, but I am the banner bearer. Also, a security position on a Lotus-class base pushes one ahead of the other junior officers."

"Even if it kills you?"

"I will not fail, which means you must not fail, either. I am your direct supervisor; your career is in my hands. This is not a job from which you want to be dismissed."

"Ten minutes ago that would have frightened me into agreeing with anything you said. However, I no longer care."

"You are an intriguing man, Mr. Fischer. You evolved from a mouse to a wolf in the space of two sentences."

"That is the perfect word: sentence. I have come to the realization that I am doomed. My position here in Yukon Station is my final sentence. My execution is only a matter of time."

"Until now I thought the Japanese were the most nihilistic race on the planet. What is your lineage?"

He barked a laugh that created a large cloud in front of his face. The vehicle cabin had yet to warm up.

"You work with the Kempeitai and you don't already know the answer to that question?"

"Not many people make me feel ignorant, yet you are doing an excellent job of it today." Her eyes narrowed to slits and her voice sharpened. "Please answer the question."

"I'm a Jew! Not a practicing one, but a Jew by blood and birth. If you were to hand me over to the Germans I would be dead within twenty-four hours. We are as hunted as the American bison were, and once shared the same multitudes. Look where they, and the Jews, are today. I was waiting for mounting Jewish heads on German walls to become fashionable, but now it's too late since we are nearly as extinct as the bison."

"Are not a few in zoos?" she asked in a small voice.

"Which, bison or Jews?"

"Bison!" she snapped.

"Damned if I know, and damned if I care."

"You sound intoxicated as well as impertinent."

"I feel intoxicated. Drunk on tragic reality."

He felt emotionally light to the point of being weightless. The sensation was not at all unpleasant and he wondered why it had taken this long for him to come to the realization of his guaranteed doom.

"Would you like to survey the areas under your responsibility?"

"Sure. Why not?"

She showed him the rail yard and the huge maintenance building with three sets of tracks running through it. Two sets of tracks went through the two-meter fence topped with something she called razor wire and were guarded by two armed sentries at each of the gates.

"Why such ample security inside already ample security?" he asked.

"Any high ranking person may visit the outside of that fence. Inside is the heart of the project."

"You are protecting it from other Japanese? I don't understand."

"Do you understand the concept of *han*?"

He shook hid head.

"It can be translated as clan, but not the way it is perceived by a *gaijin*, a foreigner. The Imperial Army is the *han* of all of its officers and enlisted soldiers. Loyalty to the *han* is the most important element in our lives after the *on* we owe the Emperor. The Imperial Navy, such as it is," she made a quick smile, "is also a *han*. Do you understand?"

"So a *han* is like a professional organization? If you are in the army you are automatically part of its han?"

"It is deeper than a mere trade union. It is a combination of family with professional loyalty which includes an emotional aspect you wouldn't understand."

"I think I understand," Levi said, wondering why he had never before heard of these things.

"This project does not meet with universal approval. There is a rather large faction of government officials who believe the project is a huge mistake in many ways. They are not without power, or spies, and they are not part of our *han*."

It never occurred to me that they would have factions of their own to deal with.

"Where did Mr. Suzuki fit into this puzzle?"

She cut her eyes away from the road for a moment and regarded him briefly before looking forward again.

"That has yet to be determined."

"Is the Kempeitai also split on the soundness of the project?"

"The Kempeitai is part of the Imperial Army, part of our *han*. Of course there are no dissidents within our ranks. We see this as a *yogei sakusan*, a decisive battle that will change everything."

"It will do that for sure," Levi said. "But who wins is still up for debate."

Captain Atsumi gave him a hard look and pointed through the windshield.

"See those buildings on the other side of the fence?"

The interior of the vehicle had warmed comfortably and the windows had finally cleared of frost. He regarded the rows of identical buildings and nodded.

"Yes, I see them."

"Those are the worker's barracks, where the Chinese conscripts live. Most Americans call them 'Chinks.'"

He stared for a moment then said, "As long as they can socially look down on someone else the average American is a contented person. Most would sell their mother for a good meal or more money in their pay check."

"You are a very bitter man, Mr. Fischer."

"Perhaps. Could you find out something for me?"

"What?" Her guarded tone nearly made him smile.

"Could you find out if Joanna Fischer still lives in Grand Island, Nebraska?"

"That's in the Greater German Reich—"

"I know that. Can you do it?"

"Probably, but not without causing more diplomatic ripples than I care to generate on behalf of one of your whims. Your ebullience might see you dead yet today! Do not forget your place or some minor functionary will test his virgin sword on your neck."

He smothered the first retort that came to mind with the cold realization that she was correct. There had to be a façade of subservience constantly maintained or he could easily die without German assistance.

"My apologies, Captain. I have been so overcome with my new view of life that I actually jeopardize it. Thank you for being so lenient."

"Are all Americans as facile as you seem to be?"

"I honestly don't know. We are an intelligent people and we do not forget a slight. However, there are many apologists among us who tone dangerous rhetoric down to a barely audible buzz."

"It must be unbearable to be a defeated nation. We Japanese have never known defeat throughout our history."

"Yet," Levi blurted.

Captain Atsumi glared at him again. "Do not forget your place, Mr. Fischer! We firmly believe that no other race is the equal of the Japanese and this is why we have persevered and conquered all peoples bordering on the Pacific Ocean."

"How do you supermen explain away the fact that Nazi atomic bombs won the war for you? Does that make the Germans equal to the Japanese?"

"I suggest you keep your questions to areas that concern you and your position here and now." Color had risen in Captain Atsumi's face, anger glistened in her eyes, and her voice held a new edge.

"I assume the power plant is where nuclear fission experimentation is being conducted and perfected."

"Yes."

"The annex is even larger. What are they doing in there?"

"Unfortunately I cannot disclose that information to anyone."

He searched her face, seeking signs of deceit and found only embarrassment. Her recent anger had completely evaporated.

"Who can tell me?" he asked in a subdued tone.

"That information is to be disclosed only by those with a security clearance higher than mine."

"So there is a clearance higher than Lotus."

"Two, actually; Chrysanthemum and Imperial. Only three people here are cleared for Imperial. I have no idea how many carry Chrysanthemum, since that is also classified above my clearance."

"Who handles manpower needs in the annex?"

"All I know is that it is not you."

"Okay, so much for work. Where do I purchase my food and other articles of living?

"We have a commissary but it is woefully inadequate and the food barely ranks above atrocious. There is a general store in Wolf River operated by a Negro woman that is surprisingly well stocked and a lodge where excellent meals can be had, all are much more expensive than the commissary, of course."

"The Indian village isn't off limits?"

"Wolf River? No, any of us can go there. I know that all the non-Chinese workers patronize the store and the lodge as well as a few Japanese."

"Are you one of those patrons?"

"Sometimes."

"How many Chinese laborers are currently on Yukon Station?"

"I don't know. However, I do know that we have over 300 at our disposal, so it's more than that."

"How do you personally feel about the project?"

"We all serve the Emperor, Mr. Fischer, and I suggest you do the same."

"You haven't answered my question, Captain."

"Which question?"

"Tell me the nature of my duties and how much I honestly must accomplish in order to create the illusion that I am competent."

She laughed. "Keep the railroad running efficiently, the runways and roads maintained. Do not snoop into areas where you have no need. Become a proficient agent for the Kempeitai."

"That last one. I have absolutely no idea how to achieve that goal. The rest is a lead pipe cinch."

"A what?"

"A situation I guarantee will happen."

"But, lead pipe? I don't understand the term."

"We Americans are an inscrutable race," he said with a grin. "However, I am not, nor ever have been, a secret police agent."

"You will learn, Mr. Fischer. I shall see to that."

CHAPTER 7

"On this road

where nobody else travels

winter nightfall."

— Matsuo Basho

WOLF RIVER VILLAGE, ALASKA PREFECTURE

"Why were you not the successor of Mr. Suzuki?" Doubtful Thomas sipped his tea.

"I don't know," Gunther Charles stared at the glowing wood stove. "I really thought I would be selected for the job. I was next in line."

"Have you met this Fischer person before?"

"Yeah, a couple of times. He blends into the woodwork he's so quiet. You'd think he was hiding."

"Perhaps he is. What do you know about him? Is he part of our group?"

"I don't know much about him and, no, he's not part of our group to my knowledge. He's been on the job longer than I have, but always farther south. He was the assistant down in Livengood. His boss had a heart attack a few weeks ago."

"Heart attack? Did they examine the body to determine that?"

"No idea. The Japanese took over and I'm not about to ask them anything."

"Do you think he will work with us?"

"I don't know, Doubtful. What little of him I've seen hasn't given me many hard facts, I honestly don't know what makes the guy tick."

"We have to tread very carefully now. The Japanese may suspect something is in the wind and this Fischer person could be a plant. Have we heard from any of those inside the project?"

"No." Gunther drank the last of his tea and peered into the cup. "I'm not sure they are alive. It's been over a week since any of them reported in."

"If they were apprehended, I hope they used their cyanide pills."

"Chin would have. She lived in total dread of being discovered. I don't know about the other two, they're pretty stoic."

They sat for a moment in silence.

"I think I should invite the new foreman to dinner," Doubtful said. "What do you think?"

"You're the Chief of Wolf River so you can do anything you want on a social level."

"Yes," Doubtful said, finishing off his own cup of tea. "I think I'll have Mr. Fischer over for dinner. When can you arrange it?"

"How about I just bring him over and you invite him to dinner?"

"I would like that."

CHAPTER 8

YUKON STATION

WHEN LEVI ENTERED HIS OUTER OFFICE THE NEXT MORNING, GUNTHER Charles sat in the guest chair chatting with Tomiko Watanabe. Both stilled when they saw him. Levi shut the door behind him and Gunther shot to his feet.

"Mr. Fischer, I am so sorry I couldn't be here yesterday. I was in the field."

Levi stared at him for a moment and then wordlessly nodded toward his private door. Gunther held the door for him. As he divested himself of his outerwear Levi studied Gunther openly. He slid into his chair and pushed the intercom button.

"Miss Watanabe, would you please bring us some tea?"

As soon as he heard the outer office door close he stared into Gunther's eyes. He knew they had met prior to this, but then it had not been important to take stock in Gunther Charles. Now it might matter a great deal.

Gunther gave all indications of being a capable man. Levi wondered if he could trust him.

"Have a seat, Mr. Charles. What were you doing in the field at minus forty degrees?"

"I was inspecting railroad crossings. They tend to fill with snow and ice. We've had a few trains derail. So I check them every other day and get a crew out to clean them if needed."

"That makes sense. I freely admit I don't know all the intricacies of maintenance yet. Why did Mr. Suzuki go to Livengood?"

"I have no idea. He is, uh, was, Japanese and questioning their actions can be bad for one's career."

"He didn't tell you anything?"

"Only that he was going south and planned to be back the next day."

"Any idea why someone would murder him?"

"Not really. He was a pretty quiet person and kept to himself."

"Why didn't they give you his old job?"

Gunther laughed. "I have been wondering the same thing. I thought I was the most logical choice."

Levi grinned. "I happen to agree with you and I admit that this *promotion* is not only unwelcome, it scares the crap out of me."

Gunther's face radiated instant disbelief. "*Scares* you? Why?"

"I think I am a pawn in a game with no rules, at least any rules I understand. My predecessor was murdered. To top it all off, just yesterday I discovered this station is a secret military project that even some Japanese don't want to succeed. Further, if the Germans get wind of this project we will all probably end up atomized. I don't want to sound too much like a madman, but you bet your ass I'm scared."

"You make some good points, Mr. Fischer. I—"

"That's another thing. Unless there is a Japanese officer above the rank of major present, I am Levi. Okay?"

"Works for me, whatever you wish, Levi. How much did they tell you about the project?"

"That it is really a nuclear power plant and they are developing a bomb."

"That's it?"

"There's more?"

"How about we go for a ride?"

"Right after we drink our tea."

Once it was served, neither man finished their cup.

Gunther Charles owned a large four-wheel-drive Mitsubishi truck complete with a heavy-duty winch mounted on the front of the chassis. Once they slammed the doors against the bone-numbing wind Levi looked over at Gunther.

"Does the damn wind ever stop?"

"Oh yeah. Sometimes it's so still you can hear a moose fart two valleys away."

"I'll look forward to that. What do you want to tell me that you don't want the Kempeitai to know?"

"You're learning fast. There's someone I want you to meet. In fact, he wants to have you over for dinner."

"As a guest or as the main course?"

Gunther laughed. "Guest, Athabascans aren't cannibalistic."

"Who is this person and why should I go?"

"Doubtful Thomas. He's the head man of Wolf River village."

"Doubtful?"

"His mother was a very religious woman and wanted to name him after an apostle."

"I thought it was 'Doubting Thomas.'"

"I understand her hearing had never been good, and that's how she heard it. It's too late to bring it up anyway; she's been deceased for over twenty years."

"Why should I go?"

"You need all the friends you can get, that's why."

"Okay, I accept. Now tell me what else is going on here that I don't already know about."

"What do you know about the Annex?"

"Absolutely nothing. Even my boss, Captain Atsumi, won't tell me what they are doing in there."

"Atsumi is your boss?" A lewd smile slid across his face.

"Yes." He studiously ignored the man's expression. "What are they doing in there?"

"Even though you have worked out of Livengood for years, I need to know more about you than the fact that you aren't Japanese. Where are you from down in the states?"

"Nebraska. Came to Alaska in '49 when I was fourteen years old."

"With your parents?"

"Alone."

"Alone? Why?"

"I was living with my aunt in Colorado and a friend of hers offered me a job up here for the summer. I've been here ever since. I'd lived with my aunt since '45 when the Germans were on their way and my mother wanted me safely west of the Rockies."

"Safe, from the Germans? I don't understand."

"I'm Jewish."

"Why didn't she come with you?"

"She promised my dad she would wait for him in Nebraska. We didn't know if he was alive or dead. Now I don't know if either of them are alive or dead."

"Damn, and I thought I had it rough." Gunther stared into his eyes. "The Japs are building a rocket in the Annex."

"A rocket? What kind of rocket? For what?"

"They want to establish a moon base of their own."

"Seriously? What the hell for?"

"Because the Germans did it. That is the only conclusion I can come to. I really don't know. But just knowing about it can get you dead in an hour, so keep it to yourself."

"How do you know this is true?"

Gunther's face lost all humor. "How about we wait and see if we are both alive tomorrow? Nothing personal, but I didn't get this far by taking anyone at face value."

"Works for me." *At least I know he's not an over talkative idiot,* Levi thought.

While they talked Gunther had driven out of the project area and down a road paralleling the Yukon River. The surface of the river looked tortured and impassable, yet out in the middle ran a smooth pathway barely visible between up-thrusts of ice.

"Is that a trail?"

"Yeah," Gunther said. "Indians run dog teams from village to village down the Yukon."

"This is my first real look at the river. How thick is that ice?"

"At least twelve feet. Sometimes they drive trucks on it."

The came up behind an Imperial Army lorry and Gunther reduced his speed. A few hundred meters later the truck turned down a side road toward the river.

"Where are they going?"

"It's time for shift change on the anti-aircraft gun emplacements," Gunther said.

"Gun emplacements? Why would they have manned anti-aircraft up here?"

"Y'know, Levi, I could never figure out a good enough reason to ask about it from someone who would know. We suspect they are here to guard the Project. What's interesting is that besides the Japanese, and the bush pilots, the only other people with aircraft are the Germans, and they are allied with the Japs."

They passed a small house of which the south side lay completely covered with a snowdrift starting at the north side of the roofline. More houses appeared out of the blowing snow and Gunther pulled up in front of a much larger building, most of what had been a huge drift had been removed.

"This is the Wolf River Lodge."

They climbed out of the truck and bent into the wind, trudging through blowing snow to the door. Just as they got to the door it swung open and Levi followed Gunther into the dim interior. They immediately stamped the snow off their feet and opened their parkas. The door slammed shut behind them and warmth quickly dissipated the cold fog.

"You're in luck. I just got the tea water to a boil," a cheerful voice said.

Levi pulled his hood back and glanced around while taking off his parka. The room seemed cavernous when compared with other log buildings he had seen in Alaska. In the middle of the room, radiating massive amounts of heat, sat a huge wood stove with "U.S. ARMY" cast into the iron front above the door. On the flat surface above the door a teakettle whistled shrilly.

The atmosphere in the room hung rich and redolent with the odors of cured moose hide, elusive herbs, gun oil, and a hint of ozone left over from the outside frigid air. It was the most nasally exotic room Levi had ever experienced and he loved it.

"Doubtful," Gunther said, "I would like you to meet Levi Fischer. Levi, this is Doubtful Thomas."

Doubtful stepped forward with a smile that displayed good dental hygiene and shook Levi's hand. His rather ragged hair was mostly white interlaced with bits of dark here and there. Lines had been carved into his face from decades of long subarctic winters and his dark eyes sparkled with intelligence.

"So this is the guy that got your job, huh?"

"Well, that's one way of looking at it," Gunther said with a wide smile.

Levi smiled grimly and nodded. "I was quite content with the job I had, to be honest."

"Are you both staying for supper?"

"You're not cooking, are you?" Gunther asked as if alarmed.

"My word, no. Thelma is cooking tonight."

Levi frowned questioningly at Gunther whose smile returned even wider.

"Thelma is his youngest daughter. Both she and Theodora are excellent cooks."

"Who inherited their skills from their late mother," Doubtful said as he crossed himself in the Russian Orthodox manner.

"Don't we have to go back to the office?" Levi asked, trying not to frown at Gunther yet again. This seemed far too enjoyable to be part of his job.

"You're on official business. Doubtful is the man to talk to for getting Indian laborers for whatever job you have in mind. Get used to the idea that you're one of the bosses. You don't have to ask permission for everything you do."

Despite the lack of any current projects demanding laborers that he knew of, Levi happily nodded. "Thank you for the viewpoint. I'm still new at this *boss* thing."

"You are an enigma, Mr. Fischer," Doubtful said as he poured tea for the three of them. "The Japanese picked you for a very important position here and yet I understand this is your first trip to Yukon Station?"

"How do you know so much about me?" Levi asked, feeling cautious yet desperate to affect an off-handed manner.

"There exists no communications system faster than the mukluk telegraph. Your record in Livengood is above reproach."

"Do you also know I have decided that I am a doomed man?"

"No, *that* is new information. How did you come to that conclusion?"

"Because the Germans are going to discover what is going on here and they will destroy all of it, probably with an atom bomb."

"You are an incredibly pessimistic person, sir. If you are that sure of destruction why don't you just cut your throat and be done with it?"

Levi laughed. "The thought has occurred to me, but I am also a very curious pessimist. I've paid for the ticket and I want to see what happens next."

Gunther regarded him with an odd expression. "Have you ever had a psychiatric evaluation done?"

"Gunther, in this place and at this time, I am probably one of the sanest people you can find. I firmly believe we are all doomed and the rest of you think everything is fine."

"He has a point there," Doubtful said.

They all drank tea.

The outer door swung open and a blast of cold air swirled across the room, fogging instantly. When the fog cleared, two young women carrying jute bags stood chatting and laughing. They had already pulled off their parkas when they noticed the three men.

"Oh, sorry, father," said the taller woman. "We didn't know you had a guest."

"You didn't see my beautiful truck out there, Teddi?" Gunther asked.

"Oh, we knew *you* were here, we just didn't know that you brought someone else." Both of the women smiled and Levi felt his heart lurch.

Doubtful didn't rise, but Levi did as the older man said, "Teddi, Thelma, this is Mr. Levi Fischer, the new head of manpower on the Yukon-Fairbanks Railway."

Teddi nodded and politely smiled. Thelma, smiling widely, stepped forward and extended her hand.

"Very pleased to meet you, Levi."

He caught the scents of jasmine, worked leather, and healthy woman: all equally intoxicating. He felt a physical attraction as compelling as gravity and, not having all that much experience with this sort of thing, allowed himself to be pulled in.

"And I am pleased to meet you, Thelma," he nodded to her sister, "Teddi."

Levi had been with few women over the past fifteen years after his first initiation into sex with an older woman in Anchorage. Her husband was in a German prison camp somewhere in Europe and she wanted be with a man who would appreciate her. Levi had very much appreciated her.

Despite infatuations here and there, including one memorable week at Denali Lodge with a visiting German hiker who wanted to experience as much of Alaska as she could, he had never fallen in love. Years ago he came to the conclusion that either love didn't really exist or perhaps he was one of those people unable to expend the necessary trust demanded by the condition. It remained merely a concept and he felt that it was behind him at this point in his life.

Suddenly his closely held beliefs evaporated as he smiled into

Thelma's wide, brown eyes while they shook hands. He realized he *did* give a damn and the realization intensified his sense of terror. The Kempeitai major's words sliced through his mind; *Being single and seemingly without family, the only hold we have over you is your very life.*

Despite the immediate attraction and yearning he felt for this young woman he knew he could not pursue the situation. It would not only potentially endanger him; it would also endanger *her*.

All of these thoughts cascaded through him in a few seconds. He went from astonished arousal to giddy realization and finally sorrowful avoidance in the length of a handshake.

He released her hand, lost his smile, and dropped back into his chair.

"Are you ill?" Gunther asked. "You've gone white as a ghost."

Levi made a weak smile. "I'm fine. Perhaps I stood too quickly."

Thelma's wide grin had settled into a wry smile and she continued to look at him while Teddi hurried off with their sacks of groceries.

"We were able to get a lovely moose roast from Audrey over at the store." Teddi's cheerful voice lit up the room. "Glen Bassett came through with a load of meat so this is very fresh."

Doubtful and Gunther both turned to look at Teddi as she chatted. Levi and Thelma still stared at each other.

"Will you be staying long, Levi?"

"In Yukon Station?"

"No. Here, tonight."

"Gunther and I are staying for the evening meal. Your father invited us."

"Oh, that's good." Her smile grew wider.

Levi felt he stood outside his body and watched as an observer rather than a participant in the interaction between himself and this lovely Athabascan woman. Even with his pathetically small hoard of experience with the opposite sex, he felt sure he detected a matching interest in him from her. He also felt torn in half and the two sides instantly warred with their negative twin.

Thelma glanced at his hand then refocused on his eyes. "You're not married?"

"No. Never was. You?"

"Gosh, no. I've never met anyone–"

"Thelma, you gonna help me in here or not?" Teddi called from the kitchen.

"Be right there!" she called. In a lower tone she said, "I'm very pleased you are staying for supper." She turned and walked toward her sister.

Levi refocused and found both Doubtful and Gunther regarding him with identical grins.

"Come on back to Earth, Levi," Gunther said.

"I believe you and my daughter have discovered a kindred spirit in each other."

"You have lovely daughters, Doubtful, but I am sure you knew that. Thelma does seem to be an extraordinary person." He picked up his tea with a trembling hand and drained it feeling frightened and exhilarated at the same time.

The meal, Levi later decided, was the best he ever ate. The perfectly herbed moose roast was medium rare, the baked potatoes (where did they get potatoes in the middle of winter?) were exquisitely al dente, and the freshly made bread seemed ethereal. Of course he realized the company had something to do with how much he enjoyed the meal.

Both of the Thomas daughters made the room brighter merely by their presence, and their rambling, high-energy table talk lifted his heart further than it had been in years. He could not remember the last time he had smiled, and laughed, so much. Then, just as they were all feeling full of camaraderie in their satiation, the door slammed open.

The usual gust of cold-fogged air swirled across the room and the door slammed shut. A figure wrapped in a beautiful parka, moose hide pants and carefully beaded mukluks staggered across the room toward them.

"Shit, I've gone and missed supper!"

"Glen?" Doubtful said, rising from the table and moving toward the man. "Are you drunk?"

"Oh, hell yes! I'm so drunk Audrey threw me out of the store! Did ya leave anything for me to eat?"

"I didn't expect you. I'm sure we can find something to soak up a bit of that beer."

"Hell, Doubtful, I've worked hard on this here drunk and I don't want to end it now."

"Well, my friend, it is either sober up or move along to some place else."

"You're throwing me out, *too?* I thought we was friends!"

"We are. I offer you hot coffee, good stew, and a place to sleep.

Nothing else."

Glen fell on his face and started snoring.

"I think he just needs a place to sleep, father," Teddi said with a judicious nod.

The good mood in the room had evaporated along with the fog of cold air.

"We need to be getting back," Levi said.

"Let's move Glen out of the way first, okay?" Gunther said. "You grab his feet."

They carried his surprisingly heavy weight into the closest room the lodge offered for visitors. They dropped him on the bed and Gunther began taking Glen's parka off.

"Pull off his mukluks and as soon as I wrestle him out of this we'll cover him with a blanket."

"Does he do this a lot?" Levi asked as he unlaced the footgear and pulled them off.

"Glen leads a solitary life. If he didn't have the bush he would probably be dead from drink by now. Don't get me wrong, he's a good man, but he has his weaknesses."

Levi wrinkled his nose. "He sure could use some clean socks!"

Gunther laughed, stood up straight and threw a blanket over the snoring man.

"Okay, let's get back to our hosts."

As Levi put on his cold weather gear, Thelma came up and helped him find the right lashings.

"I enjoyed having you here, Levi. Will you please come back and visit?"

He stared into her lovely dark eyes. "Do you really want me to?"

"Yes, very much. Please be careful."

He watched her move across the room and felt nearly suffocated by emotions unfamiliar to him. For the moment, fascination had trumped fear.

CHAPTER 9

FAIRBANKS,
ALASKA PREFECTURE

MAJOR KATSU MIAMATSU GRUNTED APPRECIATIVELY AS THE HOT WATER penetrated him to the bone. In the bath next to him Major Akio Sakura echoed the grunt.

"I appreciate this, Katsu," Sakura said in his gravely voice, "but I sense that you have an ulterior motive for this generous afternoon soak."

"You know me too well, Akio. However, all I wish from you is some information. A little bit of history."

"Pertaining to what?"

"The death of an American by the name of Mathieson."

Sakura turned his head to stare at his friend and colleague through the steam.

"Why are you asking about him?"

"I sense this is a touchy subject, but I believe it bears on an investigation I am conducting. You were the officer in charge of collecting the body, were you not?"

"You are twisting a dragon's tail, Katsu. The file on Mathieson has been given Chrysanthemum status."

"I do not wish to see the file. I only wish to know if the man indeed died a *natural* death."

"Well, I know his heart stopped. Doesn't that usually result in death?"

Miamatsu looked over to see Akio's grin. "So I have been told. Do you know what stopped his heart?"

Sakura glanced around the small room. As the door had not opened since their attendant left, Miamatsu thought the action telling.

"He appeared to have suffered a heart attack. However, the autopsy revealed an injection site on his neck and potassium chloride in his body. If you tell anyone I told you this it will mean both our heads."

"Who uses potassium chloride for assassination?"

"The SS, the Tokkō, and us. That completes the list, I believe."

"I would ask more questions but I do not wish to strain our relationship."

"Be careful, you are in the dragon's lair with this line of investigation. I would hate to lose you. Good drinking companions are difficult to find in this frozen place."

"I appreciate everything you have said. I will be careful."

CHAPTER 10

"If you're an oak
you don't pretend
you are a flower"
— Matsuo Basho

YUKON STATION

THE GROUP OF MEN STARED AT LEVI WHILE HE FERRETED OUT ELUSIVE words from his swirling brain. Their faces held nothing but a stoic "now what?" expression. A mixed lot, one large black man, a couple of Athabascan Indians, and four white men of whom one was definitely Italian and an Irishman. The other two were a toss up.

"I'm in over my head here," he continued. "I inherited a position that seems to be wider than my grasp. Because of that I ask each and every one of you to help me be a supervisor who can make a difference to you and your life.

"Any advice or pointers you can give me will be greatly appreciated. They surprised me with this job and not much choice about accepting it. I'm positive there were better choices.

"The one thing I can pledge is that if you give me an honest day's work every day, week after week, I will stand behind you and champion your needs as much as I am able. We are all in this together and that's how we need to face the world we live in."

More than a few of them nodded at his words and Levi felt the first flush of success he had experienced since arriving in this strange place.

"What happened to Suzuki?" The question seemed to come from the air itself.

"He's dead."

One of the beefier men shifted his stance, glanced over his shoulder and said, "Yeah, we know that." He had a slight Irish accent. "What happened to him?"

Levi shrugged mentally. "He was murdered in Livengood."

Most of them hadn't expected that answer. Some actually stepped back a pace with shock evident on their faces. Levi tried to memorize the faces of the three who didn't recoil.

"Did the Japs say that?" Levi couldn't tell who asked.

"I saw his body. Somebody had put holes in him, don't know how."

"They catch the murderer?" the beefy man asked in a more subdued tone. He had stepped back.

"No. Not yet."

"How was he killed?" a tall, thin-faced fellow asked.

"Either shot or knifed. He came into my office, fell down, and died. Now we are all on the same page as I know nothing further about the event than that."

"Why'd they give you his job?" the beefy man asked. His tone had altered from belligerent to curious.

"I wish I knew. Like I said, I feel that I am in over my head. I was the assistant down in Livengood until six weeks ago when my boss died. I was just getting used to being in charge there when they sent me up here."

"Sounds like somebody either really likes you or hates your guts!" the thin-faced man said.

Everyone, including Levi, laughed harder than the joke called for. It also broke the ice.

"You don't have to worry about us," the beefy man said. "We know our job and we've got yer back."

"What is your name, sir?"

"Timothy Keegan. I am the rail crew foreman. Mr. Charles is my boss." He nodded at Gunther who stood next to Levi.

"I really appreciate your help on this. I wasn't kidding when I said I was in over my head. The less I have to worry about the better."

"You from the territory originally?" Keegan asked.

"No. I lived in Nebraska until I was ten, then I came north."

Keegan nodded. Further inquiry into his background was pushing societal bounds, and everyone knew it.

"Thank you all for your time," Levi said, forcing a smile he didn't feel. "I really do appreciate it."

As one, they all turned and wandered back through the cavernous shop, stepping over two sets of rails between huge sliding doors. On either side of the building squatted large pot bellied stoves demanding constant attention. Off to one side sat a dismantled steam engine in the middle of the rebuild process.

The atmosphere lay heavy with the odors of bearing grease, wood smoke, and massive, cold metal. Despite the obvious insulation on walls and sliding doors, errant puffs of cold air randomly penetrated the area. Yet the overall feeling Levi had in this building was strength.

I'll have to sort that one out later, he thought.

"You ready to go, boss?" Gunther asked.

"Yeah, what's next?"

"I need to give you a tour of the Project Building. After that you're on your own."

"How long have you been here?"

"Hired on to the Project in '60 and worked in Fairbanks for two years, then got promoted to this job in late '62."

"Going on five years," Levi said. "I can see why everyone thought you would get this job."

"Including me," Gunther said with a quick laugh that could have been interpreted as a bark.

"You might still get it." Levi nodded toward the door and pulled his parka hood over his head. "Let's get this over with."

They pushed out into the frigid, windy afternoon.

CHAPTER 11

"Come, butterfly

It's late—

We've miles to go together."

— Matsuo Basho

KEMPEITAI HEADQUARTERS
YUKON STATION

"Yᴏᴜ ʀᴇqᴜᴇsᴛᴇᴅ ᴍʏ ᴘʀᴇsᴇɴᴄᴇ, Mᴀᴊᴏʀ Sᴜᴍᴍᴀᴛsᴜ?"

"Yes, Captain Atsumi. Please take a seat."

She straightened from her three-quarter bow and primly sat on the wooden chair.

"How may I serve the major?"

She kept her tone military and official, yet she knew it affected him more than that. She was the only young Japanese woman north of Fairbanks. She dared not show a hair's width more attention to any one man here over any other, as the results would be disastrous for her career.

"It is time to begin training Mr. Fischer in the fine art of investigation. He has had a week to meet all of the personnel under his direction and we must forge his resolve before his attitudes harden."

"Other than what I have already done, how should I proceed with his education?"

"First, discover what he already knows. Keep in mind that what we really need is a spy, not an investigator. Try to infuse a sense of Bushido into his being. Above all, we must keep him sufficiently motivated throughout."

Captain Atsumi's face allowed a slight smile to surface before regaining control.

"I firmly believe he knows nothing other than his job of adding numbers and making the columns balance. Fear has always proven to be an excellent motivational tool."

Major Summatsu awarded her a quick nod.

"The fact that he is a Jew in an anti-Semitic world is at the core of his psyche. Self-preservation dictates he keeps this fact secret. Use the threat of extraditing him to the Gestapo only as a last resort."

"Do you think he would actually call our bluff?"

The corners of Major Summatsu's mouth twitched once, the closest thing to a smile as she had ever seen on his face.

"Of course he wouldn't. He is a rabbit."

"I will begin his training tomorrow morning."

"Keep me apprised of his progress."

As she left the office, Captain Atsumi wondered why she had not told the major of Fischer's nihilistic attitudes and statements. Retaining that observation of his mental make-up might give her an edge over her superiors in the future.

Perhaps I am guilty of amae, *anticipating unofficial indulgence on the part of Levi Fischer. This makes me a conspirator*, she decided. The thought gave her a secret thrill of pleasure mixed equally with apprehension.

CHAPTER 12

"Come, see the true
flowers
of this painted world."
— Matsuo Basho

YUKON STATION

AFTER PASSING THROUGH THE FIRST GUARD POST, LEVI KEPT HIS IDENTITY card in his hand. It saved time.

He and Gunther had finally progressed to the outer door of the huge project building.

"Papers!" the Japanese corporal snapped while the alert private flanking the door kept his machine-gun pointed at the ground in front of them.

The corporal examined their documents carefully and then handed them back.

"Please to sign here," he said in a heavy accent.

He stepped to the side to reveal a small desk with an open ledger and a ballpoint pen. They signed their names, recorded the time of entry, and in the space for "Reason for Entry" both wrote, "Inspection."

The corporal read the ledger and looked up at them. "Wait here." He turned and walked through the door.

The passageway between the front arctic entry and where they now stood was marginally warmer than outside. Levi shivered and pulled his parka tight again. He had anticipated a great deal more warmth by this time.

The door opened and a sergeant major walked in, trailed by the corporal.

"I am Sergeant Major Fukita. I am the senior non-commissioned officer at Yukon Station and in charge of security. What, exactly, do you plan to *inspect*?" His English was so perfect that Levi felt each word had been chiseled from granite and then flung at them in sentences.

He felt an overwhelming urge to bow to the man but also knew he was probably superior to him in status. His stomach churned with indecision.

"Sergeant Major Fukita, I am the new head of personnel for the project railroad. My assistant," he nodded, "Mr. Charles, is giving me a tour of the project so I may better perform my tasks."

"Then you are merely *observing*, not *inspecting*. Is that not the case Mr. Fischer?"

"That is true."

"Very well. Corporal Shogi will accompany you while you are in this building." He vanished back through the door.

Levi felt his sphincter relax.

"Right," Gunther said. "Let's get on with it." He walked past the corporal and pushed through the door. Levi followed closely.

Corporal Shogi kept exactly a meter between his wards and himself. He also pointed his machine gun at the floor between them, his arms and hands anything but relaxed.

"This part of the building is safe in that you don't have to wear a radiation suit." Gunther waved expansively at the large hallway whose walls echoed their steps. "Up there, where there are red lights over the doors, it is lethal to enter if you are not protected."

Next to the door was a huge window where they stopped for the view. Levi noticed the window was made of very thick glass with five identical panes set in the frame separated about two inches from each other.

"The walls are lined with lead," Gunther said. "Nothing can leak out. This window has two panes that contain lead sheeting."

"Why can we see through it?"

"Ask the Japanese, it's a state secret."

They both glanced at Corporal Shogi who stared blandly back at them.

"How many people who work in this structure are part of my crew?"

"None, really. I wanted you to see what was in here in case you were ever asked to detail workers to these welcoming walls.”

"Gunther, I have come to the conclusion that you are dangerous."

"Levi, we are *all* dangerous! Right Corporal?"

Corporal Shogi's mouth bent in the semblance of a smile. "Of course you are. Why else would I be here?"

Gunther laughed and Levi smiled. He wasn't used to a Japanese soldier with a sense of humor, however slight.

Levi stared through the window where two people in bulky white coverings were carrying a third person.

"What's happening in there?" Levi asked.

"It is time to leave this place," Corporal Shogi said in a hard voice.

"I think we've seen all that we can here, Levi. Let's go find a beer." He carefully nudged Levi.

Levi didn't want to leave; he had questions. After further consideration he quietly followed his subordinate toward the door.

CHAPTER 13

WOLF RIVER GENERAL STORE

"I'D LIKE ANOTHER BEER," LEVI SAID.

Audrey popped the cap off another Borealis and sat it on the bar between them.

"That'll be a dollar, Mr. Fischer."

Levi pulled a grimy bill from his pocket and let it fall next to the beer.

"Even their money looks wrong," said Gunther with the hint of a slur in his voice.

"Everything about the Japanese is wrong. Same goes for the damn Nazis." Levi had perhaps imbibed more beer than was healthy. If the wrong person heard his words he would be dead within a week.

"Too bad there's nothing we can do about it," Audrey said, staring intently at Gunther.

Gunther returned her gaze and both turned to regard Levi.

"Would you ever consider doing something to weaken the Japanese up here?" Gunther asked.

Suddenly looking much more sober, Levi glanced from one to the other. "Are you two talking to *me*?"

"Yeah."

"There isn't much I could do other than sabotage the railroad. Then they would shoot me, fix the railroad and that would be that, but I'd still be dead."

"How about the project?" Gunther pressed.

"How the hell could I hurt that? They have massive security and are well armed. They would just kill me. This whole place is already doomed if the Nazis get wind of its purpose. Why hurry our deaths?"

Silence settled on the room for a time.

"What if you could help destroy their project once and for all?" Gunther all but whispered the words.

"Gunther, they own our damned world. They would figure it out and I, and anyone else involved, would face a long and painful death."

"They don't own the *whole* world!" Audrey said.

"True, they only own half and the Germans own the other half. Either way we'd all die."

"They don't own the bush, Levi!" Audrey snapped. "Out there they are lost and vulnerable."

"So am I," Levi said, finishing off the last of his beer. "I think I need to go home now. I have a big day ahead of me tomorrow."

"Consider being part of something that could change things. Think on it, okay?" Audrey said.

"Yeah, I'll do that. Thanks for the company. C'mon, Gunther. You're driving."

The door slammed behind them and Audrey poured herself a beer. She cleaned up the bar and carefully put the empty bottles in the wooden case in the back room. The brewery bought them back, cleaned, and refilled them.

"Damn it!" she said out loud. "If we can't win him over, we're going to have to kill him."

CHAPTER 14

WOLF RIVER LODGE

"Glen, you're gonna get someone killed, probably yourself, if you keep drinking so damn much."

"Don't gotta shout, Doubtful, I hear you loud and clear." Glen Bassett drank of the rest of his tea and held the cup up toward Teddi who refilled it. "And I've got a splitting hangover."

"Three-day drunks will do that to you. I'm surprised you didn't end up frozen in a snow bank."

"Thanks for seeing to my dogs. I really appreciate it."

"Thank Thelma. Once we saw your condition she went out and tended to them. They're staked out in the dog yard. You owe me about 32 pounds of dog salmon, so far."

"There was somebody else here when I barged in the other night, wasn't there?"

"Levi Fischer, the new personnel boss for the project."

"The *whole* project?"

"The part he knows. Actually, everything outside the security wire."

"Does he know what's going on in the annex?"

"No."

"Then he might be worth recruiting."

"Gee, why didn't *I* think of that?"

"Okay, Doubtful, you can cut the crap. I apologize for coming in here and acting like an asshole. I've been out there alone for over six weeks and I had to make up for it."

"*Had* to?"

"I *wanted* to. That all right with you, reverend?"

"We had him getting philosophical when you busted in here. In the long run maybe it's better that it happened. At least now he has something to think about and hasn't committed himself yet."

"Was that a long-winded way of saying 'You're forgiven, Glen?'"

"Sure, if that makes you feel better."

"What's he like?"

"He's complicated to say the least. When he first got to Yukon Station he was scared of being in the spotlight—"

"Why?"

"Don't interrupt me, dammit. Probably because he's a Jew."

"Oh, hell!"

Doubtful glared at him and plowed on. "Then he found out what they are doing up here and he sorta came unglued. Says he's in the middle of a huge bullseye and he's doomed no matter what, so he no longer gives a shit."

"His words?

"Yes."

"He's correct, you know."

"Of course he is. That's why we have a real opportunity here. A key to a heavily locked door."

"He can go places Gu–, er, others can't?"

"If not now, definitely later."

"How are you going to persuade him to our side *all* the way?"

"I think that's already in the works."

Glen waited. He rubbed his head and winced.

"Okay, you want to tell me how?"

"I would bet good money that he and Thelma are attracted to each other."

"Already?"

"When they saw each other it was like a load of firewood toppling over. The rest of the evening they stared at each other no matter what else they were doing."

"Well, he has good taste in women."

Doubtful's face softened and he made a wry smile.

"Sorry, Glen. I know you were interested in her, but I don't think *she* ever noticed."

"Yeah, you're right. Damn, I could sure use a beer!"

CHAPTER 15

YUKON STATION

"How would you recognise a saboteur, Mr. Fischer?" Captain Atsumi asked, standing in front of a blackboard.

Levi thought her question ludicrous.

"Big black beard and crazy eyes, holding a bomb?" He ventured a smile.

Captain Atsumi's face stiffened into a frown. "Do you find this a joking matter? We have one of the most important endeavors in all of history taking place here, and vigilance is of utmost importance. If you cannot find the maturity to address potential problems perhaps we made a mistake in bringing you up here."

He realized if they kicked him out of Yukon Station he was a dead man. He already knew too much. Her admonition a few days ago flashed through his mind, *"This is not a job from which you want to be dismissed."*

"I apologize for the levity, Captain. However, I have no idea how to recognize a saboteur."

Her frown dissipated and he continued, "I have deduced that you are a member of the Kempeitai and don't understand why you won't admit it."

"For this reason; to see if you would not only make that deduction but also if you would tell me when you did." She awarded him a wry smile.

"If saboteurs all did fit the caricature you mentioned our task would be much easier. Unfortunately, they look as normal as we do. You discover their hidden side by observing their actions.

"In a way you are in a perfect position to detect an enemy of the state. To carry out your public duties you are obligated to meet and learn the particulars of each of those employees who would have access to secure areas. Once you have met them you will have a working knowledge of their mannerisms and attitudes.

"If any of those things change you will be able to note them and alert your fellow Kempeitai agents so the person can be more closely observed. Quite simple, really."

"Why do you believe there is a saboteur here?"

"Three reasons. First was the murder of your predecessor, Mr. Suzuki. Second was the murder of your former supervisor."

"Barney Mathieson was murdered?"

"We believe so. After a careful examination of his work reports, personal habits, interests, and medical records we came to the conclusion if he indeed died of a heart attack, it was induced."

"The third reason?"

"Connected to the second; we have under close surveillance the functionary who ordered Mr. Mathieson's cremation."

"Why not arrest him and interrogate him?"

"Because he is a member of the Tokkō and we can't touch him."

"The Tokkō? I am not familiar with that organization. What is it?"

"The Tokkō, often referred to in the Home Islands as the 'thought police,' is responsible only to the Home Ministry, who in turn advises the Emperor. We Kempeitai are part of the Imperial Army, responsible to the Prime Minister, who in turn advises the Emperor."

"They have the same status level as the Kempeitai."

"Now you see the problem."

"How do we identify who is a member of the Tokkō and who is not?"

"The same way you identify a member of the Kempeitai; when they tell you so, or are wearing an arm band."

"Why is there bad blood between the Kempeitai and the Tokkō?"

"Politics. The Home Minister is an old man who has forgotten the underlying, inescapable basis of the Greater Pacific Co-Prosperity Sphere. There are many young Japanese who share his defeatist attitudes and would have Japan roll over and offer its placid belly to the Third Reich and any other threat that manifests itself now or in the future."

"They are against the Project?"

"Yes. We touched briefly on this subject in our first interview, the one where you experienced your epiphany."

"Go on."

"These are the Japanese who disagree with the avenue we have taken. They are a slowly growing minority, but a very vocal and powerful minority. Very little of this political discussion reaches North America. It is, to quote a quaint Americanism, 'a housekeeping' matter and we usually deal with it in the Home Islands."

"Yet we suffer the consequences here in the middle of Alaska."

"Alaska Prefecture is the only military controlled prefecture in the Empire of Japan. If we were to cause the Emperor a loss of face this all could change in the wink of an eye. We do not wish for his imperial eye to wink."

"I see. You are gambling on a man who has embraced his own extinction to save a military project that is probably already doomed."

"No!" She slapped the blackboard hard enough to shake dust from its surface. "This project is *not* doomed. It is a whole new beginning where the Empire can take its rightful leadership role in a modern world."

"Captain Atsumi, please forgive my impertinence, but I think you are more frightened than I am."

"We have spies, saboteurs, and assassins among us. We *all* need to be frightened. If whoever killed your predecessors decides *you* are in his way, no amount of levity will save you. You must discover who these people are before you become a target."

"Frankly, Captain, I am more frightened of the Greater German Reich and the Empire of Japan than I am of anyone skulking about around here. At least with a potential assassin I might see them first and be able do something about it. With the other two I am only a pawn.

"I will be alert for potential problems. However, I am but one man in a situation totally new to me. I can't promise I won't miss something."

"That will be adequate for now," she said. "Return to your duties."

CHAPTER 16

In the twilight rain
these brilliant-hued hibiscus...
A lovely sunset
— Matsuo Basho

WOLF RIVER LODGE

Thelma Thomas read through the terse wording carefully for the second time, letting her enthusiasm grow. No matter what her personal preferences, she had to get this right or a lot of people could die. Despite her fears, it was all good news.

The Livengood agent had sent everything available and all of it was positive. Smiling, she got up from the table and moved over to the large wood stove. In moments the report burned to ash and she stirred all the ashes together.

She allowed herself to dwell on Levi. What was it about him that she found so intriguing? She knew men in their scattered community who were more handsome, wealthy, and even more prominent. There had been something about him that had made her heart skip a beat when she first saw him.

All of her life she had been the cute, younger sister to the real beauty in the family. Thankfully it was not something that Theodora actually thought about, let alone flaunted. However, Thelma had realized her sister's beauty from an early age.

Young men had buzzed around Teddi like bees at a rose bush. Many, after Teddi gently turned them down, would then approach Thelma. She never gave them the time of day.

Was that it? Do I feel this way about him because he barely glanced at Teddi and focused his attention on me?

She liked to think that she was more mature than the concept made her feel, but it probably didn't hurt that he immediately warmed to her. Suddenly she felt her mother's presence and her heart swelled with emotion. Thelma had been twelve and Teddi thirteen when cancer took their mother.

The last thing she said to them was, "Take care of your father and each other." The memory brought tears to her eyes. Emily Thomas had been a beautiful soul, inside and out.

She had told her daughters to avoid men who held them back; that a woman could do anything she put her mind to and worked at it. She taught them how cook, butcher salmon and moose, split a moose hide and tan it to supple softness. Emily explained men and women to her girls in a matter-of-fact way.

They were functioning adults when she left, she had made sure of that. "There will be boys and men who will fill your ears with words and your minds with longing, but all they wish is to rut or treat you as a possession. The longings are real, they are natural, and they are hard to endure at first. The hard part is to wait for the right man."

"How will we know the right one when we meet him?" Teddi had asked.

"He will look into your eyes rather than stare at your body. He will ask you questions about yourself rather than boast of his deeds and ambitions. Most importantly, he will treat you as an equal."

Thelma remembered Levi getting lost in her eyes, and her attraction to him magnified. She fervently hoped he felt the same way. She thought he did, but certainty eluded her.

Someone tried the door–she had locked it while reading the report–and then knocked once, waited ten seconds and knocked three times. Thelma hurried over and opened the door to find her father smiling at her.

"Doing Pack work, lovely daughter?"

"Yes!" she said with a wide smile. "He's what he says he is. We can trust him."

"I think that might be more important to you than it is to me at this point."

"We'll see," she said and blushed. "He's an honest, good man."

CHAPTER 17

The summer grasses—
For many brave warriors
The aftermath of dreams.
— Matsuo Basho

SS HEADQUARTERS, NW BRANCH, FORT St. JOHN, DEUTSCHE COLUMBIA, GREATER GERMAN REICH

"OBERSTLEUTNANT HOFFMANN, WE HAVE A MESSAGE FROM OUR AGENT in Alaska Prefecture."

Deiter Hoffmann looked up from a subordinate's poorly written report, tired of laboriously wading through it, and gratified to have a distraction.

"Excellent news, Sturmbannfüher Zimmer! Has it been decoded yet?"

"Just now, sir. I brought it to you straight away."

The Sturmbannfüher stiffened to attention, his highly polished boot heels snapping together smartly, as he held out the red folder with the SS Death's Head emblazoned across it.

The Oberstleutnant took the folder and gave his subordinate a wry smile. "Do be at ease, Rudi. We are so *very* far from New York here, not to mention Berlin."

"Thank you, sir." He went to a stiff parade rest.

Hoffmann sighed and began reading the report. After a moment he glanced up at the Sturmbannfüher.

"You've received your top secret clearance, haven't you?"

"Of course, sir. Otherwise I could not have had physical possession of that message."

"True. Please sit down, I want two brains working on this one."

"My privilege, sir."

"You must keep in mind that our agent is rabidly anti-British and looks down upon the Japanese as an inferior race. To that end we have much in common."

Both men laughed.

He read the message out loud, "Japanese garrison less than 400 effectives. Fighter jets present. North perimeter poorly guarded. Jap progress close to what US had in late '44. Urge action sooner as opposed to later. Please advise if sabotage indicated."

Zimmer frowned. "Progress in *what*?"

Hoffmann stared at his subordinate and wondered if anything this dolt might say would be worth the effort of listening.

"They are building atomic weapons, Rudi. They are also building a rocket capable of carrying little yellow men to the moon."

"In Alaska?"

"How did you obtain this posting?"

"I, uh, was offered it, Oberstleutnant Hoffmann."

"What was your other *offer?*"

"North Africa."

Hoffmann realized he had made a mistake in accepting this idiot for his staff. He thought hard and fast.

Who recommended him? Strauss, it was Strauss. He must have still been angry about the Cuban thing. What a trusting fool I have been!

Erwin Strauss in Berlin had to have held an overwhelming grudge against him for nearly nine years to send this fool to such a sensitive post as this, no matter how inclement the weather.

"Thank you, Rudi, that will be all."

The Sturmbannfüher shot to his feet and saluted.

"Very good, sir." He performed a parade ground about face and left the office.

Now how do I get rid of him and obtain someone with a working brain?

He picked up his phone and hit three numbers.

"Georg? Deiter here. Can I have about an hour of your time? Right now. Thanks."

By the time Hoffmann read through the transcript again his door swung open.

Georg Hoyt filled any room he entered. The Nazi Party had used his full-length photo on a poster in 1955. They believed he epitomized the perfect Aryan male. At 6'7" with thick blonde hair, piercing blue eyes, and a physique honed from three hours in the gymnasium on a daily basis, he had the pick of any woman who saw him.

"How may I rescue you today, Oberstleutnant Hoffmann?" he said with a wide smile that displayed superb dental care.

"I merely seek your august opinion on a top secret matter, Oberstleutnant Hoyt."

"Really, top secret?"

One of the things Deiter appreciated about Georg was his ability to instantly focus on a situation. It also helped that he was an excellent strategist.

"Yes, top secret, Herr Superman. Here, read this."

Georg accepted the message and dropped into a chair while he read it.

"Where is this Japanese garrison? Progress in what?"

"Yukon Station, Prefecture of Alaska, is the first answer. Atomic weapons, is the second answer."

"Please open your map."

Deiter rolled the large map down until it covered the wall in his office.

"Right here. Note the only ways in are the railroad, the rudimentary road that parallels it, which both bottleneck through Fairbanks, and the runway for their rather large aerodrome."

"Or one could get there on the Yukon River." Georg briefly glanced at Deiter. "What is the timeline on this?"

"That is yet to be determined. We have a full battalion of SS *Fallshirmjäger* here and getting bored with arctic training. Paratroopers are not noted for their patience. Obviously speed is of the essence."

"Is New York or Berlin behind your plan?"

"This base was placed here in the frozen north to watch our little yellow allies. As far as I know the Reich is solidly behind our 'Instant Strike' concept. Yesterday a squadron of heavy transports was ordered here for arctic training.

"I have kept New York and Berlin informed of every step, every jot of intelligence gleaned, and it and they tell me nothing in return. However, they *are* building us up."

"Is your Alaska agent trustworthy?"

"As trustworthy as a spy can be. This one hates the British and thinks the Japs are sub-human."

"He sounds perfect to me. Who is your commanding officer?"

"Standartenführer Schwenkle down in Regina. He just became adjutant to Brigadeführer Baumann. Do you know either of them?"

"I know both of them, they are equally venal. Convince them that this will be the one episode in their careers that will outshine anything we did in the war and they will press New York and Berlin to back anything you want to do."

"You make it sound easy."

"It will be, you'll see. Both are incredibly arrogant men, pitiless as a Jüden money lender, and stupid as a Pole."

CHAPTER 18

Ungraciously, under
a great soldier's empty helmet,
a cricket sings
— Matsuo Basho

YUKON STATION

"HOW LONG HAVE YOU WORKED FOR THE YUKON FAIRBANKS RAILWAY, Mr. Smith?" The tall, gangly man was second to last of the long list of employees.

"Got hired as a heavy laborer in the spring of '59, coming up on eight years now. Did I do something wrong?"

"No, not at all, your work record is excellent. I just wanted to have a chat with everybody I'm responsible for. What is your job now?"

"I work in the maintenance shed as a pressure tank specialist. I always joke that I work under more pressure than anyone else." He made a toothy grin and Levi dutifully chuckled.

"And here I thought I had that record."

Smith laughed.

"What happened up here last fall? The train derailment, I mean." Levi kept his tone as nonchalant as possible.

Smith's grin dropped into a frown. "All I know is that one of the trains out of Fairbanks jumped the track and a bunch of chinks ran off into the woods. The wreck killed some of them, too."

"What do you think caused the derailment?"

"From what I could understand, there was some sort of frost heave that moved the track out of true, made it wider than the engine could handle."

"Was it cold enough for a frost heave to occur?"

"I'm no expert on that, Mr. Fischer. I know they happen every year and there ain't a darn thing you can do about them."

"How many Chinese do you think got away?"

"No idea. A bunch is all I heard. The Japanese didn't give me any numbers, if you know what I mean."

Levi leaned back and gave Smith a level stare. "I didn't think you had any official information. I was just wondering about rumors or hunches you might have had."

The corner of Smith's mouth twitched, and Levi suspected the next thing he said would be a lie. "I didn't hear nothing about numbers at the time. Didn't think much on it afterwards, neither."

That makes fourteen.

"Well, thanks for coming in. You won't be docked for the hour you spent here."

Smith's smile returned and he unfolded to his feet and shook Levi's hand. "Good luck up here, Mr. Fischer. We're all pretty impressed with you so far."

When the door shut Levi dropped into his chair. He felt exhausted, and wondered why Captain Atsumi wanted to know about numbers of Chinese hiding in the forest.

Hell, they're probably all frozen to death by now!

A soft knock sounded and he recognized it as that of Tomiko Watanabe.

"Come in."

She looked in and said, "The last man on the roads and grounds crew is still here, Levi."

"Oh, good, please send him in."

Levi stood before the man walked through the door. He stood taller than Levi, had handsome Athabascan Indian features and seemed very sure of himself. Most of the others had been slow to enter his office, but not this man.

"Mr. Fischer, I'm Eddie Hildebrand, from Nulato." He smiled and held out his hand.

Levi grabbed his hand and shook. *Why don't I remember him?* "Eddie, I'm Levi, okay? How long have you been on the crew?"

"It'll be a year next month. Why do you ask?"

"I don't remember seeing you before this."

"I kinda hung back when you came through the shop and I never got sent to Livengood for anything."

"Why did you hang back?" Levi lifted one eyebrow.

"I wanted to see you with the others first." Eddie shrugged and smiled.

"Why?" Levi's other eyebrow lifted.

"Well, to see if you were an asshole, mainly. Lots of new guys the Japs bring in tend to be assholes."

"That's reasonable," Levi said. "So what did you decide?"

Eddie grinned. "If you were an asshole I wouldn't still be here."

Levi laughed before he could stop himself. "Thanks for the vote of confidence, I appreciate it! You're a very direct man, I'm not used to that up here."

"From an Indian, you mean."

"No, from anybody. Only one other man on the roads and grounds crew was as direct as you are; *that's* what I meant."

"Sorry, I'm so used to hearing 'dumb Indian' remarks that I tend to take everything that way at first. I learned a long time ago that being direct saved me time and effort. Usually if someone has a question they already know the answer–or know what they want to hear."

"I'm somewhere in the middle there," Levi said. "I have questions but not answers, which is why I ask. You seem more sure of yourself than most of the crew and I suspect it might be due to education, right?"

'My father was headman at Nulato and my mother worked in the school, I didn't have any choice about getting educated by the nuns. And for the record, I am very grateful for *everything* that I learned, and not just what the nuns wanted to teach us."

Oh great, Levi thought, *he's a Catholic, just what a Jew needs.*

"Nulato, that's down closer to the mouth of the Yukon, isn't it?"

"Yeah, around here I'm a 'downriver Indian' and to me everyone here is an 'upriver Indian.'"

"Does that make a difference, what part of the river you're from? I've never heard anything about this before now."

"A hundred years or so ago some villages fought with other villages. It all got sorted out in the end. But the Yukon River is pretty long and there are a lot of villages that don't get as much salmon as others."

"Huh? I'm sorry, but what does that mean?"

"I should be the one apologizing; that's something my father told me. See, when the Russians came to Alaska two hundred or so years ago, they came up the Yukon River. The farther they went up river, the percentage of *exploring* Russians dropped down to almost nothing."

"So the fewer Russians that made it up river resulted in less influence over the villages," Levi said.

"They told me you were smart. It's my opinion that the villages at and near the mouth of the Yukon are distrusted by villages farther up." Eddie grinned.

Levi nodded.

Eddie continued. "When I was a teenager I realized that the people in my village had a subtle distrust for anyone from an upriver village because they were probably not as *smart* as we were. Of course anyone from a downriver village was considered culturally tainted by the Russians, or by the missionaries later, and didn't understand the *real* way to do things according to our ancestors."

"So what do people think about your opinion?"

"I never talked to other Dené about this theory of mine; I just kept asking people what they thought of this person and that person. So far every one of them has proven me right."

"So you think each village feels the same way about all the other villages."

"Yeah, whatever village they're from, they think they're smarter'n upriver people and don't trust folks from downriver. Most other people don't see any difference, but they also didn't grow up on the river."

"Do you know anyone in Wolf River village?"

"I got a few friends over there. Don't get me wrong. We don't have any problems with people marrying folks from other villages, or trading up and down river, that's been going on a long time.

"It's just that I noticed this difference and I thought it was interesting. You're not from the river and I think you are an intelligent person, so I thought I would run it by you and see what you thought."

"I'm new to the Yukon and its people. There is a lot that I don't understand, and I think you just gave me a whole new way of looking at things. Thanks."

"So why are you meeting with everyone on the crew?"

"Because I don't know them, and I want to."

"Why?" Eddie said.

Levi grinned. "Do you know that you are first man to ask me that straight out?"

"I'm also the only one who knows he can live here without someone paying him a wage."

"I'm still impressed. I want to get to know everyone because I'm responsible for you, your work, and your welfare. It's all part of my job."

"Word on the track says you're a spy. Are you?"

The abrupt turn in the conversation mentally tripped him for a moment. "What? Who the hell– no, I am not a spy! Like I told everyone down in the shop that day, I'm new and in over my head. You said you were in the shop that day?"

"Yeah, back near the dispatch shack. I don't think you saw me."

"Well, that was the truth then and it is now. I didn't ask for this job, I wasn't trained for it, and I frankly didn't want it. Yet here I am."

Eddie nodded and Levi felt like he had just passed an exam.

"What do you do on the crew?"

"Heavy laborer, gandy dancer, track layer, whatever they tell me to do."

"Why?" Levi asked.

"Because I need a job?" Eddie blurted, then he grinned. "That won't work, will it? I already told you I didn't need a job."

Levi laughed.

"Let's just say that I find this job interesting and it might help my future."

"What can you tell me about the train accident up here last year?"

Eddie abruptly sobered and gave him a hard look. The newborn warmth between them cooled noticeably.

"Why are they still asking about that? We talked to people about that for six damn weeks!"

"I don't know who *they* might be, but *I* am asking because *I* wasn't here, and *I* don't know the story. And for the record, every other member of your crew has acted like it was something they just heard about and 'don't know nothing other than it happened.'"

Eddie nodded. "I understand. But until I know you better, just for the record, I don't know nothing other than it happened."

Levi smiled. "I can't ask for more than that right now. Thanks for coming in and you won't be docked for the time you were here."

Eddie stood and smiled back. "That's what we're here for, that paycheck." He winked and walked out the door, shutting it behind him.

Levi stared after him, his mind racing.

Tomiko Watanabe knocked on his door.

"Come in."

She entered the room, stopped when she saw him standing. "There are no more people waiting to see you, Levi. I have two phone messages for you." She handed him two slips of paper covered in her precise, neat script. He wondered if she had ever trained as an artist.

"Thank you Tomiko. You may leave for the day if you like."

"Thank you, Levi. The weather is warming nicely and the river ice is beginning to show signs of breaking."

"Do you watch the river a lot?"

"Everyone does, especially this time of the year. When the ice finally goes out it is an incredible display of nature's force and energy. I know of no other place in the empire where one could watch something equally spectacular."

"I've heard that it is a sight everyone should see if they get the opportunity."

"That is true, sir. I will see you in the morning."

Levi watched her leave, wondering if she had been that formal with Suzuki. All of his adult life he had believed that the Japanese only allowed a portion of their true selves to be seen by others and working this closely with them had not changed his belief.

As far as their motives go, nothing is seen until it is too late. He decided to change his focus; turn it to something more enjoyable.

Abruptly Thelma was in his mind and he wondered how much he didn't know about her. He had been to the Wolf River Lodge at least three evenings a week for the past two months. She always seemed delighted to see him, and he had given up on trying to mask his interest, but he offered her no encouragement.

He wondered who Eddie Hildebrand's friends were in the village.

In the parking lot he admired his new utility. Well, new to him. He had purchased it from one of the workers who had been transferred down to the railhead at Seward.

His increased pay scale allowed for things like this. Even better was that his fuel expenses were borne by the Imperial Army. He drove to the lodge and parked.

As he stepped out of the truck, the door of the lodge swung open and Thelma stood smiling at him.

"I was hoping you would visit today, Levi."

The wind had abated a day earlier and the crisp air had warmed to 20°F above zero, almost balmy for the Interior.

Levi walked up to her, stopped and stared into her eyes.

Her smile subsided and she stared back.

"Levi, you *do* know that I like you. Don't you?" The softness of her voice could have lulled a feral cat.

"Yes. I mean, I thought you liked me. You've always seemed happy to see me. And I'm always happy to see you!"

Her smile returned.

He smiled back and said, "Is there somewhere we can talk, alone? There's something I need to explain."

She led him to the same guest room where he and Gunther had deposited a drunken Glenn Bassett months ago. She shut the door behind them. Levi sat in one of the two chairs next to the small table and Thelma eased into the other one.

"So, talk," she said.

"I grew up on the plains of Nebraska. I don't remember much from before the war but in 1945 I was ten years old. My dad was in the army in Europe when the Germans bombed Washington.

"Everybody was in a panic because President Roosevelt, the White House, Pentagon, and all the top generals and admirals were gone," he snapped his fingers, "Just like that."

Thelma watched his face and didn't even nod.

"When Vice President Truman, who had been home in Missouri when it happened, sued for peace with the Axis, my mother went crazy. She started talking about my Aunt Maisie out in western Colorado and how that would be a safe place to 'ride out the storm,' as she put it.

"I didn't argue when she told me to pack everything I ever wanted to wear or see again in two suitcases. That took me two days, and I ended up leaving a lot behind, including her."

Thelma made a small, hurt sound in her throat and in his peripheral vision saw a tear slide down her cheek. She cleared her throat. "Why did she stay behind?"

"She told me she had to wait for my father. When he left for the war she told him she would wait right there in Grand Island until he came home. I didn't know she wasn't going with me until we got to the bus. She hugged me tight, kissed me, and said she loved me. Then she made me get on the bus."

Levi paused to squeeze away a tear of his own. There were many painful reasons why he rarely talked about his past to anyone.

"Did you like the aunt you went to live with?" Thelma asked.

"Aunt Maisie was actually my great aunt, my grandmother's sister. If I hadn't had her to lean on I would have probably gone insane."

"I'm glad she was there for you, Levi."

"She was the one who told me that my mother wasn't Jewish, only my dad was. Since I was half Jewish and the Germans would be running Nebraska, I had to stay out of their reach. My mother might have been safe, too. I've been hiding from the Nazis ever since."

"It must have been hell for her to send away one of the two people she loved most in the world just to be there if the other one came home." Thelma pulled a handkerchief from her pocket and dabbed at her eyes. "How did you get to Alaska?"

"When I was fourteen the husband of one of Aunt Maisie's friends offered me a summer job in Alaska. His company had been hired to build a road from Livengood to the Yukon River and he needed a lot of people.

"I asked him how the Japs felt about the undesirables the Nazis were gassing. He said the subject had never come up because to the Japanese all white people were barbarians anyway." Levi smiled at the memory.

Thelma mirrored his smile. "What did you do on the job?"

"He taught me how to operate trucks, earthmovers, even a steam shovel. I never went south again. Every now and then I get a letter from my aunt, but neither of us ever heard from my mother again."

Thelma put her hand over his where it rested on the table and he relaxed muscles he hadn't realized were tense.

"The key sentence back there is, 'I've been staying away from the Nazis ever since.' I have lived my life in fear of someone pointing at me and screaming, 'Jew!' and then being hauled off to be gassed to death. I am a professional coward, and I'm very good at it."

He stared into her eyes and tried to frown. Her eyes were full of tears and she grabbed his hand with both of hers.

"My God, Levi, you're not a *coward!* You are hunted and you are haunted, yet you continue getting through life, and are doing a damn good job of it."

"Thelma, I already felt like a huge target and now I find I am in the middle of an even bigger one. That's why I wanted to tell you all of this. I can't make any promises just now. I can't see my personal life improving at the present time, and I can't... but I am *very* much interested in you."

Her smile dimmed and she brushed at her eyes again.

"I'll take what I can get." She squeezed his hand again. "Let's go say 'hi' to the others."

She bounded up from the chair and preceded him out of the room.

CHAPTER 19

TOKKŌ HEADQUARTERS
ANCHORAGE, ALASKA PREFECTURE

"I FEAR WE ARE RUNNING OUT OF TIME."

"Please explain, Inspector Fukawa," Tumassa Shikita said, staring keenly at the older man's face.

"With the loss of our conduit into the military project, we are without eyes or ears at a crucial moment. We know they are close to achieving what we most fear, yet we are rendered impotent."

"I wonder why he was so far from where he was supposed to be. What did he have to tell us that required him to leave Yukon Station?"

"Something about Chinese workers is all I know."

"Would it indicate anything other than a manpower report?"

"Who can know? However, once again, why would anyone care? The last thing the Empire of Japan will ever lack is a ready supply of disposable slave workers."

"You make an inescapable point, Inspector Fukawa. So how do we stop the army from starting World War III?"

"We do not have a force as strong as the army to subdue them by arms. Even the Imperial Navy would find it difficult."

Both men smiled at the statement. The Imperial Navy, once equal to both the Imperial Army as well as the Tokkō, had lost its war before the Imperial Army won theirs. Even today, over twenty years after the Glorious Victory, the Imperial Navy struggled to regain their losses from the Pacific War in an economy dictated by a disdainful Imperial

Army.

The Navy was one *han*, the Imperial Army another. The Navy accepted whatever largess it could garner.

"Perhaps we can arrange to embarrass them so they lose face with the Emperor," Shikita said, his mind still on the fate of the Imperial Navy.

"How do you propose we do that? Create a demonstration that looks like they aided the so-called Liberty Underground?"

Shikita laughed. "If you could find a representative of that mythic group you would have accomplished far more than the Kempeitai have in a decade. In all of the years we have been here we have apprehended one drunken Indian who claimed to be part of a resistance group."

"Until he sobered up," Fukawa said with a snort. "Then he wouldn't even talk under torture! Besides, I do not believe the Emperor would appreciate us giving aid to a supposed, perhaps non-mythic, enemy."

Shikita pointed through the window at the bustling Japanese workers and military. "I don't see any sedition out there."

"Our *real* enemy is Germany, and the Quiet War is a state secret," Fukawa said.

"However, an open one. Perhaps we can use the Germans to discomfort the Kempeitai."

"How?" Fukawa asked.

"Leak the information to the German delegation here in Anchorage that there is a Jew working on the Yukon-Fairbanks Railroad. They will immediately demand his extradition under the Racial Purity Treaty."

"They have a Jew on the railroad?"

"Yes, one Levi Fischer. He filled the vacancy left by Mr. Suzuki's demise."

Fukawa's smile returned and widened. "That's brilliant."

He returned to the window. Fourth Avenue, completely rebuilt since the massive earthquake of 1964, looked like a small copy of Tokyo's Ginza district, which gave him hope for the future of this massive sub continent. The new Wako Department Store, a branch of Tokyo's oldest establishment of its kind, served as a proud benchmark for postwar Alaska Prefecture to emulate. A coolie passed by pulling a rickshaw; the passenger was an American.

"If only we didn't have all of these other barbarians to deal with," Fukawa mused aloud.

"I will place the call," Shikita said. "Then we will watch developments."

CHAPTER 20

THIRD REICH DELEGATION
ANCHORAGE, ALASKA PREFECTURE

"WHY ARE YOU TELLING ME THIS?" GERHARDT RABNER SAID INTO THE phone. "Hello? Hello?" He slammed the instrument down on its cradle.

"Who was that?" Rudof Swink asked, looking up from his week-old copy of *Der Stürmer*. The banner headline extolled the engineering marvels of the recently finished Berlin to Moscow autobahn.

"A good citizen, or so he said, who wanted to report the location of a Jew."

Swink laid down the tabloid. "Really? A Jew *here*?"

"Not here. He works up on the railroad that supplies the Jap secret bomb works."

"Well, that puts paid to it, eh?" Swink said in his best English accent. He went back to his copy of the *Der Stürmer*.

Rabner stretched and arched his back until two vertebrae popped. The large man did his best thinking while standing or exercising.

"Perhaps not. The person who called was a Jap, even though he tried to sound like an American."

"If this Jew is working for the Japs on a secret project, how would our informant know unless he was also a part of the secret project, or privy to the classified knowledge of it?" Swink asked without looking up from his magazine.

"That's why I put up with you, Rudi. You have a wonderfully analytical but devious mind. So why would they be telling on themselves? What could they gain?"

Swink put the paper down and squinted at his fellow agent, "There is always that wonderfully Asian commodity of 'face.'"

"True. But why would a Jap want the Kempeitai to lose face?"

The two men stared at each other and in unison both said, "The Tokkō!"

"There is more to this than just making the Kempeitai lose face," Swink said. "Somewhere behind this intra-racial pissing match is a real reason to commit treason."

"The Japanese are maniacs when it comes to pushing their viewpoint. Our last information about the bomb project was that they were still months away from a workable device," Rabner said. "Maybe that has changed."

"Maybe it was dreck to begin with." Swink stared out the window at the mountain that locals called the Sleeping Lady across Cooks Inlet. "Maybe they are close to arming the damned thing. We should alert Berlin about this."

Swink stared down at the streets of Anchorage, four stories below. Despite Japanese domination it remained a vital, American frontier town. They weren't cowboys, but the woodsmen and farmers held as much frontier distinction as the men on horseback farther south.

There were even Indians here, but Swink found them a poor comparison to the once-proud rulers of the Great Plains. He wished he could have seen America before the war. The stories he heard about the Alaska Bush were enticing, but a visit would have to wait until the Japanese were subdued.

"I think you are correct, Rudi," Rabner said. "I also think you should go apply for a job with the railroad."

"Why me?" His reverie popped like a soap bubble.

"Because you can pass for an Englishman or an Irishman. I damn well can't do that."

"True. However, if they caught me, I would lose my head."

"We need to know if they have atomic bombs right now. You know that as well as I do."

"Well, the concept suddenly became a lot more personal."

"You are a decorated member of the Gestapo. If anyone can pull this off immediately and flawlessly, you can. I have faith in your abilities."

Rudi Swink swallowed and briefly glanced off to the side before staring at Rabner.

"I want both of us to have those new compact radios to maintain contact. I also want the Luftwaffe's guarantee that they'll pull me out of there if I scream for help."

"I believe that can be arranged. The dossier with all of the information from our agent is in the day safe. Go get into character." Rabner smiled with the beauty of his idea.

CHAPTER 21

*"How admirable!
to see lightning and not think
life is fleeting."*
— Matsuo Basho

KEMPEITAI BARRACKS
YUKON STATION

Sergeant Major Isu Fukita strapped on his sword while reflecting on the weapon's journey. In thirty years of service to the Emperor, he had used the two-hundred-year-old sword in many places and against many people. His uncle, a veteran of the Russo-Japanese War had solemnly placed it in his hands with the admonition that he now carried the *kami* of his ancestors, with all of the *giri* that entailed. Isu regarded it as his personal Shinto shrine and venerated his ancestors on a regular basis.

As the seventh generation of his family to carry the weapon, he felt symmetry in its service to him, first using it in the China campaign after being promoted sergeant in the late 1930s. Now in the middle 1960s he once again used it to direct the Chinese in their service to the Empire. He had led a charge against the American Army in the Battle of Kiska with the sword.

The Imperial Army had not prevailed that day but instead had been evacuated to fight elsewhere in the Pacific. Then, while still a mere senior sergeant, Fukita had covered himself in glory to the point Prime Minister Tojo had asked the newly promoted sergeant major what honor he wished at the end of the war.

Thus it came about that Isu Fukita, as the most heavily decorated NCO in the Imperial Japanese Army, was given the honor of taking the head of U.S. General of the Army Douglas MacArthur following the surrender ceremony in Brisbane, Australia. The five-star general had protested that a mere non-commissioned officer should not be awarded such a high honor. Although it was appreciated that General MacArthur understood the singularity of the situation, he was ignored. Fukita still possessed the silk scarf with which he had cleaned the blade that day.

Now he commanded the enlisted troops in Japan's most prestigious endeavor since becoming master of the Pacific. The Chrysanthemum Project would put Japanese feet on the Moon. The thought of such an achievement gave him gooseflesh.

More conscripted Chinese laborers were expected in a few days. He must lead by example to them and his own men. In his opinion the warrior spirit of Bushido had faded over the past few years and demanded constant stimulus.

The recent official mandate to alter the way conscripts were trained seemed absolutely insane to him. As a recruit, and later as a non-commissioned training officer, physical punishment was the universal result of mistakes or non-compliance. From where did those fools in Tokyo think their victorious soldiers had come?

Peasant boys had been hammered into a well-trained army that would die for the Emperor rather than even consider surrender. Japanese soldiers had never heard the term "surrender" until they met the Americans and the British. To train them as mere technicians would weaken the fighting muscle of the Imperial Japanese Army.

The Nazis would love that!

He meant to re-instill the spirit of *kokutai*, the national essence of racial purity, in all of them. It galled him that Americans held positions of trust and honor in the hierarchy of the Project. General Yamashita himself had told Fukita that even though the whites were a beaten race, the Empire needed their skills and expertise until Japanese could be trained to replace them.

Sergeant Major Isu Fukita was not convinced. To surrender was to give up all rights as a human. The Americans had surrendered not only to Japan, but also to Germany.

They could have no honor as they had no *giri* to anyone other than themselves. To treat them as equals of good Japanese citizens was nothing less than a personal affront to him. It was not their proper station nor would it ever be. He watched the round-eyes carefully. Victory rewarded vigilance.

Everyone in Alaska Prefecture were beneath the Japanese people, however the native Indians made his skin crawl. As a small child he had been taken to Hokkaido to see the Ainu. The animals called themselves the first Japanese; how could the Sun Goddess start their great race with those creatures?

Yet North American pre-humans worked on this very post and received payment for doing so. To make matters even worse, the Imperial Army had allowed women to become soldiers. Captain Atsumi was an affront to the fighting men of the Imperial Japanese Army, a joke of the worst possible taste. Yet there she was in full uniform, and *he* had to salute *her!*

He knew it was time for him to retire and buy himself a small farm in the Home Islands where he could take a young woman as wife and sire many children before he joined his ancestors. But first he had to see the Chrysanthemum Project through to the end, to help put Japanese men on the surface of the Moon. Then he could rest. But, until then he would endure all of the indignities the spirits could manifest—he was a Japanese soldier.

CHAPTER 22

"Nothing in the cry
of cicadas suggests they
are about to die"
— Matsuo Basho

WORKER HOUSING,
YUKON STATION

The knock on his door was just loud enoughto pull Timothy Keegan from his whiskey reverie. He staggered to the door, picked up his axe handle, and stopped.

"Who's there?"

"A supplicant," came the muffled voice of a man not wishing to shout.

Keegan cracked open the door, keeping the axe handle in his right hand out of view behind his leg.

"Supplicant is it? Who are ye and what do ya want of me? If yer looking for a job go to the personnel office in the morning."

"Mulligan sent me." The man's voice sounded tight with fear.

Keegan felt his heart skip a beat as he searched his alcohol-fuddled brain for the response.

"The one who made the stew?" he finally croaked.

"That would be his uncle."

"You need a password." Steel stiffened his backbone and edged his responses.

"Finian, would you believe?"

Keegan opened the door enough for the man to fit through.

"In. Now!" He quickly shut the door behind his unwelcome guest.

The man stepped into the living room and stopped, facing

Keegan. He was smaller than Keegan but few weren't.

"Are we finished with the cloak and dagger crap?"

"Who are you? What do you want?"

"Pleased to meet you, too, Mr. Keegan."

The fellow had a well-kept smile and a good build on him. Timothy put him in his mid-thirties and the lad seemed sharp enough to cut.

"And you are...?"

"Thomas Alan Riordan, at your service." He made a mock curtsy without losing the smile.

"Why are you in my living room, Mr. Riordan?"

"Our mutual friends thought you might need an able assistant at this auspicious moment."

Keegan's mind sorted out the code words as his mind trudged through a field muddy with alcohol. The biggest problem with serving more than one master was keeping the bastards straight. He felt an unholy thirst.

"Would you like a touch of the good stuff?"

Riordan's grin grew wider. "Well, I *am* Irish and it's a bit nippy out there."

Keegan made a slow show of pouring drinks and thought as fast as he could.

"You must be new to the Interior. It's downright balmy out tonight at long last."

"Can we dispense with the verbal chess game?" Riordan asked as he accepted a half tumbler of whiskey from his host.

"Sure. Since you started this dance, why don't you lead?"

"How close are the Japs to having a functioning weapon?"

"To my knowledge, some months away. Do you know something I don't?"

Riordan's smile all but vanished. "When did you last hear from your source inside?"

How did they know?

"It's been a few weeks," Keegan admitted, not liking the uneasy feeling stealing over him.

"Our *other* source went silent the same day Suzuki died. Was he your source, too?"

Bewilderment washed over Keegan. "Suzuki was a spy for–"

"Shut up, you damned fool!" Riordan said with a nod toward the wall.

"Fuck," Keegan spat, feeling stung. "If they're listening they already have enough to hang us both. I have gone through this shack with a magnetic detector. If there is a bug in here it's a lot more modern than most of this project."

"And why would they waste it on someone they don't suspect?" Riordan said with a faint sneer. "If they're closer than you think, they will be upping the stakes of this little horse race. They can't afford to *not* watch everyone."

Keegan stared into the distance. "Y'got a good point there, Thomas, me lad. What do you propose we do now?"

"Tell me how the secret part of the project gets its supplies."

"Well, that will take awhile. What else?"

"Get me a job somewhere in that process."

"That part will be easy."

"I'll also need quarters in the last row of houses. The farther from the guards, the better."

"That might be more difficult, but I'll do what I can. Now, there are a few rules you must agree to follow."

"What could you possibly tell me that I do not already know?"

"To start with; that you're an arrogant bastard, Mr. Riordan. The Japs aren't as dumb as they look. Do watch your ass."

"Not to worry, Timothy me boy, not to worry."

CHAPTER 23

YUKON STATION

"IF YOU AND I DO NOT KNOW THE FULL SCOPE OF THE PROJECT, HOW CAN we do our jobs to the best of our abilities?" Levi asked as he and Captain Atsumi walked slowly along Chrysanthemum Road, one of two roads into Yukon Station.

Both were in shirtsleeves and a warm breeze wafted out of the south bearing the aromatic bouquet of new leaves and budding plants. They had passed a couple of anti-aircraft gun mounts

A Fuji fighter jet shrilled over for a landing on Runway 1 and was lost to view behind the Administration Building and Project structures. They followed the jet's progress only by sound. A company of sweating soldiers ran past in undershirts and athletic shorts, accompanied by a seemingly unaffected, screaming sergeant in full uniform flailing the slackers with a bamboo baton. Levi silently watched them.

"We do as we are told," Atsumi said, bringing him back to the conversation. "If the general wishes more of us, we will be directed on how to achieve his desires."

Before Levi could respond a train whistle blew in the distance. He waited for the double blast to recede but it continued.

"Three longs and a short? What does that mean?"

"Observe." She nodded to where guards were opening one of the huge gates into the compound around the huge worker's barracks.

A company of armed Japanese soldiers stood waiting for the arrival.

"That's a first for me," Levi said. "What's going on and how often does this happen?"

"It happens whenever the Project requires more workers. That is the signal for a load of new Chinese and East Asian workers. Don't stop, let us continue our walk and our discussion."

"Is there a problem with us watching the process? Is it classified?"

"It is not classified," she said, staring into his eyes, "but I suspect that you will find it disturbing."

"Now I definitely want to watch."

Captain Atsumi frowned at him but nodded in acquiescence. "Very well."

The train slowed outside the Project area and came wheezing into the rail yard at a walking pace, bell clanging. The guards had already thrown the switch to shunt the monster through the fence. The train slowed further and, with an ear-splitting screech, ground to a stop a few feet short of the barrier at the end of the spur. The bell clanged to a stop.

From the Kempeitai building, Sergeant Major Fukita marched out to the rail siding; head back, bellowing at his subordinates who instantly reacted. Shouts tore through the air. Guards threw open the sliding doors on the boxcars and people tumbled out of the cars and onto the ground.

Some landed on their feet, many fell like sacks of dirt and didn't move. The guards screamed at one and all, kicking and prodding with clubs, herding the ambulatory into shifting lines between the tracks and the barracks. Those that didn't land on their feet were kicked or prodded with batons wielded by the screaming soldiers.

At least two-dozen still bodies lay unmoving along the tracks.

"What's wrong with the people on the ground?" Levi asked.

"They are either dead or close enough to be assisted to finish the journey."

"Where did that train come from?"

"Seward. They have been in those cars for at least three, maybe as many as five, days." Captain Atsumi spoke matter-of-factly and without inflection, as if reading a shopping list. "They are a commodity and some wastage is anticipated."

"They're people, not potatoes! That is beyond inhumane even for the Japanese!"

She gave him a bland glance. "That is something you should never say to any Japanese, other than me of course, if you don't want to immediately die."

"Does this not bother you?"

The freight car doors were slammed shut and the train slowly backed out of the compound. Once the engine passed the gate, the soldiers shut the opening and replaced the heavy lock.

The guards had now kicked and beaten the workers into a dozen ranks that gained a degree of symmetry. As Levi and Atsumi watched, the workers were herded off in different directions towards various barracks. A few workers fell along the way and Levi clutched his chest when Sergeant Major Fukita flicked out his samurai sword and decapitated one of the fallen Chinese.

The sergeant major then stared directly at Levi for a long moment.

"My god! Is that permitted?"

"Mr. Fischer, keep in mind who won the war. There is a method to official brutality that trains and educates all observers. It even has a name: *seishan*. It is the military version of *Bushido*. They know we are watching. They know who you are."

"Do you mean that man would still be alive if I hadn't been watching?"

"It was a woman, and who is to know? We are all part of the painting whether we add color or not."

"There must have been three hundred people on that train. Where will they get shelter?"

"There is adequate room in the barracks else they would not be here. Are you finished being provincially horrified? We have much yet to do."

The worker's barracks were outside his responsibility, and further investigation on his part would be considered, at the very least, insubordination.

Levi bit back his first response and gave Captain Atsumi a withering look. "I thought karma was an Asian concept."

"It's actually Indian and Shinto does not have a correlating concept."

"So none of you will ever answer for this kind of thing?"

"Have we yet?"

Her smile angered and chilled him. It was at this moment that he began to hate her.

CHAPTER 24

"The temple bell stops
But the sound keeps coming
out of the flowers"
— Matsuo Basho

CONSCRIPT BARRACKS
YUKON STATION

BAO LI WATCHED THE NEW PEOPLE SOBBING AND WAILING AS THEY poured into the barracks, bleeding and bruised. He knew exactly how they felt, and sympathized with their fear and agony. However, they had to overcome their emotions and learn the rules quickly or they would be dead very soon.

"Give me your attention!" he shouted in Mandarin. It always amazed and saddened him how quickly they complied. "You are all going to die if you do not remember my words here today. The Jap considers you less than an animal. You are all more expendable than a dog."

He watched the effect of his words sink into their thoughts and, in a few, recognized awareness.

"The work here can be deadly and it can also be life giving, therefore choices must be made. I am an old man, probably the oldest man in this building. The Japanese made me honcho in this barracks because I make their domination of us easier, at least that is their belief.

"We must grow our own food with the exception of rice. Between the barracks we have gardens, chickens, and hope. A new fragrance is in the wind and it might promise freedom.

"For now you must listen to me, understand that I am trying to save as many of us as possible, but also realize there must be sacrifices for the good of the whole. Some of you will have to work in the Annex; the large building you can see from the barracks door. I tell you now that all who work in there die far ahead of their normal time. That is why I ask the older people to volunteer for those jobs.

"We need the younger people to prepare for the day we leave here as fighters and avengers. Those who are left behind will be venerated as the heroes they are. They will not be forgotten.

"Now find a place to sleep. I am here to answer questions and help where I am able. Do not forget to bow to every Japanese you encounter or you will instantly lose your head."

He felt gratified as they all hurried to do as he said. Hope continued to keep his spirit from bending and he knew there had to be a path out of here.

CHAPTER 25

WOLF RIVER LODGE

Levi pulled into his usual parking spot outside the lodge. Two other vehicles sat parked close together. One he recognized as belonging to Gunther Charles and the other was a sedan he had never before seen.

"Business must be picking up," he muttered as he walked up the steps. Until the spring thaw commenced he hadn't realized there were steps in front of the lodge. As it turned out, there were four.

The snow certainly hadn't looked that deep.

With the warm weather everyone was making bets on when the ice would go out on the Yukon. Traffic on the road down the middle had ceased weeks ago. He had asked Thelma why the traffic ceased when all of the ice was still there.

"The river doesn't wear away the ice on the bottom evenly. There can be places where the water is almost at the surface. If that happened where someone was driving a truck, or a car, or a dogsled they could go right through the weak spot. It has happened before."

"Is there any way to save them?"

"Levi," she had replied gently, "the river still flows beneath the ice. The current is very strong. If someone goes through, and is even able to get out of the vehicle, there's no way they can make it back to the hole where they went in."

The mental image of drowning while tumbling in a frigid torrent beneath unbreakable ice had stuck with him. He understood now that the Yukon River was more than just water. It provided life and also took it from the unwary or careless.

He pushed through the door and Thelma rose from a chair at the table where a number of people were sitting and drinking tea. One of them was a Japanese wearing civilian clothes. Having just left the arrogance of Captain Atsumi's presence, he was not pleased to see an unknown Asian.

"Levi, I hoped you would come over tonight. We have some guests we would like you to meet."

"How nice." He kept his voice and face neutral.

Gunther nodded to him and stood.

"Levi, I would like to introduce you to a couple of friends."

As he moved toward the table Levi realized the room had gone still. He searched his mind for any reason the Kempeitai would want to arrest him and came up with nothing. He forced a smile and nodded back.

Doubtful Thomas, sitting on the far side of the large table, grinned at him. "This isn't a trap, Levi. Quite the contrary."

Both of the visiting men got to their feet. The Caucasian, well into middle age, spoke first.

"Hello, Levi. I am Jacob Rose. Before I changed it, my last name was Rosenblum. Like you, I am a Jew hiding in plain sight."

For a long moment Levi was aghast that everyone in the room now knew he was a Jew, finally Jacob's words sank in.

"How long have you been here?" Levi asked.

"I've worked on the Chrysanthemum Project from its very beginning. I helped design the complex and the annex back in '59. Prior to that I was in New Mexico with a second office in Tokyo where I conferred with the Imperial Army High Command."

Despite himself, Levi's eyebrows shot up in surprise. "They must think a lot of you, Jacob."

"Please, call me Jake. This is my colleague, Dr. Jerry Hyakawa. He is a medical doctor and the most intuitive mathematician I have ever met."

The Japanese was at least a decade younger than his companion. Levi started to bow.

"You don't have to bow to me. I'm as American as you are." His accent was pure California with no trace of Japanese inflection.

"Pleased to meet you, Jerry." He turned to Thelma. "Could I please have a cup of tea? I think I am going to need it."

Everyone at the table silently waited as Thelma went into the kitchen.

Levi looked around. "How do you know the Japanese don't have any listening devices in here?"

"They have never had the opportunity," Doubtful said. "In addition to that we go over the entire building with a radio frequency detector every week just in case some nasty visitor infected us with a bug. Anything larger than that would be very obvious to us."

Teddi gave Levi a warm smile. He felt awkward and surprisingly out of place. Thelma brought him a cup of tea and sat down next to him.

Jake glanced around at the others and then gave Levi all of his attention.

"I have worked long and hard to make this project succeed. We have spent many lives on it and not all were Chinese conscripts. For the record, I believe what the Japanese Army Occupation Force is doing here is nothing less than criminal.

"However, I have diligently worked on this project, helped the Japanese Empire perfect an atomic bomb, actually *two* atomic bombs, with two more on the way, for a very good reason." He stopped talking and just stared at Levi.

"Okay, I'll bite. Why?"

"Revenge on the Nazis."

"Won't that just give the *Japanese Empire* the upper hand in the world?"

Jerry Hyakawa nudged Jake to get the floor. "My turn. We would have won the war if the Germans hadn't developed the bomb first."

"First? Who else had it?"

"We did, the U.S. Army. It was being developed down in New Mexico where I worked on it initially. That's where the Japanese got their technology, they stole it from us. The Germans didn't know about the Manhattan Project, that's what the U.S. called it, until years after the Japanese had spirited it away to Alaska."

"So we came that close to winning the war?"

"The Allies were kicking Axis ass until the Ardennes Breakout and then the dual Heinkel He-390 atomic bombings of Washington and the Russian front, all in the span of three days. We still had months to go before our bombs would be operational."

"Why are you both telling me this history stuff? What can I do about it?" He took a sip of tea.

"Let us tell you a bit more and then we'll answer your questions," Jake said.

"Okay, I'm listening."

"The Japanese have also built the Chrysanthemum Rocket—"

"Yeah, to go to the moon," Levi said. "Why they would want to go there is beyond me."

"They don't want to go to the moon," Jake said. "They want to destroy Berlin using the rocket."

For the first time in his adulthood Levi felt a jolt of hope.

"Is that really possible?" he asked in a whisper.

"Very much possible. They also want to drop an atomic bomb on New York City to wipe out the headquarters of the Greater German Reich in North America. The bomber would depart from Prince Akihito Aerodrome south of Fairbanks once the weapon arrived from the Yukon Station Project. The plane would be airborne before the rocket was launched."

"Why wouldn't they just take off from here with the bomb?"

"It's too heavy. They need to use a B-29, just like the U.S. Army was going to do back in '45. The runway here at Yukon Station isn't long enough for a fully loaded B-29 to take off, so they plan to ship it on the railroad to Akihito Aerodrome and load it there."

"It would certainly set the Third Reich back," Levi said.

"General Yamashita told us he wants to bomb the Germans back to the Stone Age," Jerry said with a smile.

"That would still leave the Empire of Japan running the world, even if war broke out between them and what was left of the Third Reich."

"That's where all of the organizations that make up the Liberty Underground come in," Gunther said. "We are planning to apply a bit of misdirection."

"Liberty Underground?" Levi blurted. "I thought that was a fairy tale!"

Gunther said, "Actually it's an army in hiding. There are independent units throughout North America, they might not all call themselves the same thing, but they all have agreed to work together when the time is right. Right now, you are sitting with one of the unit leaders in central Alaska."

Gunther wiped his brow. "We were going to leave you out of the equation since you were an unknown, in terms of security and politics, that is."

"You thought I would side with the Japs!" He glanced at Jerry. "No slight intended."

"I'm Nisei, no worries."

"We know you are supposed to be an undercover Kempeitai agent just like your predecessor," Doubtful said. "We also know that if you are you aren't a very good one."

Even Levi laughed.

"They told me that I was Kempeitai, but what they really wanted me to be is a spy. I am supposed to watch for workers under my supervision who behave oddly."

"Around here that would make for a long list," Gunther said dryly.

"So why did you change your mind about me?"

Everyone looked at Thelma who blushed and smiled.

"Thelma told us you were okay, 'an honest, good man' as she put it. That's good enough for us," Gunther said.

"What do you want me to do?" Under the table he gave Thelma's hand a squeeze. She returned it.

Jerry cleared his throat.

"We'll get to that. The rocket has to be on the clock in launch preparation eighteen hours prior to the bomber taking off to hit New York. The Japanese plan is to wait until the rocket pilots are sealed in before sending the second weapon south on the railroad. We want the second weapon to detonate right here."

A wave of cold fear rushed through him.

"What? What about the village, all of the people?" It took all of his will power not to add, *what about me?*

"We will be gone, headed down river in our boats. Most of the villagers have already left," Doubtful said. He looked grim.

Jacob nodded and said, "We know from studying the blast effects of the Washington bomb that the prevailing wind is an important factor. In spring the wind here is mostly from the south-southwest which would blow it into Germany's Yukon Territory."

Levi shook his head in disbelief.

"Do you really believe the Germans don't know about this plan?"

"They know there's a bomb." Jerry said. "They think it has about six months to go before it becomes operational. They also know there is a rocket but they believe, as you did, that it is destined for a moon shot, the crew are even called *Tsukiyomi pilots. Tsukiyomi* is the Shinto spirit that lives in the moon according to the Japanese."

"The Germans are considering attacking the Yukon Station Project," Jacob said. "Our double agents have carefully fed them enough disinformation to throw them off our true schedule."

Jerry laughed. "At the last moment one of the agents will tell them about moving the weapon by rail. We think they will launch their attack at that point."

"I once heard a rumor that the District of Columbia is a dead zone, as well as the Potomac River," Levi said. "Wouldn't the same thing happen to the Yukon, all the way down?

Jake frowned but said nothing.

"We'll do the best we can," Gunther said. "Of course, there are a thousand things that could go wrong, but this is the only chance we have as a people to get out from under the double yoke of the Axis."

"What about their armies, their navies, their air wings? Are they all going to get caught in the blasts too?"

"The Imperial Japanese Navy lost its fleet and political face in the war. The Imperial Army has kept the Navy under its heel since the war ended. We have nothing to fear from their navy.

"The organizations that make up the Liberty Underground have been in existence since the day the Germans bombed Washington, D.C. and all have been quite active. The veterans of the U.S Armed Forces hid their weapons and equipment including massive amounts of arms and mechanized armor, and waited for this day. Some of our Navy guys managed to hide vessels as large as destroyer escorts and smaller craft before they scuttled the larger ships. All of this equipment has been well maintained. In some places it has almost attained the status of a religion." Gunther looked around the room.

"Once we pass the word, sabotage will commence all across North America. After the bombs go off, every German and Japanese military installation will be attacked by trained men and women who are just as desperate as we are. The occupation forces have grown complacent. They think we are sub human and beaten. They are wrong."

"I agree. Still, what about Alaska?" Levi glanced at each of them in turn. "That bomb could kill the whole Yukon River."

Doubtful, looking troubled, asked, "Is that true, what he said about the Potomac River? I thought the bomb would just destroy Yukon Station, not the heart of our land."

"We've heard all sorts of things," Gunther said. "We don't really know."

"So what do you want me to do?" Levi asked. The sensation in his chest seemed to swell by the second. He finally realized this was what hope really felt like.

"First we want you to take a boat ride with a couple of us. After that you will understand the scope of what we can field right here on the Yukon."

"Don't the Japanese patrol the river?"

"Yes, but poorly. Most of the time the patrol boat is tied up on the bank out of sight of the project. Besides, you have the authority to go where ever you wish."

"When do you want to make this trip?"

"As soon as the ice goes out," Doubtful said.

"I'm betting that's less than three weeks from now," Gunther said.

"Closer to four," Doubtful said. "I've already taken your bet. I've been watching this river a long time and I'll also happily take your money." Levi noticed the man's humor didn't reach his eyes.

CHAPTER 26

"Cormorant fishing:
How stirring,
How saddening"
— Matsuo Basho

YUKON STATION

"THAT'S A HELL OF A STOREHOUSE," THOMAS RIORDAN SAID, FORCING admiration to supersede awe in his tone.

The huge Negro walking beside him nodded. "There are things in there that would unhinge your mind if you knew what they could do."

"Barnes, you have a better vocabulary than our parish priest does back in Boston."

Barnes slowed and gave him a look devoid of expression. "Not that I care, since it's not polite in Alaska to inquire into a man's past, but you are not from Boston."

Riordan felt his heart race and he nearly stumbled. "What do y'mean, not from Boston?" he said, thickening the brogue a little more.

"Don't push it, Thomas, if that's even your real name. All I ask is that you don't insult my intelligence. If you *are* Irish you're from the Midwest, not the East Coast."

Riordan opened his mouth to argue and thought better of it. *This Schwarzer is quicker than most of our intelligence section!*

"And you're smarter, too," Riordan said. "So what's in here that would unhinge my mind?"

They stopped in the middle of the large building. On the far side an entrance to the power plant complete with an armed guard was the only other way out. Barnes carefully looked about them.

"Do you know what they are doing on the other side of that wall?" Barnes asked in a low voice.

"Word has it that they are building an atomic bomb. Is that right?"

Barnes nodded his head. "They're building more than one. They have two finished and have started on the next two."

Riordan felt the blood rush from his head. "Finished? Two bombs finished? Are you sure of that?"

"Why does that upset you? Why do you care?"

"Oh, I'm not, I don't, but I am surprised. It's just, just that the lads told me the Japs were months away from completing their first one and now you tell me they've got two in the pram and more on the way."

"You're doing it again, Thomas. You're insulting my intelligence. You were not only surprised to hear about the bombs, you were also dismayed."

"Dismayed? What the hell kind of a word is that?"

"Clear English, but you know that."

"Look, would you stop with the cross examination? You take apart everything I say like it was a broken watch."

"We have work to do," Barnes said. "We have to count the barrels of bearing grease and solvent. If our numbers don't match what we have already used in the shop, somebody is going to lose their head."

"What would anyone do with a barrel of bearing grease?"

"You can sell anything on the black market. You know that."

"But up here?"

"Anything you can sell in Seward, Fairbanks, or Anchorage you can sell up here. You take that row and I'll take this one. Then we'll trade and verify each other's count."

"They really don't trust us, do they?"

"Who, the Nips?"

"Isn't that why we're doing this, because they told us to?"

"No. They only check every six months or so. We're doing this because the last warehouse crew who couldn't account for everything lost their heads, every one of them. Sergeant Major Fukita demonstrated his mastery of the samurai sword. He proved to be very adept with his blade."

Riordan felt a chill run down his back. "I've heard he's a real son-of-a-bitch."

"He's a lot worse than that. Now get to work."

Hours later, Thomas Riordan stepped from his cabin and stretched. During his stretch he managed to survey everything in sight. The late evening held enough spring twilight to show a complete lack of movement around him.

He sat down on his porch steps and pulled out his pipe. After carefully filling it by touch while his eyes surveyed the area again and again, he struck a match and puffed the bowl to life. Leaning forward he angled his face toward the ground as if pondering the meaning of life while his eyes continued to flick back and forth as far as peripheral vision permitted.

Standing up, he buttoned his light jacket and pulled his hat on at a jaunty angle. Following the well defined path to the commissary store, he hesitated near an electrical pole, knocked the dottle from his pipe, and leaned against the post long enough to pull an object from a hiding place beneath one of the three large, wooden braces holding it upright.

Continuing toward the commissary he veered off into a thicket of brush and trees next to the road. Riordan quickly unwrapped the waterproof oilcloth from around the miniaturized radio and, with another quick glance around, pushed the power switch. He unwrapped the cord connecting the small microphone and earpiece to the set.

After adjusting the earpiece he spoke into the microphone.

"This is Stellers jay. Two eggs in the nest and two more on the way."

After waiting a full minute for a response and not receiving one, he switched off the set and carefully rewrapped it. On his return to the pole he detected no other movement than his own. Everything seemed fine. There was nothing out of place or unusual.

One cannot be too careful, he thought. He surreptitiously replaced the radio in its hiding place and ambled back to his cabin.

Now it's all up to Gerhardt.

CHAPTER 27

YUKON RIVER

ALL THE PREVIOUS NIGHT THE THAWING SURFACE OF THE RIVER CREAKED and groaned. The constantly moving water beneath the ice along with the wind and sun above had melted and abraded its thickness from twenty feet in places to less than a foot. Thicker areas still existed but were not sufficiently wide enough to hold the structure a moment longer.

A thin edge of water separated ice from shore as increasing heat in the air and shoreline melted the connecting ice. Just before noon a massive crack snaked down the old roadway and abruptly fissured out in all directions. The corresponding snap of the breaking ice sent birds fleeing into the sky and brought people out of cabins and buildings. All activity along both banks ceased as every eye fastened on the shuddering, frozen expanse.

A massive floe, pushed from beneath by the hydraulic force of the river, broke free and crushed through a few feet of thinner material. It became the loosened linchpin that had held the mass together.

Huge chunks of floes cracked apart, shifted, and smashed against each other as the entire river slowly inched into motion. Thunderous fractures filled the air with noise and crystalline clouds of tiny ice shards. Wide sheets, pushed by the larger floes, ran up onto the shore to cut through mature trees and brush like giant, cold razors.

Meter-thick sections of ice reared into the air until they broke from their own weight or angled sideways enough that they slid down beneath the rest. The crashing, slamming, breaking action rapidly achieved the decibel level of an artillery barrage. New banks were created as the ice sheared off earth, brush, and trees.

Even cabins and caches, built in years past prior to the erosion effects of many springs like this one, now sat too near the edge and fell beneath the massive onslaught.

The slumbering giant had awakened.

The cacophony would lose volume after a couple of days and the Yukon would take weeks to shed its winter mantle. The sight mesmerized everyone, even those who had witnessed the event scores of times throughout their lives.

Pieces of ice filled the now swiftly moving water. Some small enough to pick up, and pieces large enough that twenty stranded caribou easily stood on them and drifted past watchers on the shore. All were drawn to the grandeur and spectacle of the strength of the mighty Yukon River. True Spring had finally arrived in the Interior of Alaska Prefecture.

CHAPTER 28

"Teeth sensitive to the sand
in salad greens—
I'm getting old."
— Matsuo Basho

TOKKÖ HEADQUARTERS
ANCHORAGE, ALASKA PREFECTURE

"Why has nothing changed?" Inspector Fukawa shouted, instantly regretting his unprofessional outburst.

"Inspector?" Tumassa Shikita said in a hushed tone, looking up from his desk across the room. "What do you mean?"

"It has been weeks since we alerted the Gestapo to the fact that there is a Jew working on the railroad. So why has nothing changed?"

"We do not know if anything has changed or not. We no longer have a conduit into the Project."

"What became of our conduit *outside* of the Project?"

"The agent only reports when he has information. We have had no word from him in weeks."

"Would it be possible for one of us to go view the situation on our own?"

"Inspector," Shikita said with a nervous frown, "in an official sense; no. Were either of us to attempt a clandestine visit it would not only end in failure, we would cause the Tokkō to lose much face and result in unwanted, and impossible *giri*."

"We *have* to know what they are doing. If they perfect this abomination and use it, we are all lost."

"There is nothing we can do! Is there?"

"We could send in a specialist."

Fukawa stared at his subordinate while he thought about the suggestion.

"To what end? How can one man, no matter how dedicated, trained, and competent kill an entire project?"

"We must eliminate either the top Army technicians or the rocket pilots." Shikita, his eyes bright and shining, licked his lips. "This would have to be done *before* they are ready to launch their weapon."

Fukawa nodded. "Who is available?"

"I believe we a have at least four from which to choose, inspector. We have no time to waste. Should this be done in the name of the Emperor?"

"Yes. Summon all four."

"At once." Shikita turned to his telephone and dialed.

CHAPTER 29

FAIRBANKS,
ALASKA PREFECTURE

MAJOR KATSU MIAMATSU WASLKED DOWN SECOND STREET reveling in the warm spring breeze coming off the Chena River. He ambled along at a slow pace to give the illusion he was merely out for a stroll and even nodded at people who passed him. His stomach ached from the tension he knew he must hide.

He carefully wandered into the park the army had built in 1955. Covering four full city blocks it was the showpiece of Japanese culture in Interior Alaska Prefecture. Topiary had been grown to create mazes, additional earth and rocks created hidden glens with benches where lovers could sit. Three koi ponds with connecting streams were crossed by six small bridges. Other cultural features, including a pagoda housing an eating establishment, all combined to create something seemingly out of a Hiroshige woodcut.

A walled compound dominated the very center of the park. Two public gates in classic tori style allowed access to a beautiful, three-part Shinto shrine. The large structure held the *haiden*, the public hall of worship, the *heiden*, the hall of offerings, and finally the *honden*, the main hall of worship that only the high priest may enter on a regular basis.

Major Miamatsu would not be entering the shrine today; his objective was not pure enough. He liked to come here to relax, knowing that this was as close to Japan as he would ever be again. There was nothing for him in the Home Islands and he had come to appreciate this massive subcontinent of Alaska.

He had planned to travel down to Southeast Alaska when he retired. The seasons there were even more reminiscent of traditional woodcuts, and the weather more temperate for a man in his later years.

That day is so close I feel I could touch it, he thought.

A young Japanese woman in a kimono quietly pushed a pram holding a sleeping child. He nodded to her as he passed and she gravely nodded back. He stopped at a kiosk, purchased a small bag of popcorn, an acquired taste since coming to North America, and continued his walk. A man sat on a bench next to a pond, dropping flakes of fish food on the water while admiring the huge koi as they came up to take it from the surface.

Miamatsu sat down at the other end of the bench and finished eating a mouthful of popcorn before speaking.

"Might you be Mr. Homma?"

Without looking up the man replied, "That is one of my names, yes. You must be the inquisitive detective, Major Miamatsu."

Neither man looked at the other. Both watched the koi as they talked.

"Who did you ask about me?"

"A mutual friend who said you could be trusted, else I would not be here. What do you want?"

"In the space of six weeks two men were killed in Livengood."

"Mathieson and Suzuki, yes, I am aware of their deaths."

"Did you kill them?"

"Do you think I would be foolish enough to admit that even if I had? Besides, why do you care, was one of them a personal friend?"

"No. I never met either one of them. They are merely pieces of a puzzle I need to understand."

"Why do you need to understand this puzzle?"

"It is my *giri*, surely you can understand that."

"Professional or personal duty?"

"It doesn't matter," Miamatsu said. "I need to understand this, even if it means my undoing."

"You are a rarity, Major Miamatsu. Most Japanese, especially those in North America and Alaska Prefecture, are not nearly as obsessed with self-obligation and traditional duty as are people in the Home Islands, yet you seem to be."

"Understand that I have no wish to incriminate or pursue you legally, I just need to know what happened and why."

Homma dropped more fish flakes on the pond and both men admired the sleek, colorful fish as they fed without fear of predation.

Homma lowered his voice to such a degree that Miamatsu had to strain in order to hear him.

"Mathieson was removed because it was determined he was part of an underground organization. I was hired for the task and carried it out. I have no idea who killed Suzuki, or why. I only know it was the work of an amateur or a bungled job."

"I see. Thank you for the information."

"It is my pleasure to assist a man with classic attitudes about his obligations. I caution you on bringing up Mathieson's name in the future. People are watching you."

"I understand. Now I owe you *giri* and will look for a way to repay it."

Homma smiled. "Never fear, I will need your help somewhere along the path. It is the nature of my existence."

Miamatsu stood and made a second-degree bow. "I look forward to the day I may repay you in kind."

Homma had stood at the same time and returned the bow without further words.

Miamatsu turned and sauntered out of the park munching the remainder of his popcorn, the tension in his stomach had nearly vanished. He smiled in his mind. Now he only had to ferret out the rationale behind the death of Suzuki and all would be in balance in his world.

CHAPTER 30

"Blowing stones
along the road on Mount Asama,
the autumn wind."
— Matsuo Basho

WOLF RIVER VILLAGE,
ALASKA PREFECTURE

Doubtful Thomas drove slowly thrugh Wolf River Village, giving Levi the opportunity to look at houses and people he had never before seen. The lodge was one of the first structures in the village and this was the first time Levi had traveled farther than that. Dogs barked as they passed, straining at the chains and ropes staked in front of their individual shelters.

"Why are they all tied up like that?"

"Those are sled dogs. If they were allowed to run free they wouldn't pull sleds like they're supposed to. This way, once they're in harness, they'll run for miles just for the exercise. They're not pets, Levi. They are working animals."

The utility turned toward the Yukon and Doubtful pulled up to a large log lying parallel to the water before shutting off the engine. He put the gearshift in reverse and opened his door.

"C'mon, we're going for a boat ride down the Yukon."

They walked down a steep bank that Levi judged to be at least fifteen meters high. Two men he had never met before stood waiting, each holding the flat-bottomed riverboat against the bank with an oar.

"Fellows," Doubtful called out as they neared the men, "this is Levi Fischer. He's one of us now. Levi, this is Boston Titus and Bill Frederickson. They're both cousins of mine."

"Welcome to the club," Boston said with a smile.

"You need to wear one of these, Levi," Bill said holding out a life vest.

"Is there a chance we'll sink?" Levi asked.

Boston nodded at the river. "That water was ice and snow yesterday. It's not only cold enough to kill you in fifteen minutes, it's also full of silt."

"Silt. Why is that bad?"

"That glacial silt is finer than flour," Bill said. "If you fall in the river it will permeate your clothes, making them about five times heavier than they are dry. You wouldn't have more than a minute to get out before you went down, unless you had some floatation."

"Thank you," Levi said, reaching for the life vest. He took in the boat, decided it to be eighteen to twenty feet long and four to five feet wide. Two outboards bolted to the stern, one three times the size of the other, were canted forward so their propellers hung above the water surface.

Doubtful motioned him forward and Levi carefully sat on the bench in the middle of the boat. Doubtful sat on the bench behind him and Boston and Bill pushed the boat away from the shore. In moments Bill had the large motor in the water and burbling. Then they were moving smoothly down the river.

"What is the little motor for, emergencies?" Levi shouted over the engine noise to Doubtful.

"That's as good an explanation as any."

Somehow, Levi reflected, *the river is much larger from this angle than viewing it from the shore.*

Two Japanese soldiers waved in greeting from the far bank. They rested on the shore, their boat tied firmly to a beached log. They made no effort to detain them.

"So much for Japanese security," Doubtful said behind him.

Wind beat on their faces with occasional dashes of spray as the boat ran down the flat middle of the wide Yukon. Levi leaned back to Doubtful.

"How far are we going?" he yelled.

"That's a military secret!" Doubtful shouted and laughed.

As they passed Stevens Village people on the shore waved. All four men in the boat waved back. The throttle remained open for another hour, the constant noise driving Levi back into himself.

I wonder what the point is in of all this? I hope this doesn't turn out to be imaginary rather than reality.

The roar abruptly dropped to a purr and the boat angled into a slow turn toward the north shore. Levi peered over the bow and saw a small tributary dumping fresh, green water into the brown Yukon.

"Where are we?" Levi asked Doubtful.

"At our destination. Keep an open mind and don't jump to conclusions."

The boat slowly motored into the tributary. The bottom sparkled clearly visible, no more than four feet beneath them. The creek, wide where it met the Yukon, narrowed to less than twenty feet in moments.

"Who are you?" a voice shouted from the dense thicket on the shore.

"Fellow voyagers," Doubtful shouted back, "bringing a friend."

"Proceed slowly. Do you have weapons?"

"Yes!" Boston and Bill shouted in unison. "We both have machine pistols," Boston finished.

The bank went quiet and Levi's apprehensions climbed when they drifted into a clearing. At least twenty Asian faces stared at them over the rifles each of them carried. Despite the fact that none of the weapons were aimed at them, he felt his heartbeat quicken and his hands trembled.

"Don't jump to conclusions," Levi mumbled to himself despite the awful certainty arrowing though him that he had just been betrayed into the hands of the enemy.

The group parted and a bearded white man wearing rough clothing hurried down to the little dock fashioned from driftwood and sisal cord.

Bill goosed the motor and the bow of the boat surged up onto the bank. Boston stepped off the bow and shook the man's hand.

"Things are looking good here!"

"Thanks, Boston. We've all been training hard."

Doubtful nudged Levi in the ribs. "This is our destination. You can get out now."

Glad that nobody could see him blush, Levi stood and carefully walked toward the bow, slowing to remove the life vest and to also allow his cheeks to lose color. He stepped ashore wondering what this was all about.

"Mr. Fischer, I am so happy to finally meet you when I wasn't drunk on my ass." The man grabbed Levi's right hand and pumped it vigorously. "I'm Glen Bassett."

"The hunter," Levi blurted. "Yes, I have heard much about you, and you're heavier than you look."

"That's right, you helped Gunther put me to bed, for that I thank you. But don't believe all the bad things you hear. I am a much misunderstood man." Glen changed his focus. "Doubtful, my friend, so good to see you. Did you bring anything beer flavored?"

"No, Glen. Not until this thing is over. It is so good to see you active and involved."

"Are those replacement words for *sober*?"

"That too. Show us the operation. Levi has no idea what we brought him to see."

"Wow." Glen moved back to Levi as he waved at Bill. "Mr. Fischer, I—"

"Mr. Bassett, Glen, please call me 'Levi,' okay?"

"Sure, Levi. This set up is really going to knock your socks off."

Levi glanced around. "Are all of these people Japanese deserters?"

"Don't ever call them Japanese," he said in rapid whisper. "They are Chinese and Vietnamese with a Filipino here and there. They all hate the Japs even more than we do."

"I find that difficult to believe, frankly," Levi said in a low voice.

"Have the Japs chopped off the head of a white man in front of you? A man that you knew and liked?"

Fukita's samurai sword flashed in his memory and he instantly felt like a fool.

"Migawd, I apologize. No, the only decapitations I have witnessed have been those of Chinese workers. I honestly can't image the degree of their hate."

"You are very quick. I like that in a person," Glen said. "I want to introduce you to someone I greatly admire and who is the linchpin of our whole operation here."

An Asian standing off to the side watched them approach. His bearing seemed more professional to Levi than any of the others around them. His uniform also seemed different. More people moved out of the trees to get a look at the visitors.

"Levi, this is Captain Vu Dinh Doan. He is a Vietnamese and is the commander of our Coprosperity Battalion."

"Our what?"

Captain Doan smiled and held out his hand. "That's Glen's feeble attempt at humor, Levi. My Chinese colleagues have deemed us the 'Righteous Fist,' which seems more appropriate now than when their grandfathers used the term in 1900."

"Where did you go to college, Captain?"

"Please, call me Vu, I insist. I went to a secret Jesuit school in southwest China. The priests ran an orphanage and I lived there from the age of three until I left at twenty years.

"It would be impossible to not become educated in a place like that. We had some brilliant scholars as well as some very peculiar men. I firmly believe that the apex of education is to know when to quit and get on with one's life."

"He talks like that all the time," Glen said and elbowed Levi gently in the ribs.

"What are you doing here? Who are you all going to fight?"

"Japs!" Vu and Glen said at the same time.

Vu continued, "With very few obvious exceptions, every person here was a slave of the Japanese Army. All of us escaped, some individually and after one wonderful accident on the railroad, over two hundred people were able to get away. The Liberty Underground has provided us weapons, and the Dené Army has been training us. When the time is right we will make the initial assault on Prince Akihito Aerodrome south of Fairbanks."

"You are going to assault what?" Levi said. "Are you insane? They'll cut you to pieces!"

"Levi doesn't have the whole picture," Doubtful said to Vu.

What the hell?

"What is going on here? Who are the Dené Army? I thought you guys already told me everything."

"Easy, son," Doubtful said. "The part you actually *did* know but what you *didn't* understand is the enormity of this whole operation. The Dené Army are all Athabascan Indians who work hand-in-hand with the Liberty Underground."

"How many groups are there?" Levi asked, trying to put everything into perspective.

"Oh, hell," Glen said, "There's probably at least a few hundred individual groups across Alaska, Canada, and the Lower 48 States. Everything is kept pretty insular for security purposes–people can't talk about things they don't know about."

"Here in Alaska," Doubtful said, "there are at least five groups, and that doesn't include Southeast Alaska. We have no idea what the Tlingits, Haidas, Tsimshians, or even the whites are doing down there."

"So how does this all fit together with what is happening here?"

"The Liberty Underground has created a shortwave communications link with all of the various groups, elements, armies, whatever they call themselves, and got them all to agree to act together, in *concert* was the term I heard, when the time is right. The UL has shared information in all directions and while the rest of the elements don't know *what* is going to happen, they know that *something* is going to happen."

"We're going to blow up the Interior of Alaska, right?" Levi asked.

"When the bombs are delivered we are going to hit the Japanese and Germans with everything we have stored up, both physically and emotionally," Glen said. "We are going to kill those bastards and take back our country. Right after that we are going to retool and take back the world. Liberty will not be complete until the Nazis and the Japanese military are annihilated."

Levi looked around at all the resolute faces, male and female, and realized the hope he had felt earlier had strengthened into determination that eclipsed his former mute acceptance to the outcome.

"I am honored to be a part of this," Levi said. "I just wish this had happened in time to save more of my people. I'm probably one of the last Jews in North America."

"The Liberty Underground and other groups have saved thousands of American Jews from death camps," Glen said. "There are a large number of Jewish fighters training along with the rest of our troops down in Montana and Idaho." He stopped for a moment and gave Levi a searching look. "You had no idea, did you?"

The amount of hope swelling in his breast frightened him. There might be a lot more to lose here than he had ever imagined.

"No, not even a glimmer."

Doubtful smiled. He nodded toward a row of trees. "If you don't mind, we all have to talk."

Levi and Doubtful followed Vu and Glen as they led the way. Once past the row of trees a camouflaged compound of sorts took shape. The area wasn't cleared of brush and it took him a moment to pick out the small cabins all around the area despite the small trails leading to each.

In the middle of the minimal clearing a medium-sized cabin blended with its surroundings. Vu and Glen went through the door and, although he wanted to, Levi didn't hesitate as he followed them. As they moved toward a table with many chairs, time seemed to expand and Levi experienced his second epiphany.

There is no rational point in hesitation. This is the only future in which you have any choice about your destiny; you need to stop dragging your feet.

Levi pulled out a chair and dropped into it. "What do you want to talk about, Doubtful?" he asked.

"Please tell them," he waved at Vu and Glen, "what you said at the meeting last night about poisoning the Yukon River."

Levi slapped Doubtful on the shoulder and grinned. "I am so glad that someone took me seriously!" He regarded Glen and Vu.

"Last night I got to see the big picture, the whole bomb plan and everything. When they said that one bomb was going to be detonated right there at Yukon Station, I was appalled."

"Why?" Vu asked with a frown on his face.

"Have you heard anything about the Potomac River, the one that flows through what *was* Washington, D. C.?"

"No," Glen said. "What have you heard?"

"That it is dead and probably will be for about a hundred years."

"What?" Doubtful exclaimed. "You didn't say that last night!"

"I knew they didn't want to hear it, or anything else that would change their precious plan. They're all focused on a war, not the peace that will hopefully come at some point."

"So that bomb would kill the Yukon for a *century*?" Glen said.

"At least."

"That's just your opinion, right?" Vu asked.

Levi shook his head. "Before I went to work for the Yukon-Fairbanks railroad, back when I was pretty young, I spent one summer at the Denali Lodge. Mr. Lauesen trained me to wait tables, assist the cook, scrub the floor, and listen to everything I possibly could. People from all over the Empire came to see the mountain and enjoy the pristine beauty of the place.

"One day three cars full of Japanese in gold-braided uniforms and two Europeans in three-piece suits arrived to have a conference. We fed them a couple of meals, made sure they had all the drink they wished, then watched and listened.

"The only language they had in common was English. They talked about the devastation that still marked Washington, D.C. and some place in Poland. They said the land and rivers were still *radioactive* and unfit for humans.

"I didn't know what the word meant until four years ago when a soldier told me not to approach one of the trains going north as it was radioactive. When I asked what that meant he said it was poison in the air around a thing and it would kill you." Levi softened his tone and looked into Doubtful's eyes.

"Now *you* understand everything."

"You know Elstun Lauesen?" Glen asked.

"Yes. Haven't seen him in many years; since that summer at Denali Lodge in fact. His dad was my boss."

Glen laughed. "Elstun's running the Denali Rangers. They cover everything from south of Akihito Aerodrome all the way to the Paxson cutoff."

"What is the point if we have to trade our land for victory in a war?" Doubtful asked. "We can live a good life under the Japanese if we just ignore their posturing and rules. They don't come too far down river anyway."

"Yeah, but they want you to live by *their* rules, pay attention to *their* desires, do everything *their* way!" Glen said.

Doubtful gave him a level look. "To be honest, Glen, the only thing that has really changed for *my* people is the language of the invader."

Vu laughed. "I know what you mean. First we had the Chinese as enemies, and then suddenly the Japanese were attacking all of us! Once this is all over I hope we won't have the Chinese as enemies again because we're training them to fight."

"I'm sorry, Doubtful," Glen said. "As usual, I didn't think before shooting off my big mouth."

Doubtful nodded but said nothing.

Levi said, "All I remember is war and occupation. I am tired of being afraid and I like Alaska Pre–, Alaska. I want to live here if we ever have a country that's really ours. That's why I think this is a bad plan and I truly believe we have to come up with something else before it's too late, before we kill the heart of a beautiful place."

"Wow," Glen said, dropping his face into his hands. "We would need to get to someone in the command structure."

"I am a member of the Wolf River Pack and the Dené Army War Council," Doubtful said. Once we get back to Wolf River I can talk to two other members as well."

"We can't just tell them to change their plan without offering a better one," Glen said, spreading his hands.

"Then let's get busy and come up with one," Doubtful said.

"Are we just going to write off all the Chinese laborers at Yukon Station?" Levi asked. "They have to hate the Japs as much as we do."

"They do. Much of China was overrun long before America got into the war; many of those people were born slaves. We have a group of former slaves who have been training to rescue them from the beginning of our planning," Vu said. "We were going to get them out of the camp and down river the day before the bomb detonated."

"That's a great idea," Levi said. "Over three hundred fighters with nothing to lose could be a real boost to our effectiveness."

"Not to mention our morale," Vu said quietly.

"Wow," Doubtful said, running his hand over his face. "We have a *lot* of planning to do, and it's got to be good!"

"If we don't explode the bomb, the Japs will still have it," Glen said, frowning.

"Not necessarily," Levi said. "I've been thinking a lot about this thing and came up with a plan. I need someone to tell me why it won't work, if you can."

CHAPTER 31

"A caterpillar,
this deep in fall—
still not a butterfly."
— Matsuo Basho

WOLF RIVER GENERAL STORE

AUDREY HUNG THE FADED *Taking a Nap!* SIGN IN THE DOOR WINDOW AND pulled the blinds down over it. She went to the door, shot the bolt, and turned back to her cash register. She loved the machine originally built in 1921. It had been modified in 1951, right at the beginning of her service with the Wolf River Pack.

She held down the Total key and reached behind the ornate, etched metal body to a screw on the back. With a hard tap on the screw the front of the machine lifted up, keys and all, to reveal a shortwave radio.

She turned on the power switch and waited a moment for it to warm up. After picking up the tiny microphone she held it to her mouth and spoke in flawless German.

"This is Big River Rose. The fellows are close to completing their hobby. I will contact you again as soon as more information is available. Out."

She switched off the radio, replaced the microphone and lowered the front of the machine back into place. Keeping the messages short, sending them on a certain day at a scheduled time that varied from week to week, made for slight chance of detection by the Japanese. At least she hoped that to be true.

As a single woman of color she had faced many challenges during the war. When the Axis suddenly won she had gravitated toward the sparser parts of the country. She arrived in Alaska in 1947, fluent in German, and with a valise full of money she had lifted off a drunken, egotistical SS colonel who liked to go slumming in Kansas City.

She used the money to buy a trading post in the bush. Her thinking was that even if the Kraut figured out where she went, he wouldn't have enough pull with the Japanese occupiers of Alaska to get at her.

Within a year she realized she had come home. The Athabascans were friendly, open, and generous with their advice and help. She knew she wouldn't have made it through the first winter without them.

When the Imperial Army showed up and started building the Yukon Station Project, she saw a way to mess with the occupiers on both sides of the mountains. An added surprise occurred when young Tim Botkin appeared on the scene and recruited her into the Liberation Underground. He hadn't stayed long, but he brought Doubtful Thomas into the fold at the same time.

The night before Tim returned south they sat around a bottle of scotch one of the Japanese officers had left at Wolf River Lodge.

"I think you should be a spy," Tim said, looking at Audrey.

"For who?"

"The Greater German Reich of North America, of course."

"Why would I give those bastards information?"

"Because it would be inaccurate, at the very least. We, uh, *you* would have to give them factual intelligence to establish your veracity. After that we could tell them pretty much anything we wanted to fatally alter their perceptions of Alaska Prefecture."

"My reason for doing all this would be what?" Audrey decided she liked scotch.

"To feed them disinformation and keep them off balance long enough to play the Japs off against the Krauts, and vice-versa. We'll feed you the information through Doubtful here, and he and his team will dissect anything they send to you. It's a lot like fishing."

Audrey enjoyed playing the Nazi agent. All carefully worded messages she sent to the Krauts were the work of the three-person Intelligence Group of the Liberty Underground working in concert with the Dené Army, and Doubtful was the only one who knew her identity as the conduit. The best thing about running a general store and tavern was that nobody wondered about the presence of people at any time of the day or night.

Since she was a woman of color she was effectively invisible, even to the Japanese. Thus far everything had gone well. She had no evidence that those circumstances would change.

CHAPTER 32

"Coolness of the melons
flecked with mud
in the morning dew."
— Matsuo Basho

KEMPEITAI HEADQUARTERS
YUKON STATION

"Do you know why you are here Mr. Riordan?" Major Hakari Summatsu asked in a pleasant tone. He sat at his desk with his hands out of sight in his lap.

His heart hammering in fear, Riordan licked his lips and hoped for the best. "To work on the railroad, Major."

The major's solemn expression did not change. "No. Do you know why you are in this office in front of me?" The tone didn't change; the man was still being nice.

"I have no idea, Major. Is this part of the orientation to Yukon Station?" He glanced at the sergeant major standing against the wall. The man wore a samurai sword and was flanked by two armed privates as back up.

That must be Fukita. This doesn't look good, Riordan thought.

"You possess much hubris, Mr. Riordan. You thought you could do anything you wished without anyone noticing your subversive actions."

"Subversive! I haven't done anything—"

Summatsu tossed a something on his desk for all to see.

Riordan swallowed despite himself. It was his radio, earphone and all, completely disassembled and useless.

"You were under close surveillance by one of our officers from the first day you arrived. You were observed using this device. When we brought it in and analyzed it, we discovered it to be a link to the Third Reich delegation in Anchorage. Which, of course, is actually the Gestapo, isn't it?"

Riordan felt like weeping. The damn Jap was correct–he had way too much hubris and it would probably cost him his life–and soon.

"What do you want to know?"

"Why are you here?"

"To gain information on your bomb project, of course."

"Who are your allies in this place?"

"Allies?" Riordan said.

"Before you answer consider this: you can die quickly and cleanly, or you can linger for days, perhaps weeks, in anguish and torment. The choice is yours."

I'm dead no matter what I do. Maybe I can piss them off enough to kill me outright. Why the hell didn't I have a cyanide pill ready for something like this?

Riordan raised his head and stared into the major's eyes. "Why do you think I'm not alone? Aren't any of you little yellow bastards smart enough to do something on your own hook with–"

The blow smashed him to the floor, breaking his nose and splitting his lower lip. The buzzing in his head took a few minutes to dissipate.

"So you have chosen torture," Major Summatsu said with a heavy sigh. "Well, that will make Sergeant Major Fukita happy. It has been a long time since he was given leave to ply that part of his trade at which he is so adept."

The two privates lifted him to his feet and dragged him toward the door. He shook his head violently, knowing his time was rapidly running out. It took all of his willpower and energy to kick the side of the right-hand private's knee, breaking it instantly.

"No!" he screamed hoarsely.

The world abruptly went dark.

A thousand years of agony later, Rudof Swink surfaced through his pain and suffering. His universe consisted of agony from one end of his ravaged body to the other.

"Ah, you have returned to us, Herr Swink. Your torment will end when you tell us what the Third Reich knows about our operation here." Major Summatsu sat across the blood stained, scarred table from him.

A rope held Swink in the chair, not that he could move of his own volition, but to keep him upright. Both of his broken arms hung useless, dislocated at the shoulders and any attempted motion would send lightning waves of soul ripping pain throughout his muscular system.

"Don't know," Swink muttered through split lips and broken teeth, "other than atom bomb and moon rocket."

"If your government knows that much about the project, why have they not attacked us?"

"Waiting… for something. Don't know what, or who…" Swink wanted it to be over. Anything to end his universe of pain and silence his shrieking nerve endings.

"I think we can dispense with your now, Herr Swink. Your information has been quite helpful. Your head will be forwarded to your office in Anchorage."

Rough hands grabbed each arm and he screamed in agony as they hauled him outside into the sunshine and dropped him on the ground. He lay sobbing, smelling the dirt and clean air. He was pulled to his knees and his head pushed forward.

The polished boots of Sergeant Major Fukita stepped into his vision. The naked blade of the samurai sword hovered in front of his weeping eyes.

"Any last words?" Major Summatsu's voice floated about him.

Rudof Swink took his last deep breath and shouted, "Fuck you!"

The sword swished out of sight and abruptly all of his pain ceased.

CHAPTER 33

Heat waves shimmering
one or two inches
above the dead grass."
— Matsuo Basho

SIXTY MILES NORTH OF
FORT YUKON

Mɪɴɪᴍᴀʟ ʀᴀɪɴꜰᴀʟʟ ᴄᴏᴜᴘʟᴇᴅ ᴡɪᴛʜ ʜɪɢʜ sᴜᴍᴍᴇʀ ʜᴇᴀᴛ ᴅʀɪᴇᴅ ᴏᴜᴛ ᴛʜᴇ brush, trees, and taiga of Interior Alaska. Cold north winds collided with unstable warm air from the southwest and created storms that produced only a token of moisture, but generated massive amounts of thunder and lightning.

The lightning strikes ignited forest fires, scores of them. The Japanese did not bother fighting fires that didn't threaten their immediate infrastructure. In past years entire Athabascan villages had been lost due to Japanese indifference.

With inadequate tools and minimal supplies, the village crews did all they could to halt the flames. It was never enough, and they and their families suffered.

The summer of 1967 saw 109,000 acres burned before the weather changed and the unprecedented rain extinguished every flame, only to precipitate an entirely different threat. The Japanese were not prepared for the new situation either.

CHAPTER 34

The dragonfly
can't quite land
on that blade of grass."
— Matsuo Basho

ROADS & GROUNDS MAINTENANCE BUILDING
YUKON STATION

"Don't ya think things have gotten more pissy since they put that Jew in charge?" Ed Heine said as he sipped his coffee at morning break. "I feel like the Japs are behind me every time I turn around."

"What Jew?" Timothy Keegan asked. He swallowed coffee and his mind moved to other thoughts.

"Fischer, who else?"

"He's a Jew?" Keegan's focus sharpened instantly. "I thought the Krauts killed them all."

"From what I've heard there's another one over in the Annex," Shorty Ferranti said, puffing on his rank cigarillo.

How did I miss that? Keegan wondered. It didn't matter to him that Fischer was a Jew, but the Krauts might give him a bonus for letting them know. You had to look out for number one in this world, even if it meant playing both ends against the middle.

"I don't think anything has changed since Levi came on board," Eddie Hildebrand said, favoring the oblivious Heine with a frown.

"So what does him being a Jew got to do with anything?" Barnes asked. He held a small porcelain teacup in his huge black hand. "I thought the Japanese welcomed all races in the Greater Pacific Co-Prosperity Sphere."

Everyone in the crew laughed.

Ed Heine said, "You're the smartest nigger I–"

"Ed," Barnes interrupted in a gentle voice, "I don't like that word, it's demeaning and hateful. I am a Negro, Colored, Black, or even a Spook. But don't ever call me that again, okay?" He sat down his cup, interlaced his fingers and loudly cracked them all at the same time. His huge biceps flexed correspondingly, showing plainly through the sleeves of his work shirt.

"S-sure, Barnes. I didn't mean nothing by it. My daddy always used that word. It's just how I was raised."

"Well it is long past time that you were educated. I'm sure you are smarter than your daddy, aren't you?"

"That's for damned sure!"

Not for the first time, Keegan wondered where the huge black man had formerly called home. His massive build made him a perfect gandy dancer. His speech patterns and vocabulary hinted at education well beyond high school. Barnes was a potentially explosive, quiet enigma that nobody on the crew had the guts, or suicidal tendency, to rile.

"Hey Tim, where the hell is that Riordan fellow you hired? He's missed work for two days now," Ed Heine said, obviously anxious to change the subject.

"He must have caught the train south. I checked his room, and nothing seems to have changed." Tim wondered if he was right. He thought Thomas would check in with him before he went haring off someplace else.

"Was his winter gear still there?" Shorty asked. "Nobody leaves without their winter gear if they're not coming back."

"Yeah," Timothy said, suddenly feeling queasy. "His winter gear *is* still in his room."

All of his alarms seemed to go off at once. He glanced at the big clock on the shop wall.

Two hours and the northbound gets here, an hour later it heads south again. I think I'd better be on that train.

"Okay, let's get back to work, fellows. I need to go talk to the boss."

He left the shop and rapidly walked through the rain toward his small house. He silently cursed himself for not realizing that Riordan was not just playing at espionage; the Kempeitai had caught him doing something stupid.

If they have had him for this long he's probably singing like a damned canary. If they think I helped him they'll tell that bastard Fukita to chop off my head.

Sweat broke out on his brow and relief washed over him when he reached his front porch. Just before he would have touched the doorknob, he heard voices inside–they were speaking Japanese. Keegan quietly dodged around the corner of the small cabin and pressed against the wall in the constant downpour. The scent of newly split firewood wafted across his nose and his fingers explored the rough, weathered wood of his cabin.

When the hell would it stop raining?

More than anything, he wanted to scream. He leaned against the wall, terrified, his heart pounded loud enough to hear. A quick glance around revealed no troopers outside.

They were waiting for me to walk through the door. Probably would have killed me on the spot. No, they would have hauled me off and tortured me to see what I knew.

Sweat ran down his forehead. Fear stomped through his mind and kicked at his spine. Terror became something tangible enough to grasp and inspect like some type of rare creature.

Thomas Riordan, or whatever his real name was, had talked, no doubt about it. He had told them everything he knew and probably added a lot of bullshit on top of it. One thing he no doubt repeated at high volume was the name of Gestapo agent Timothy Keegan.

He quickly walked across the small sodden yard separating his cabin from that of Bill Brody, who bossed another gang specializing in building roadbed. Brody was away for the whole week with his men building a spur near Livengood.

For a moment he considered hiding there until dark.

No, that wouldn't work, he decided. Ten minutes after the shift whistle blew and he hadn't returned, the Japanese would conduct a house-to-house search. Their searches were fanatically thorough.

He changed shirts, putting on one of Bill's favorite checker patterns. Keegan swapped his hat for a porkpie that Bill treasured. He found a different slicker than the one he had worn and shrugged into it.

Nightfall would not occur for hours at this time of year and he didn't have the leisure of waiting any longer.

Keegan walked out of the house, followed the well-trod and now rain slick path over the embankment that supported the inbound loop of the tracks. Every step of the way he anticipated the impact of a bullet. As he walked down the other side of the tracks and out of sight of the cabins, he wanted to weep with relief.

The shift whistle wouldn't blow for another half hour and he encountered no pedestrian traffic. At long last he crossed Chrysanthemum Road and passed the first row of rain-lashed willows between the Project and Wolf River Village Road. Once on the well-used path he immediately felt safer. For the first time in two hours he believed he might actually get away from them.

The shift whistle blew and he broke into a trot through the storm. It was only a little over a mile to the village.

CHAPTER 35

Wrapping the rice cakes,
with one hand
she fingers back her hair."
— Matsuo Basho

WOLF RIVER GENERAL STORE

As soon as Levi left work he drove straight to the store. People were waiting. Only two other vehicles sat in the rain soaked parking lot and he wondered if the meeting had been called off. He heard a motor and recognized the sound of a riverboat coming up the Yukon.

He walked over to the bank and watched the approach of a boat he hadn't seen before. It beached directly below the store and three men in raingear clambered out and tied the boat up. Levi turned and walked into the store. Audrey sat at the bar talking to Thelma, and Doubtful sat at a table conversing with three men, one was Gunther Charles, Levi didn't know the one whose face he could see, and the other had his back to the door, but seemed oddly familiar.

"Here's Levi!" Doubtful said.

"Good afternoon, ladies, and gentlemen." He smiled first at Thelma and then the others in the room. "There are three more people coming in who just arrived by riverboat."

"That's everybody," Doubtful said in a tone of finality.

The three men filed though the door and pulled off their rain gear.

"How good to see all of you!" Doubtful said and moved across the room to shake the hand of each man. "Please, if everyone would sit at the big table."

As he moved toward the table, the man whose face he hadn't

seen moved up behind him.

"How are things going, Fish?"

Levi whirled around and looked up into the face of Jim Spreter.

"Jimbo! What are you doing here?"

"Business, just like you," he said with his signature grin.

Everyone took a seat and Doubtful glanced around.

"Since all of you don't know each other I'm going to ask everyone to introduce themselves." He nodded to one of the three men who arrived by riverboat.

"I am Dexter Williams from the Galena Scouts." He flashed a friendly smile. "Member of the War Council."

"Daniel Sherry, Minto Warriors, War Council."

"Charlie Esmalka, Huslia Hustlers, also War Council."

"Mike Christenson, Fairbanks Irregulars, War Council."

"Jim Spreter, Livengood commander of the Fairbanks Irregulars, War Council."

"Gunther Charles, Yukon Station Underground, War Council."

Then it was Levi's turn and he gave his name and added, "Guest."

Thelma smiled at Levi and said her name, adding, "Wolf River Pack, War Council."

Levi was so surprised by her response that he didn't hear the first two things Doubtful said, and only hearing him say "Levi Fischer" pulled his attention back to the table. Thelma had smiled at him the entire time.

"I'm sorry, "Levi said. "What did you say, Doubtful?"

"I asked that you tell everyone here what you told us the other day."

Levi reiterated what he knew about radiation, the Potomac estuary, and ended with, "I honestly think that detonating the bomb in the Project building will kill the Yukon for the foreseeable future."

"How can *one* bomb do that?" Charlie Esmalka asked, disbelief strong in his voice. "Maybe it would leave a big crater, but *kill* the Yukon?"

"Charlie," Doubtful said, did you hear what he said about the radiation and what it did to the Potomac?"

"I ain't seen that river, and I never heard of this radiation thing," Charlie said. "If we want to get rid of the Japs this is the best way we can do it."

"I agree with Charlie for the most part," Dexter said. "But do you believe this radiation stuff, Doubtful?"

"I never heard of it before, but I don't disbelieve it."

"Is there any way this thing about the Potomac can be proven to our satisfaction?" Daniel asked.

Doubtful looked at Levi. "Any ideas on that, Mr. Fischer?"

Levi thought hard. The only possibility gave him the shivers just to contemplate it. "There might be a way, but it could get someone killed if it goes wrong."

"Just as long as it ain't me," Charlie said with a laugh.

"Who–" Doubtful began.

"Me," Levi said.

"Then don't do it," Thelma said instantly.

"We might not have a choice if we want to save the Yukon," Levi said gently.

"This plan has been in the works for almost two years," Dexter said. "We have consensus across the board with all the other War Councils. People down in the states are waiting for the word from us. The Japs ain't gonna wait for us to figure something else out before they go ahead with *their* crazy plan."

"Dexter makes a good point," Gunther said.

Mike Christenson raised his hand. "Some here don't know it, but I am a medical doctor. We use radiation every day at our office in Fairbanks, x-rays. It is dangerous for you to get too many x-rays and we know they can mess up your sperm or eggs, depending on your sex. That's why we have lead aprons for the technicians, and cover the parts of you that we don't need to see inside.

"Years ago when I was in medical school we were shown a movie about radiation burns. It was made by the Third Reich and had images of men and women who had been on the edge of the bombings in Washington, D.C. and Poland. The burns were horrific to say the least.

"One thing they mentioned in passing was that these people had been far enough away from the center, from what they called 'ground zero,' not be atomized or killed outright. The film also said the casualty rate extended far beyond the time frame of the bombings as many hundreds died each month from the ongoing effects of the radiation. The film didn't address the Potomac or what was left around Washington."

The room went silent for a while.

"I really don't see any way around keeping to the original plan," Jim Spreter said. "We have to act when the Japs do. It will be our only real chance."

Doubtful caught Levi's eye and raised his eyebrows for a moment. Levi nodded back and Doubtful cleared his throat.

"Okay, let's call that Plan A. We have come up with a 'Plan B.' Would you all like to hear it?"

"Of course we would!" Dexter said. Everyone else nodded.

"It's a little more intricate and would take more time, but we wouldn't risk killing the Yukon," Levi said.

"We're all ears, Levi," Thelma said and gave him a dig in the ribs with her elbow.

He started talking.

CHAPTER 36

"Midfield,
attached to nothing,
the skylark singing."
— Matsuo Basho

WORKER HOUSING,
YUKON STATION

LEVI WOKE TO SOMEONE POUNDING ON HIS CABIN DOOR. HE ROLLED OVER, sat up on the edge of his bed, and glanced at the clock–three in the morning....

What the hell?

"Just a minute," he yelled, pulling on his robe. This had to be official and he rapidly rushed through the possibilities for a visit this early in the morning. No idea other than fear proffered itself.

He opened the door to a steady downpour. Sergeant Major Fukita stood glaring at him, three armed troopers flanked the NCO, glistening in their dripping rain gear.

"Yes?"

"Clothe yourself," Fukita shouted. "You are to accompany us immediately."

Knowing better than to shut the door, Levi turned to his closet and grabbed trousers and a shirt off hangers. He shrugged off his robe and tossed it over the bed before slipping into underwear. He had no idea if the Japanese watched or not; he really didn't give a damn.

The conviction that they had penetrated the Yukon Station Underground and were hauling him off to be executed overwhelmed him. What else could it be? He pulled on his raincoat and hat as he trudged toward the door.

He sat helpless in the back of the lorry between two of the guards. Opportunity for escape did not exist. He wondered why cyanide pills were not an option for the organization.

The lorry raced through the checkpoints without slowing, windshield wipers slashing back and forth. He felt he was in deep shit, as Jimbo would say. He hoped everyone else had escaped the Japanese net. The lorry lurched to a stop outside the Kempeitai headquarters building.

This would be Levi's first visit to the structure. He wondered if it would also be his last. The fact that he had not been manacled or otherwise secured in any way gave him a glimmer of hope despite his understanding of Japanese tactics.

The guard on his right quickly jumped out of the lorry and then nodded to Levi.

They have yet to touch me, he thought.

Sergeant Major Fukita preceded the group through the rain and into the building. By the time Levi went through the doors all of the NCOs in the foyer were at attention for Sergeant Major Fukita. Every one of them stared through him, piercing his soul, assaulting his self-confidence, and trying to read his mind.

The entire operation elicited no sound save for footsteps and water dripping off rain gear. Levi wondered if he would walk out of the room they were about to enter, or would he be dragged out feet first.

Fukita opened a door and then stood to the side. The guards moved Levi forward with a subtle gun butt. Inside the room, squatting like a massive toad behind a small desk, sat the corpulent bulk of Lieutenant General Tomoyuki Yamashita.

Levi snapped to attention and performed a first-degree bow, holding it until the general sniffed, before standing upright.

"What have you learned about your workers, Mr. Fischer?" The low voice instantly gave Levi the mental image of a massive iron door grating on its hinges.

"Nothing of interest, General Yamashita." He spoke carefully so he wouldn't stammer.

The general hadn't aged well. At the venerable age of 81 he had gone to fat and obviously had given in to a sedentary life. His hand quivered slightly and the general moved it to his lap, hidden by the desk shadow.

"*We* have discovered a worker who was spying for the Germans. We are sure he was an agent for the Gestapo. He was a member of your railroad crew."

For a horrible moment Levi thought he was going to lose control of his sphincter. He strained to show no emotion, especially fear. He frowned as if in concentration.

"What is his name?"

"The name he used *was* Thomas Riordan. His real name was Rudof Swink."

"I don't know anyone named Riordan or Swink."

"He was new and arrogant. He thought no one paid him any mind as he sent radio reports to the German legation in Anchorage. He gave us a number of names before he died.

"Unfortunately most of the names were elicited in his final, raving state and carried little if any context. Yet your name *was* one that he shrieked. What I wish to know is why *you* didn't discover this enemy agent before *we* did?"

"I am a single agent in a position and situation still new to me. I am carefully making friends and observing all that I can. It would be difficult for me to follow any given person, let alone a number of them."

"You could contact the duty officer and have as many field personnel as you need within minutes. We also notice that you have made more friends in Wolf River village than here in the Project. Why is that?"

"The people in the village do not work for me, therefore they are more forthcoming with observations than would any of my workers. My crew would do or say nothing incriminating in front of me because I am their supervisor. I must admit that so far I have not discovered any covert activity among the roads and grounds crew."

The general stared at him at length. Levi fantasized a long tongue whipping out of the wide mouth, wrapping around him, and pulling him screaming into a suddenly wide, cavernous maw.

"Should we discover another subversive without your aid we will be impelled to thoroughly examine your mind. You would not appreciate, nor enjoy, the experience."

Lieutenant General Yamashita nodded to Sergeant Major Fukita and a rifle butt painfully rapped Levi in the middle of his spine. He immediately bent into a first-degree bow and held it as the general and a few others slowly exited the room. When the door closed he straightened, the sergeant major leaned within inches of his face.

"I am confident that you will fail," he screamed, spittle flying. "I look forward to causing you great agony before relieving you of your head."

Levi returned the man's stare and said nothing. He understood this man hated him and would work hard to discredit him. He had absolutely no concept of Sergeant Major Fukita's motives or the rationale behind his constant animosity.

Fukita's eyes shifted to the right and he snapped an order in Japanese for a private to return this barbarian to his hovel. A hand grabbed Levi's left arm, spun him around, and pushed him out the door. The rain-filled open air cleansed his mind and body. A breath had never tasted better despite his sodden state.

A corporal stood by the lorry and motioned him into the cab. Levi was so drained he had to concentrate on every move required to climb into the truck. The corporal drove him back to his house without a word.

The truck stopped, Levi stepped onto the running board and glanced back at the stone-faced soldier.

"*Arigato*, I appreciate the lift."

He jumped to the ground, slamming the door behind him. As the lorry splashed away into the night Levi began to shake uncontrollably and he realized he had just pissed himself.

And I thought I didn't care.

CHAPTER 37

The old pond—
a frog jumps in,
sound of water."
— Matsuo Basho

YUKON STATION PROJECT ANNEX

DR. JERRY HYAKAWA AUTOMATICALLY CHECKED HIS DOSIMETER AND bent over to check his math one last time. The miniaturized bomb neared final assembly inside the vehicle. Technicians on scaffolding high above the concrete floor of the Annex fussed with multiple checks on the device in the nose cone of the Chrysanthemum Rocket.

All were in awe of the two pilots who would make sure their deadly cargo was delivered to the heart of the Greater German Reich. The pilots thought of themselves as the final knights of the Kamikaze Corps.

The last tweaks and nudges had been completed on the larger bomb sitting inside a heavy crate on the flatcar in the large assembly room.

Jake Rose entered the lead-lined room and nodded to his friend.

"Are we close to completing the project?" he asked.

Jerry looked up and read the sign language that Jake rapidly delivered while keeping his back to the wall-mounted camera.

Is it time to alert the agent and summon the opposition?

"Very close. The rocket should be finished by late tomorrow."

Jerry signed, *Yes. As soon as the rocket is away the opposition needs to hit this place. We need to evacuate as soon as possible.*

"That's good," Jake said. "How soon do you think they will launch the rocket?"

"General Yamashita told me to begin the launch sequence as soon as the railcar weapon is ready to roll. That's about ten days from now."

Jake signed, *Good luck!*

Jerry responded with the same sign. He left the Annex and went through security three times before reaching the over-saturated parking lot. In moments he was driving his Mitsubishi coupe toward Wolf River village through the constant rain and sending up sprays of water every time he hit a pothole.

Much had to be done, and quickly.

What neither he or Jake realized was that their signed conversation was reflected in the window, in full view of the camera.

CHAPTER 38

"What fish feel,
birds feel, I don't know—
the year ending."
— Matsuo Basho

THIRTY MILES NORTH OF
FORT YUKON

VICTORIA CREEK, USUALLY LESS THAN A BOOT HIGH TRICKLE IN LATE summer, had swollen to twelve feet deep and fifty yards wide, all rushing downhill at great velocity. The surrounding mountains and plateaus had suffered heavily in the recent forest fire season and now lay denuded of vegetation. Forty-four days of unprecedented, incessant heavy rain had long ago doused all flames and embers.

Interior Alaska's forests were comprised of stunted black spruce in the low-lying areas because the root systems cannot descend more than eighteen inches below the ground before they reach permafrost. Permafrost had been measured to depths of one hundred sixty feet or more and consisted of ice mixed with dirt, or frozen mud.

Likewise, water running off higher points covered by birch, tamarack, and spruce could only soak in less than two feet before the ground became saturated, forcing the water to run off in ever greater volumes. By the second week of August, 1967 the creeks and feeder streams were filled far over their banks and pouring water into larger streams like the Chena, which ran through the heart of Fairbanks. From there the excess water flowed into the Tanana, and thence to the Yukon. All of the rivers in Interior Alaska Prefecture were rising over their banks.

Bridges large and small washed away, low-lying areas including vehicle roads and railroads disappeared under newly formed lakes and expanding rivers, flooded or destroyed by the unrelenting hydraulic pressure. A lake the size of the state of New Jersey grew in the center of Interior Alaska Prefecture. Disaster had cascaded down on a mostly lackadaisical Japanese government who did not understand, or chose to ignore, the meteorological and geographical mechanics of the massive prefecture they ruled.

Their indifference would now cost them much more than any of them could imagine, even on their most pessimistic day.

CHAPTER 39

YUKON STATION

Levi sat at his desk, staring at the telephone in his hand with no small amount of trepidation. He dialed three numbers and put the receiver to his ear.

"Good morning, Captain Atsumi, this is Levi Fischer. May I come up and chat for a few minutes? Thank you." He hung up the phone and wiped his damp brow.

Step by step.

He went into the outer office and nodded to Miss Watanabe.

"Tomiko, I will be up in Captain Atsumi's office for at least half an hour."

"Very well, Levi. I'll hold the fort." She gave him a quick smile.

He forced himself to hurry up the stairs. Levi tapped on Atsumi's door and she called for him to enter. She looked up from some papers as he entered.

"The failed spy catcher in the flesh," she said in a mocking tone. "What can I do for you?"

He dropped into one of the chairs without waiting for an invitation.

"That's not fair, Captain. I didn't even know the man had been hired by my foreman."

"A foreman who has *also* disappeared. For that matter we haven't been able to locate Mr. Charles for the last two days. What is going on out there in the rail yard? Where are all of your people?"

"Gunther? As our main inspector he's always out checking track and roadbed for signs of wearing, damage, or instability. I never worry about him unless he's gone more than a week."

"If he's gone more than a week you will face great displeasure from the third floor," she nodded her head toward the ceiling, "and I believe General Yamashita has already made his current displeasure known."

"I understand. Now that you've had your official gloat and I've been reprimanded once again, may I please get to the reason I dropped by?"

"If you do not show respect for my rank in this office I will have Sergeant Major Fukita explain Imperial Japanese military courtesy to you."

Levi stifled his first retort. She was right; the room was certainly bugged and he had no idea who else listened.

"My apologies, Captain Atsumi. I have a lot on my mind today and am under no small amount of distress. Even a rabbit has a temper."

She smiled and nodded. "Much better. What can I do for you, Mr. Fischer?"

He didn't change his sprawled position in the chair and gave her a wink.

"I recently remembered something I overheard some years ago and applied it to our current situation. In short, I am worried about the safety of my railroad crew when we transport the weapon to Prince Akihito Aerodrome."

"What did you hear, and when?"

He related his experience at Denali Lodge without naming Elstun Lauesen, referring to him only as "my boss."

"If that thing can kill a whole river, the radiation it, uh, *creates* must be incredibly dangerous to those handling it, right?"

"You're worried about the health of your workers?" She frowned as she spoke.

"Yes, yes I do. They're Americans, not Chinese, remember?" He was surprised at how much honest anger he suddenly felt.

"You, and they, have nothing to worry about. As I understand it the radiation is minimal until they trigger the weapon and it splits uranium atoms to release their energy. The force of the explosion is supposed to be massive.

"That is what I remember from my classes in military school. The weapon will be in a lead-lined container all the way to Prince Akihito Aerodrome. No radiation will leak out."

"Can the bomb really do what the Germans said; kill a whole river?"

"Who cares? It won't be here, it will be, well, somewhere else."

"I'd just like to know; can that thing kill a whole damn river for a century?"

"It hasn't been a century yet, merely twenty-two years. The Potomac is currently a fetid, radioactive ditch, so don't buy any real estate there."

He decided that it was her cold smirk that made him wish he could strangle her on the spot. Still, he had what he needed and he forced himself to maintain his composure.

"So the Hudson River is likewise doomed," he muttered loud enough for her to hear.

"The Third Reich capitol in North America is doomed, Mr. Fischer. Does that create a conflict for you?"

"No, Captain, it does not. I would cheerfully assist in the termination of every Nazi in North America if given the chance."

"Excellent, you may get what you wish for once we cut the head off the German serpent and are left with remnants to exterminate."

"I look forward with great pleasure to that day, Captain Atsumi. Thank you for your time and assurances."

"Any time, Mr. Fischer." She turned back to her paper work and he left her office. Once back in his office he carefully closed the door and unbuttoned his shirt. The microphone was still live and he clicked it off before pulling the tape holding the recorder off his chest.

The tape took more hair with it than anticipated and he nearly cried out with the sudden pain. The War Council wanted proof and this was all he could get, but he felt sure it would be enough.

CHAPTER 40

"Cold night: the wild duck,
sick, falls from the sky
and sleeps awhile."
— Matsuo Basho

LUFTWAFFE HEADQUARTERS,
BERLIN, GERMANY

"Mein Führer the last pieces of the Japanese solution are nearly in place."

Hermann Göring tore his attention away from a Rembrandt hanging on the wall and peered at the speaker.

"Have they launched their monkey moon rocket yet?"

"Nein. We have been apprised that they have two functional weapons and are constructing two more. Our assault troops are assembled at Fort St. John in Deutsche Columbia. Our attack will be a total surprise to the Japanese."

"Rather like a reverse Pearl Harbor?" Göring said and began laughing. The laugh quickly devolved into a hacking cough. He waved away the physician and two nurses who hovered in constant attendance.

"I'm fine, fine! Leave me be."

The aide still stood at attention.

"There is more?"

"Gruppenführer Stoltz, in the belief that events should proceed as quickly as possible from this point on, requests that you give him the clearance to proceed with Operation Lotus as he sees fit."

"Stoltz. Was he in the war?"

"He was a pilot, shot down thirty four Russian aircraft. You gave him the Knight's Cross in 1946."

"Ah! Yes, I have faith in that fellow. But if there are problems with the successful completion of the operation, it will mean his execution. Make sure he understands that."

"Yes, mein Führer."

"He is to notify us immediately when he is ready to launch his assault. We want to time our gift to the Emperor of Japan for simultaneous delivery."

"Yes, mein Führer!"

"In the meantime, notify the general staff of the situation. I will require instant action once the delivery is made."

"Yes, mein Führer!"

Göring returned his attention back to the Rembrandt. He particularly appreciated the chiaroscuro so beautifully mastered in the Dutchman's works. Göring's own career had profited from a much different type of chiaroscuro and he hugely enjoyed the irony.

CHAPTER 41

"A cicada shell;

it sang itself

utterly away."

— Matsuo Basho

YUKON STATION

"I THINK THIS WILL DO THE TRICK," JERRY HYAKAWA SAID SOFTLY AS HE slid a small, mechanical device across the desk of Jake Rose.

"What trick?" Jake murmured, still immersed in a wiring diagram.

"Detonate the device when we want that to happen."

Jake glanced around and was careful not to look at the unwinking eyes of the camera at the far end of the room.

"Great. Where does it go?"

"Inside the electrical panel with all wires soldered tight. It needs to be as integrated as possible. Do you want to come with me while I get Dr. Tommatsu's approval?"

"There are times, Jerry, when I truly believe you have a death wish."

"Jake, we're probably not going to get out this alive, so let's have as much adventure as possible."

"I can't argue with that." He pushed his chair back and followed his colleague out into the corridor.

Jake knocked on Dr. Tommatsu's door and turned the knob when he heard the muted, "Enter."

The old man straightened from his workbench. His lab coat was spotless and his Eton tie perfectly knotted.

"Gentlemen?"

"I would like your opinion on this, doctor." Jerry handed him the device.

"A radio-controlled switch," Dr. Tommatsu mused. "A switch to do what?"

"Set off an atomic bomb," Jake said in a light whisper. "We'll signal it through a series of microwave towers."

"And if a bird happens to fly by at an inopportune time," Dr. Tommatsu said, "the device won't get the signal. Do you have a backup?"

"No, sir," Jerry said. "Not unless one of us stays for the party."

"True," Dr. Tommatsu said as he sat down and stared at the device. "This is very good work. Your craftsmanship impresses me."

"Without your instruction and guidance we would have never perfected anything here," Jake said. "You are the heart of this project."

"I must sadly agree," Tommatsu said so softly the other two men had to strain to hear his words. "It wasn't supposed to happen like this, you know."

"What wasn't?" Jerry asked.

"This project, these weapons. When I met Dr. Kurt Diebner the very first time I visited Germany in 1942, I was overwhelmed by his knowledge of nuclear physics. At his side stood another mental titan, Eric Schumann.

"Between them they fought the Third Reich for everything they got in order to create the bombs that won the war for the Nazis, and the Empire of Japan. The German military tried to shut down their research time after time, claiming it had no relevance in the greater scheme of things even if it did work–which they doubted."

Jake said, "They would have lost the war if the military had won that argument."

"Of course they would have. They nearly did as it was. If the Battle of the Breakout hadn't succeeded, the bombs wouldn't have been finished in time. Who knows where we would all be today."

Jake and Jerry glanced at each other.

"Why are you doing this, working with us to destroy the project?" Jerry asked in a gentle tone.

"Because both sides have abused it. Initially we viewed it as a classic *yogei sakusan* but it now has become a club in the hands of madmen and we must start over. If I can help make that happen the act will exonerate me for all the misery I have helped create."

Jerry frowned, "Yogei... a decisive battle, Doctor Tommatsu?"

"Exactly. But that was twenty years ago.... Now I fear these weapons threaten humanity."

"You haven't told anyone else about how you feel, have you, doctor?" Jake asked.

"No, of course not. I know that if you both survive what is to come here, you need to understand your roles in a new world."

"We'll have you to help with that, Doctor Tommatsu," Jerry said, putting more enthusiasm in his tone than he actually felt.

"No, that will not be the case. I have decided that I will be the failsafe. I will remain here to insure the device is triggered when the time comes."

"That's suicide!" Jake said in a hard tone. "The situation is not that hopeless. You will be needed–"

"You do not understand, do you?" Tommatsu said without raising his voice. "I am Japanese, and soon that will be a distinct liability. I can clearly see the future, and I know that I will be viewed as an architect of death, not a liberator of conquered peoples. No, I have carefully reasoned this out.

"I owe it to those poor souls working on this project without benefit of protective clothing to end this in one clean stroke. As my heirs, you must carry this knowledge safely to your people to even the odds. Great change is coming. I will install this device while both of you prepare your exits."

"It has been an honor to work with you, Dr. Tommatsu," Jerry said. "I hope my future holds someone as brilliant as you."

"Thank you both," he said looking from Jerry to Jake. "You have been my only light in an increasingly darkening world. Please get out here while you can."

They both gave him a first-degree bow, then left without another word.

CHAPTER 42

WOLF RIVER GENERAL STORE

LEVI DROVE INTO THE WOLF RIVER LODGE PARKING LOT AND FELT RELIEF that it was empty of other vehicles. Despite the beautiful summer day he hurried through the screen door and found the large room empty.

"Hello!" he yelled.

Noise issued from the pantry in the kitchen and Thelma walked out.

"Levi, you surprised me. I thought you weren't coming over today, but I'm happy that you have."

"I'm happy about it, too. How long have you been on the War Council?"

"Wow, that's *so* romantic. Sorry, my sarcasm sometimes starts before my mind does. Why do you ask?"

"I'm sorry, I didn't mean to be abrupt. Despite keeping up with everything that has happened, there are a number of things in this situation that are still out of focus for me. Why didn't I know prior to yesterday that you were on the War Council?"

"Because you didn't need to know, Levi. We have learned over the years that the less each person knows, the better. Any one of us could be arrested by the Kempeitai and questioned. If you don't know something there is zero chance you can spill it to the Japs while they're pulling out your fingernails."

He thought about her words and realized how ignorant he must have sounded. Her clear, brown eyes remained fixed on his face as she waited for a response.

"I, I hadn't thought that all the way through. You must think that I am incredibly naïve."

"I don't know if you're naïve or suicidal. From the first moment I saw you I thought you were interesting. Yet there is something about your charge and abruptly retreat philosophy that I really don't understand."

"Charge and retreat? What do you mean?"

"Every time you come here and see me you start talking, are friendly, even flirtatious. Then you slowly pull back and wrap that shell around you. Talk about not knowing what is going on–you are certainly an enigma to me!"

Levi felt his cheeks growing warm. "I have to start talking when I see you so that I don't tell you how beautiful you are and then have to push you away when you respond."

She laughed. "See, you admit that you're doing it on purpose. However, since you brought it up, why *do* you push me away?"

"So the Japanese won't use you to hurt me, or vice versa."

"If they figure out what we are all doing in time to stop us, we will all die. So why let a little thing like that slow you down?"

"You're absolutely right," he said in a tight voice. He pulled her to him and kissed her–and she kissed him back.

"Oh gosh," Teddi said from the doorway, "I think we came home too soon, dad."

"Not at all," Doubtful said. "I would have hated to miss this."

Levi and Thelma broke away from the kiss laughing.

"I'm in love with your daughter, Doubtful, and nothing can change that."

Doubtful walked over and embraced him.

"I think everyone but you already knew that, Levi. I'm glad you finally realized it. Is that why you came over today?"

"Actually, it wasn't."

"That's right, he wanted to know how long I had been on the War Council. Before I could tell him we got off on a feeder creek."

"She's been on the War Council since she was fourteen years old," Doubtful said. "She is also in charge of intelligence."

"I had no idea," Levi said, suddenly feeling adrift from his perceptions of the world.

"You thought I was just a nice, simple, sweet village girl. Didn't you?"

"With the exception of simple, yeah. I never thought of you as simple."

"Good, that's what people are supposed to think. So, do you have something for the War Council?"

"I have something I want you all to hear, but we need somewhere less public."

Doubtful went back to the door, shut, and barred it.

"There, will that work?"

"Yeah, can we all sit down?"

Doubtful pointed to the large table in the middle of the room and Levi pointed to a smaller table.

"I want to make sure all of you can hear this."

He pulled out the tiny recorder and played the taped conversation he had with Captain Atsumi.

As soon as it finished, Thelma exclaimed, "Where did you get that thing?"

"The recorder? Captain Atsumi gave it to me the day she told me I was a Kempeitai agent."

"I love the irony of this," Teddi said.

"We have to push Plan B," Doubtful said. "How can we arrange for the rest of the War Council to listen to that?"

"Send this around by courier, let each of them hear it for themselves. If Atsumi asks about it, I'll tell her I misplaced it."

"How does it work?" Doubtful asked.

Levi showed him. While he explained, he could feel Thelma's eyes on him, and he liked the feeling.

CHAPTER 43

From time to time
The clouds give rest
To the moon-beholders."
— Matsuo Basho

WORKER HOUSING,
YUKON STATION

LAN HUANG KNELT NEAR THE PERIMETER FENCE AND INDUSTRIOUSLY pulled weeds from around the carrots and slapped at mosquitoes. Intent on her labors, she did not register the low voice until it repeated, "Sister," in Mandarin.

Carefully she looked to the side and saw a man on the other side of the high fence, lying in the small channel where the run off from the garden found its way to the river. He beckoned to her with one hand and held his other hand up with a finger to his lips. Mosquitoes buzzed around his head but he ignored them, which she found impressive.

She glanced around and saw no Japanese soldiers, which was typical. Lan moved over next to the fence and pulled at weeds.

"What are you doing out there?" she hissed. "If the Japs catch you they will kill you!"

"Who is the honcho in your barracks?" the man asked.

"Bao Li, he wears a scholar's beard."

"Can you get him out here without drawing attention from the others?"

"I will try." Lan stood and brushed dirt and mud off her rough work trousers and walked toward the barracks. Scores of Chinese worked in the garden around her. The massive amount of sunlight coupled with the record rains had fostered growth beyond anything she had previously seen.

She walked into the barracks and waited for her eyes to adjust. Bao Li sat in one corner chatting with two other men. She started toward them and he looked up into her eyes. She nodded her head to the side and he immediately stood and came over to her.

"Why are you not in the garden?"

"There is a man in the drainage ditch. He wishes to speak to you. There were no Japanese in sight when I came in."

"Walk with me," he said. "Point out something in the garden near him."

In moments they were near the spot. She pointed down at some plants and smiled into his face. "He is right over there. Here, take this hoe so you can have a reason to be there."

"You are very quick, Lan. Keep your eyes open for problems."

"As you wish, Bao."

✪

Bao Li hacked at the ground with the hoe as he quickly surveyed the area. The Japanese rarely came back to the garden unless they wanted to raid it for food or rape a woman. He edged over to the fence.

"Who are you?" he asked.

"I am Sergeant Da Chen. I am with the Righteous Fists; we are part of the Liberation Underground. I was one of the slaves who escaped after the train wreck last winter."

"How do I know you are not a tool of the Japanese?"

"You don't. Yet, I would not have chosen this method of approach if there had been an easier way." He glanced down at his mud-caked khaki uniform, shook his head free of mosquitoes, and offered a quick smile.

"I concede that you have a point. While I am overjoyed that you are here, and that the Liberation Underground truly exists, *why* are you here?"

"Everything is going to change very soon. We have waited to alert you to lessen the chances of someone in your group being an undercover agent and warning the Japanese."

"My people are all true to the cause, we have examined them carefully. We have had to kill a few people who chose the wrong words or otherwise made us suspicious. What is about to happen?"

"Very soon the Japanese are going to launch a rocket from the Annex. At that time, or within a couple of hours after the event, the Germans are going to attack this place. They do not see any difference between the Japanese and us; we all look alike to them.

"Therefore, when the attack comes we will have people along this fence who will destroy it and guide you all to safety. Have all of your people grab heavy tools like mattocks, hoes, and shovels that can be used as weapons if needed. Kill any Japanese who happen to be out here, though I doubt any will. Once through the fence you will be armed with more effective weapons."

Bao quivered with the sudden intensity of his emotions. "You have no idea how wonderful this news is to me!"

"I understand, brother. The world is about to change in ways the Nazis and the Japs cannot conceive, nor stop."

"We will be ready!"

"Good. We need you."

CHAPTER 44

"Spring rain
leaking through the roof
dripping from the wasps' nest."
— Matsuo Basho

FAIRBANKS,
ALASKA PREFECTURE

Major Katsu Miamatsu wandered down Cushman Street towards the Chena River. Some of the leaves on the birch trees had started their shift from green to yellow and the fireweed blossoms blazed crimson in all of their mature glory, the first indication of the ever-looming winter. The record-breaking rain had finally ceased and what was left of summer looked lovely. A number of people stood on the Cushman Street Bridge, one of the two bridges spanning the river as it wound through town.

He recognized a man he knew. "Good morning, Mr. Atchi. What has everyone so interested?"

"Good morning, Major Miamatsu. You are unaware of our potential disaster? Look at the river!" He pointed at the swiftly flowing, debris-laden water.

Miamatsu frowned. The water was nearly touching the bottom of the bridge. Alarm coursed through him.

"How far above flood stage is it?"

"Many feet, and it is still rising. If you have any business on the other side of town I suggest you complete it quickly. The military seems to be doing nothing about the situation other than watching it. Nothing personal, I assure you."

"Not to worry, I entertain the same thoughts myself."

However, I am not ignorant enough to say them out loud.

Miamatsu smiled at Atchi. He wondered if Sergeant Hamada was aware of the situation. He didn't care if anyone else in the office was unaware or potentially affected by this unfolding event.

He nodded to Mr. Atchi and headed toward his office at a brisk walk. Upon arrival he called for his assistant to follow him.

"Shut the door behind you, Juro."

"Yes, Major. What can I do for you?"

"Get some help. I want everything in this office moved to the second floor."

"By when, sir?"

"Tonight, before you go home. The Chena is going to flood the city by morning. I don't want anything in this office to be destroyed."

"I haven't heard anything about the river flooding the town, Major."

"You have now. Get busy."

He dialed Hamada's number. "Norio, have you seen the Chena lately? If you have anything that needs done on the other side I suggest you do it now, the river will flood Fairbanks tonight. You're welcome."

After he hung up, he considered what needed done next. He walked around to Lieutenant Colonel Akio Toragawa's office and knocked on the door.

"Enter."

Miamatsu opened the door and leaned on the doorframe.

"If you value anything in this office you should move it up to the second floor, Colonel."

"What are you talking about, Major?"

He explained.

"Why has no one else told me this?"

"I'm sure they are waiting for directions, sir. The Imperial Army seems to feel it is impervious to natural disaster. This is one time when I believe we should all think for ourselves."

"I appreciate your concern. But if I were you, I wouldn't share all of those thoughts with the people you meet, Major. On a different topic, I have been informed that you are still asking questions about the Suzuki murder."

"Of course I am. The crime has not yet been solved."

"This is one time we should let it quietly fade from our minds."

"Why is that, Colonel? Was it a sanctioned kill and we were not warned?"

"This is no longer a topic for discussion, Major. I *order* you to direct your energies elsewhere. Do you understand?"

"Yes, sir. I have a flood to prepare for which will take at least a week."

"I wish you luck, Major."

"Thank you, Colonel."

Miamatsu turned and walked away, not allowing his anger to surface in any manner.

Let the damn fools drown.

"Drown!" he said aloud. "The prisoners!"

He rushed to the intake desk and slammed his hand down on the polished wood so hard the desk sergeant jerked back in surprise.

"Major Miamatsu, what is the matter?"

"Have the prisoners been moved?"

"To where, sir?"

"Out of the basement!"

The sergeant looked puzzled, his eyes flicked from one side to the other.

"Dispense with the kabuki act! Answer my question!"

"The prisoners are in their cells, Major."

"In the basement?"

"Yes, sir, where else would they be?"

"Some place safe," he snapped, and hurried to the stairway.

The floor in the cellblock was already covered in water.

"Stop!" the sergeant of the guard shouted. "Oh! Sorry, Major, but we seem to have a plumbing problem."

"Get all of the prisoners out of here. The river is flooding. This basement will be under water by midnight."

"Where should we take them, sir?"

"How many prisoners do you have?"

"Twenty-six, Major. We have nowhere else to incarcerate them."

"Put them in rail cars and send them out of town, to Anchorage, as quickly as possible. The Chena will be over its banks within hours and this building will have water on the first floor by tomorrow!"

"I need someone superior to me in rank to give me an order in writing, sir."

Miamatsu sloshed over to the desk and grabbed an official form. He quickly wrote an order moving the prisoners to Anchorage for their safety and signed his name and rank.

"There. Now get them out of here or they will all die. You should go with them."

"Yes, sir! Thank you, sir!"

As Miamatsu left he heard the sergeant of the guard shouting at his corporals. He smiled as he pondered which step to take next.

CHAPTER 45

"Now that eyes of hawks
in dusky night are darkened...
Chirping of the quails."
— Matsuo Basho

SS HEADQUARTERS, NW BRANCH, FORT St. JOHN, DEUTSCHE COLUMBIA, GREATER GERMAN REICH

"WE HAVE FULL PERMISSION TO LAUNCH THE PROJECT WHEN *WE* DEEM IT viable." Oberstleutnant Deiter Hoffmann felt giddy with power and anticipation. "You were absolutely correct in how to approach the high command."

The two men walked side-by-side down the streets of the village of Fort St. John. Summer heat lay heavy on the wide Peace River Valley, occasionally relieved by breezes from the distant river.

"So when do we release the dogs of war?" Oberstleutnant Georg Hoyt asked.

"When the agent in place notifies us that the transport of the weapon by rail is imminent; we have to strike before that transport occurs."

An old civilian lorry grumbled past and potatoes bounced out of the open box every time it hit a pothole in the road, which was often. Young boys followed the truck and picked up the potatoes as quickly as they could. Deiter wondered if they sold them or took them home to their mothers.

"You are basing the future of the Third Reich on an agent in a foreign country?"

"This agent has been fully vetted, has no connection to the

Japanese Empire other than as a conquered individual."

"And this agent wishes to help us why?"

"She hates Japs?"

"She?"

"Yes, our agent is a woman."

"How was she recruited, Deiter? Have you met her? What are her motivations to help us against the Japanese Empire?"

"I was given direct access to this agent from SS Headquarters in New York. I am following orders as would any good Nazi."

Three giggling teenage girls passed them, all had their eyes fastened on Georg and furiously batted their eyelashes provocatively. He didn't seem to notice.

"I suggest that you investigate her bonafides as soon as possible. Your very life may hinge on the results."

"Georg, why are you suddenly questioning my intelligence sources?"

"We are preparing to commit the cream of Deutschland's paratroops on a target we have not reconnoitered, and in a hostile environment held by a fanatical enemy. I truly believe my caution to be totally reasonable, Oberstleutnant Hoffmann."

"Very formal, Georg. I understand your caution and urgency, but I honestly feel that this agent can be trusted. She has been in place for over a decade and her reports have always given us useful information."

"Sorry, Deiter, it's just a visceral reaction and I have always trusted my gut."

"I would be happy to show you her reports if that would make a difference. For what it's worth, the closest Gestapo agents, who are in Anchorage, have verified all of her information."

"It is not necessary for me to see her reports. If there exists a problem here, the blame will be placed far above your station. I am satisfied if you are."

"I am so happy they let me replace Zimmer with you. That man was a waste of skin and oxygen."

Georg laughed. "I heard they stationed him in Sudan as part of the final ethnic purification project."

Deiter didn't laugh. "There are parts of the Reich's programs that trouble me, especially this 'purification' stuff. We need diversification to be a healthy species, and I am afraid we are culling too much from the available bloodlines."

"Do you wish to have sexual congress with a Negress?"

"I didn't say that, but having sampled the local talent here in Deutsche Columbia it might be worth a try."

Georg smiled. "Ah, here we are at the finest bar in this fair city. May I buy you a glass of schnapps, or a beer?"

"Yes, you may. I am in a celebratory mood."

CHAPTER 46

WOLF RIVER LODGE

Lᴇᴠɪ ʜᴜʀʀɪᴇᴅ ᴛʜʀᴏᴜɢʜ ᴛʜᴇ ᴅᴏᴏʀ ᴀᴛ Wᴏʟꜰ Rɪᴠᴇʀ Lᴏᴅɢᴇ ᴀɴᴅ breathed a sigh of relief when he saw Dexter Williams and Gunther Charles talking to Doubtful.

"What's the verdict?" Levi asked without preamble.

Dexter turned to him, waved, and smiled.

"Thanks to you, we're going with Plan B, you've made a lot of new friends in the bush."

"I like this river, too, Dexter. I didn't want to see it dead for any reason, least of all a political point."

"Your recording convinced everybody," Gunther said. "Of course Doctor Christenson already knew you were right."

"So how do I let the roads and grounds crew know that I have the blessing of the Yukon Station Underground War Council to get Plan B operational?"

"We'll give you the code to start Plan A, and after you give it to them you tell them Plan B."

"They will believe me?"

"Yes." Doubtful said. "The code will show that you are speaking for the rest of us. By the way, you have earned membership on the War Council from here on out."

"I'm honored," Levi said.

"You're supposed to be," Thelma said from behind him. "For the record I abstained from that vote. I was highly prejudiced." Her smile warmed his soul to the bursting point.

"I'm very happy to hear that," Levi said returning the smile. "So what happens now?"

"We put Plan B into action," Doubtful said. "We have a lot to do and not much time to do it. Listen carefully, this is the code the roads and grounds crew is waiting to hear..."

CHAPTER 47

FAIRBANKS,
ALASKA PREFECTURE

THE CHENA RIVER, FAR OVER ITS BANKS, PUSHED MORE AND MORE DEBRIS under the venerable Cushman Street Bridge. The wooden structure dated from the 1930s and was long overdue for replacement, but the Japanese governor had not seen fit to allocate the necessary funds for the purpose. Traffic had been halted from both directions as the elevation of the water visibly increased.

Some streets close to the river already lay beneath a half-meter of water. Soldiers and police at either end watched helplessly as the structure shook with the constant assault of debris. Brush, entire trees undermined and washed away from eroding banks, and the remains of buildings all piled up against the upstream side. The water had finally risen to the point the increasing wreckage could no longer pass under the bridge.

One of the patrolmen watching upriver shouted to his superior. "Captain Oyama, look!"

What appeared to be an entire grove of trees nearly filled the width of the swollen Chena and flowed swiftly down towards a collision with the bridge.

Police Captain Isuoroku Oyama estimated that the force of the colliding trees would tip the scale.

With the other bridge gone, this will cut the town in half, as well as the road between Akihito Aerodrome and Yukon Station. Why was this allowed to happen?

He knew better than to voice his thoughts aloud, but he also knew it would be shouted by those with far more stature than the military governor of Alaska Prefecture. Heads would literally roll, but not soon enough to matter here today.

The trees slammed into the mounting debris pile and the far end of the bridge structure jerked sideways. As Oyama watched, the end of the bridge slowly grated downstream. Railings in the middle first bowed, then bent, and finally snapped into splinters.

The crisp smell of sap from the damaged trees and the exhalations of old broken wood permeated the humid air. Despair settled over those watching. Every person witnessing the unfolding events knew they had all waited too long to prevent, or even prepare for this disaster.

The massive roadbed of squared timbers popped apart and broke under the steady hydraulic pressure. Heavy road planking fell into the swollen river. With a huge groan, as if a living thing, the north half of the bridge rolled over and fell into the water where it became the largest piece of debris yet stolen by the flood.

Free of the pressure, the south end remained vigilant, a truncated bridge to a precarious future.

Police Captain Oyama turned away and waded over to the mustard-colored riverboat where Imperial Army Colonel Hideki sat in the warm sunshine with his staff, smoking cigarettes and watching events as though they were part of a Kabuki play.

"Colonel, I believe this crossing now falls under the jurisdiction of the Imperial Army as I have no way of building a pontoon bridge."

Colonel Hideki nodded. "I believe you are correct, Captain. If this damned river ever stops rising I will put my men into action immediately."

Captain Oyama gave him a third-degree bow and walked away, happy to not be the colonel in charge of this precinct, or the military governor of Alaska Prefecture. The breeze carried no hint of the winter that lurked no more than a month away.

CHAPTER 48

YUKON STATION

Levi parked his utility and when he got out and shut the door he saw one of the crew immediately go inside the roads and grounds maintenance building. As soon as he walked through the door all of the men on the railroad and runway maintenance crew moved toward him.

"Mister Fischer," Barnes said in his deep, soft voice, "Timothy Keegan is missing. Do you know anything about it?"

Levi carefully looked around the area. There were no Japanese he could see close enough to hear him.

"The Japs were waiting for him at his cabin but he evaded them. He is in friendly hands. Now listen carefully; this is a bad joke, but I think you'll like it."

The whole crew caught their breath at the same time.

"I'll bet I've heard it before," Barnes said, speaking slowly.

"Yes, you have."

"Get out of here, Levi," Barnes said. "You've done your part. Maybe we'll all meet again one of these days."

"Not so fast, fellows. Things have changed. We have a lot to do in a very short time."

"Wait a minute," Shorty Ferranti said around his ever-present stogie. "*Who* says things have changed?"

"The Yukon Station Underground War Council," Levi said staring at the shorter man in the face.

Does he really think I am a Jap spy?

"Does the Wolf River Pack agree with the change, too?" Eddie Hildebrand asked.

"Yeah, Doubtful agrees, too."

Why hasn't Doubtful mentioned Eddie? He wondered.

"Have they changed the plan, Levi?" Barnes asked.

"Yes, quite drastically. We need to get a crew of gandy dancers down track immediately to help Bill Brody's crew lay a new spur. The War Council requests that the people with combat experience stay here, they are going to be needed."

"Works for me," Shorty said with relish. "I was a tank commander for Patton before I collected a Purple Heart and got sent stateside to mend. If there's gonna be a fight, I want to be in it."

"Okay," Levi said, "here's what we want to happen…"

CHAPTER 49

"Wake! The sky is light!
let us to the road again...
Companion butterfly!"
— Matsuo Basho

FAIRBANKS,
ALASKA PREFECTURE

"WE NEED MORE SANDBAGS OVER HERE!" COLONEL OKAKURA SHOUTED. "Water is leaking through!"

Major Miamatsu stood in front of the Kempeitai Headquarters and looked around at the water creeping up the sides of all the buildings in downtown Fairbanks. He shook his head and went over to his commander.

"Colonel, we cannot build a wall high enough and strong enough to hold the water out. We need to get all of our files and furniture to the second floor."

The colonel gave him the wild look of a man who always insists on things going his way and suddenly realizes it won't happen this time, outrage heavily mixed with astonishment.

"Why were there no alarms? We are supposed to know *everything* that is happening in Alaska Prefecture!"

"I'll get the men organized, sir," Miamatsu said in a gentle tone. He turned and waved at Sergeant Hamada who yelled at a section of ten privates to drop their sandbags and follow him.

He wished he had possessed the forethought to have a small boat available. Before he could form another thought, a skiff the color of Imperial Army mustard burbled down the flooded street. Miamatsu shivered with the feeling that the gods had just touched him.

The four men in IA uniforms waved at the men still working around the building.

Colonel Okakura saw them and shouted, "Come over here! Be careful not to make waves!"

Miamatsu smiled inwardly and wondered if the colonel realized how his statement could be interpreted in more than one way.

As the boat neared, he saw that one of the passengers was also an Imperial Army colonel.

This should be interesting. Why don't these things happen when I have the leisure to appreciate them?

The boat colonel yelled, "What do you want?"

Colonel Okakura motioned to his assistant. "Secure that boat!"

Four soldiers carefully stepped over the wall of sandbags into the water and grabbed the skiff.

"What *is* this, Colonel?" the colonel in the boat yelled. "We are on official business and I demand—"

"Shut up!" Okakura screamed. "I am the senior officer this side of Yukon Station and I am commandeering your craft! You and the two officers get out and stay here. I am sending my men out to find more boats."

"I am Colonel Hideki of the Imperial Engineers. I was instructed by Major General Tsuji to survey the threat to the town of Fairbanks and the bridges."

"I will personally call the general and tell him that the town has flooded and the bridges are already destroyed. Your mission is complete, Colonel Hideki. Now please get out of my boat."

Miamatsu turned and walked toward the building. It would not be prudent to have either colonel see his face at this time. Colonel Hideki suddenly possessed the burden of *giri*, the obligation to clear an insult, even if the insult came from a superior. The only reason Okakura had seniority was because he was a member of the secret police, and both men knew it.

This could mean bloodshed, or a feud, Miamatsu thought. *As if we didn't have enough problems.*

"Major Miamatsu!" Colonel Okakura yelled.

He turned and faced his superior officer; not realizing the gods had just touched him again. "Yes, Colonel?"

"Take command of this boat. Choose a subordinate to go with you. You are to locate as many boats as you can and bring them back here, use force if you must!

Even though he was not in uniform he snapped to attention and saluted. "Hai!"

Colonel Hideki, now standing in front of Colonel Okakura, said, "I can find you boats. I know where they are kept."

"Tell the major their location. You are an engineer and I need an engineer more than I need a major."

Miamatsu hurried inside the building and found Sergeant Hamada directing soldiers and civilian workers in moving equipment and files from the first floor to higher locations.

"Sergeant," he said in his best official tone, "find two machine-guns and an ammunition pouch and report to me outside."

"Yes, Major," he said. "At once."

Near the severely leaking wall of sandbags two soldiers guarded the boat. One held the rope attached to the bow.

"Who was the operator of this boat?" Miamatsu asked, looking around at the small group standing idle.

"I was, sir." A corporal snapped to attention.

"Get back on the boat. You're keeping the job."

The corporal climbed back aboard. Sergeant Hamada hurried out of the building carrying two Type 100 machine-guns and a large pouch hung by straps off his left shoulder.

Miamatsu stepped up on the sandbags and carefully moved to the middle of the small boat before sitting. Sgt. Hamada handed him the two weapons and then the heavy pouch before boarding. Both Miamatsu and Hamada used the paddles lying in the boat to push away from the useless wall of sandbags.

Colonel Hideki yelled, "Near Sampson's Hardware are a number of craft."

"Thank you, Colonel," Miamatsu yelled. "I appreciate your help."

The colonel shrugged and walked into the headquarters building.

"Corporal, what is your name?" Miamatsu asked.

"Akio Asakawe, Major."

"Corporal Asakawe, take us slowly out of here and toward the hardware store."

"Hai, Major!"

The little motor started on the first pull of the cord and they slowly made headway through the flooded streets of Fairbanks.

Miamatsu was happy to be moving again and strangely relieved to be away from the headquarters building.

CHAPTER 50

"Will we meet again
here at your flowering grave...
Two white butterflies?"
— Matsuo Basho

YUKON STATION

DR. JAKE ROSE AND DR. JERRY HYAKAWA WALKED INTO DR. TOMMATSU'S office and closed the door behind them.

The old scientist looked up at them and raised his eyebrows.

Jerry put his finger to his left ear and Tommatsu nodded as he switched on his radio, flooding the room with American Swing music. The two visitors pulled up chairs and sat forward so all three of their heads were within a foot of each other.

"Is the thing to begin?" Tommatsu asked.

"Yes," Jake said, "but not the way we thought."

"Please elucidate."

"We are not going to detonate the weapon here. It will leave on the railroad as officially planned. Suffice it to say that will be the end of the official plan."

"Why change what was an excellent solution?"

Jerry spoke up, "If we use the device here it will kill the Yukon River for the next century, perhaps more. It would be better to let the Imperial Army continue running the country."

Tommatsu nodded. "I see. I wasn't sure what the long-range effects would be. I once requested an official visit to the former American capitol but the Reich refused my visa."

"We have two different sources who state that the Potomac River is dead and still highly radioactive," Jake said. "That was enough to tip the scale."

"What about the trigger we built into the device? Should we remove it?"

Jake and Jerry glanced at one another.

"I don't see why," Jerry said. "It's not as if the thing can be set off accidently."

"Well then," Tommatsu said with visible relief, "we will finish the protective structure around the weapon. It is ready for shipment to where ever it will end up."

"This also means that the three of us should get away from the Project as soon as the rocket is launched," Jake said. "The part about hitting Berlin is still very much on schedule and highly anticipated."

Tommatsu picked up his telephone, turned down the radio, and dialed three numbers. He spoke briefly in Japanese and hung up.

"We can move it south in the morning. I will notify the authorities to halt the morning train from Fairbanks; we'll want a clear track. As soon as the train leaves the yards we will begin the launch sequence."

"I didn't really think this day would ever arrive," Jake said.

"It's not over yet," Jerry said.

CHAPTER 51

YUKON STATION

"Make sure the cord is hidden by the rails, if the Japs see it we're all screwed."

"Barnes," Shorty Ferranti grated, "would you just shut the fuck up? I know what I'm doing. *Okay?*"

"Sorry, Shorty, I'm just nervous. You're doing a great job."

Shorty dug out another small trench in the roadbed gravel and carefully wrapped primer cord around the head of the rail spike. Three other crew members worked close by, digging unnecessary holes and filling them up again, doing their best to camouflage their true purpose.

Three hundred feet of track leading up to a bridge close to the rail yard had undergone the first stage of elaborate sabotage. The rest of the plan couldn't be executed until the last minute.

A few of the Japanese troops manning the anti-aircraft battery watched, but did not understand what the workers were doing or cared enough to ask questions. All they worried about was potential enemies attacking from the air or from down the track. The rest of them played a card game, making a perfect distraction for the roads and grounds crew.

"This is gonna work, right, Barnes?" Shorty asked as he carefully rose from his labors.

"It's going to be beautiful, man, just beautiful."

"I hope the guys have that new track ready by tomorrow." Shorty pulled his stogie from his pocket and relit it. "That train sure won't be able to come back here."

"I just hope the Japs haven't discovered there's a weasel in the hen house," Barnes said. "This is all going so smoothly it makes me nervous."

"We all have practiced a long time for this," Shorty said. "I just wish I could get close to the rotten kraut who ordered Patton's death."

"We'll get them all, Shorty. Just wait and see."

Shorty paused and glanced up at his friend.

"Barnes, I just gotta ask–since folks of your complexion never had much going for them before the war, why you working so hard to change things back?"

"Shorty, I'm not working to change things *back*. I'm working to *change* things."

✪

On the edge of Runway 2 Eddie Hildebrand and his crew of three carefully cleaned the valves and couplings of the fueling station. They did not detach the end of the long hose that carried the highly refined kerosene out to the hardstand where the Fuji F-1 jet fighters refueled. The ground crews would tow the jets out to the area adjacent to the huge hangar for refueling.

The flashing blue light on the cab of their Mazda utility proved adequate to keep aircraft and ground crews at a distance. The roads and grounds crew were a common enough sight that they were, in effect, invisible.

"Make sure you cover all that primer cord with tape, we don't want it to show," Eddie said while forcing himself to slow down and be as nonchalant as possible. He knew the Japs in the tower were observing them through binoculars, they always did. If they worked too fast the tower NCO might send a security detail over to check them out since that would be unusual.

The cord circled the shut-off valve and a foot of the six-inch pipe behind it. The end cap where two hoses branched out would be completely shattered according to Eddie's calculations. He almost wanted to stay and watch it happen.

CHAPTER 52

"With every gust of wind,
the butterfly changes its place
on the willow."
— Matsuo Basho

KEMPEITAI HEADQUARTERS
YUKON STATION

CAPTAIN ATSUMI PICKED UP HER DESK PHONE ON THE FIRST RING AND answered. She listened for a moment and replaced the receiver. She stared at the phone for a long moment and then picked up the receiver and dialed.

"Good afternoon, Miss Watanabe. This is Captain Atsumi, I would like to speak to Mr. Fischer." She listened.

"Where in the field, did he say? *Livengood!* Ah, when do you expect him to return?"

The pencil in her left hand snapped in two and she forced herself to relax as much as she could.

"Very well. If you see him before I do, please have him contact me at once. No, it is more than important. It is imperative."

Despite wanting to slam it down, she carefully replaced the receiver on its cradle; she didn't want to break the Emperor's telephone. After running her finger down the phone list, she stopped, dialed another number.

"Ah, Mr. Charles, I'm so relieved that *someone* is on station today! Oh, sorry, this is Captain Atsumi." Smiling, she listened patiently.

"Yes, I understand he had to go to Livengood. Any idea why?" She pulled a tablet to her and took notes with the pencil stub.

"Yes, I see. Well the reason I wanted to speak with him has to do with one of *your* employees. Yes. His name? Mr. Timothy Keegan."

She made note of the change in his voice, his increase in volume and speaking speed, and that she knew he was lying.

"I find it difficult to believe he has been in the field for an entire week. Laying track, where? Livengood! What the hell for?"

When he answered, she stiffened. "Thank you, Mr. Charles. Good bye."

She faced a dilemma. Either Gunther Charles was lying about Fischer's mission, or Major Summatsu had given him a task to which she was not privy. On one hand, she could simply ask the major if he had used her subordinate and forgot to tell her.

The problem was, if he *had* tasked Fischer and not told her, he could regard her inquiry as impertinent, unmilitary, and a blot on her career. She knew he was due for promotion to Lieutenant Colonel. Just as she was qualified to trade her shoulder boards with two wide stripes and three stars for a set with three thinner stripes and a single star, denoting an Imperial Army Major.

"What if Charles is lying and I do nothing about it?" she hissed to herself. She owed *giri* to her superiors and *chu* to the Emperor. It was enough that she did not report Fischer's nihilism when it occurred. That additional guilt pushed her to pick up the receiver again.

She took a deep breath and dialed. "Major Summatsu, this is Captain Atsumi. Good afternoon to you, sir. I am puzzled by a situation and was told you had ordered some of my civilian subordinates into the field on a classified task. I apologize for ask—ah, Levi Fischer and Timothy Keegan."

She grinned and slammed the pencil stub down on the desk.

"You didn't? Well, I thought you would tell me, sir. You say that the man was convincing—ah, that would be Gunther Charles, Major. I will notify all units immediately, sir."

She listened for a moment longer and then set the receiver down gently. Major Summatsu's words still rang in her mind.

"I realize the mental process you went through to make this call. You were very courageous and I will make note of it in your record, and on the recommendation to promote you to major, which currently lies in front of me on my desk."

She shook her head and dialed the Kempeitai barracks.

"This is Captain Atsumi, I wish to speak to Sergeant Major Fukita.

Sergeant Major Fukita, issue an alert to bring in Levi Fischer, Gunther Charles, and Timothy Keegan. Yes, I know you are already seeking Keegan. I was told he is in the Livengood section, so pass the word."

She listened, and said, "Yes. I want them capable of lucid speech. Their lives will end soon thereafter."

CHAPTER 53

YUKON STATION ANNEX

THE LOCOMOTIVE BACKED INTO THE PROJECT BUILDING AS SLOWLY AS possible. Just before the coupler on the coal car touched the coupler of the flatcar, the sergeant conductor blew his whistle and the engine immediately stopped. The couplers gently connected and the sergeant conductor waved his red flag up and down with great animation.

Moments later the locomotive moved forward out into the sunshine pulling the flatcar bearing an atomic bomb in a lead-lined metal crate. On each side of the track stretched a line of twenty soldiers in full combat gear. As soon as the car was clear of the building the great doors closed and were immediately secured.

"Okay," Jake said. The race is on. You both get out of here and I'll start the launch sequence."

Jerry nodded, but Doctor Tommatsu shook his head.

"No, Jake. You go with Jerry and I will stay and take care of things here. All of this could still fail and it is my *on* to remain and see the deed done."

"Doctor, you will be needed after all this is over. You are the only remaining nuclear scientist not under German rule. Think of the future!"

"I am. I only hope the German physicists meet the same fate I anticipate for myself. Besides, both of you know as much as I do."

"Very well, sir," Jake said. "It was an honor to work with you all these years."

Jerry stepped forward and took the man's hand. "I understand your position, Doctor Summatsu. You are one of the bravest men I have ever met." He shook hands.

"Gentlemen, this was fated. Now leave while you can."

Both men left the building as technicians and soldiers hurried back and forth on last minute tasks before the Chrysanthemum Rocket was closed up for launch.

CHAPTER 54

YUKON STATION

THE LOCOMOTIVE SLOWLY MOVED OUT OF THE PROJECT PERIMETER AND into the rail yard. As soon as the flatcar crossed over the switch the engine stopped, then backed up. The sergeant conductor had already switched the track and he walked beside the car until its rear coupler came within inches of the coupler on the armored caboose. He snapped his flag up and down once and breathed a sigh of relief when they connected.

Their job finished, the forty soldiers formed into four lines under the command of a senior sergeant.

With a self-satisfied smile the sergeant conductor jumped onto the caboose step and waved for the engineer to proceed. The locomotive moved forward, slowly picking up speed. The crew in the anti-aircraft gun mount waved enthusiastically as the engine passed them. The sergeant conductor waved his flag as he went by.

Cannon fire poured from the blister on the roof of the armored caboose, cutting down every one of the gun crew and destroying the mount. The track behind them abruptly blew up along with the vehicular bridge over the swollen creek. The gun mount swiveled and fired back at the Japanese soldiers running toward the moving train. Over half of the pursuing soldiers fell to the ground, dead or wounded.

In panic the sergeant conductor turned to the door to see a huge

American Negro pointing a machine-gun at him.

"This is your stop," the man said and pulled the trigger.

Barnes went back into the caboose.

"Okay, let's get these Nips out of here!"

Shorty swung down from the gun blister and he and Barnes threw the bodies of six guards off the train. The floor ran with fresh blood.

"Leave that back door open for a minute," Barnes said. He went to the sink and ran a bucket full of water. He sloshed it onto the floor, ran another, repeated the action, and used a broom to sweep it all down the corridor and out the door.

"You happy now, chambermaid?" Ferranti asked.

"Yeah, close the door. If we hadn't done that it woulda gotten sticky and stinky."

Ferranti grinned as he slammed the heavy door and secured it. "Well, we're still moving, so Smith must have had no problem with the engineer. Them bastards never knew what hit them! You're faster than you look, Barnes."

"I wouldn't have gotten this far if I wasn't. Now let's hope the Japanese Air Force is busy today. You just know they're hearing about us right now."

Shorty climbed back up into the roof-mounted blister and strapped himself into the seat. Twin 20mm cannons pointed at the sky and he kicked the motor into life and spun them and himself in a complete circle.

"Let 'em come. I served with Patton. I hit what I shoot at!" He puffed on his stogie and grinned.

The electrical spark that caused the destruction of the track also blew off the ends of the dual pipelines running from the huge tanks behind the Annex to the aerodrome fueling station. Aviation fuel and petrol shot out onto the sun-warmed asphalt, spreading quickly across the taxi area and onto the runway itself. With the explosions on the rail line drawing attention, nobody seemed to notice the massive fuel spill.

High-grade kerosene and petrol fumes filled the August afternoon, waiting for a spark.

CHAPTER 55

SS HEADQUARTERS, NW BRANCH, FORT St. JOHN, DEUTSCHE COLUMBIA, GREATER GERMAN REICH

OBERSTLEUTNANTS DIETER HOFFMAN AND GEORG HOYT WERE DRAWING landing zones for paratroopers on the wall map's plastic overlay when running footsteps sounded on the boardwalk outside the office. Dieter looked up just before the door crashed open and a signals orderly leaned on the doorframe, breathing heavily with sweat running down his face.

"Comms center says the Japs have st-started, the launch sequence. Sir."

Both of the men straightened and grabbed their helmets and battle jackets, they already wore combat gear.

"Return to the communications center and tell them to radio Berlin and New York immediately. We should be over the Japanese installation within four hours. If they can deliver the second punch to coincide with our attack it will make things easier for all concerned."

The orderly finished scribbling on his pad and read it back to Hoffmann.

"Perfect! Deliver the message!" He turned to Hoyt. "Mein Gott! It's really happening. The 'Quiet War' is finished and now it's going to get loud again." He moved toward the door.

"Yes, for better or for worse, my friend. Aren't you going to take your Maschinenpistole?"

Dieter blushed.

"Thank you! I would have looked idiotic to appear in front of my Fallshirmjäger Brigade without it."

"Is this your first combat, Dieter?"

"Does it show?"

"Only to a veteran of firefights. Don't worry, you'll do fine."

"Thank you, Georg. Your friendship and support has made a world of difference to me and I appreciate it."

Hoyt smiled. "Happy to help. Besides, you rescued me from the propaganda ministry and put me into a combat outfit. Believe me, I appreciate *that!*"

They went out to the muddy street where a command car waited. In moments they were speeding down the edge of the runway where hundreds of troops filed into four score turboprop transports. The command car reached the lead aircraft and Hoffmann and Hoyt jumped out, pulled their gear from the boot, and jogged toward the plane.

They stopped and pulled on their parachutes, each checking the other's straps and buckles. They went over to the loading ramp on the huge Heinkel He 400. A master sergeant gave them a crisp, old-style "Hitler" salute to welcome them aboard.

Dieter glanced at the man's left arm and saw that he had 28 years in the Luftwaffe; he had been in the War. Deiter made his way toward the front of the aircraft and stuck his head in the cockpit.

"Gentlemen, I am pleased to be riding with you today. What are the weather conditions over the target?"

"It has finally stopped raining and the air temperature is in the seventies on the Fahrenheit scale, Herr Oberstleutnant, so we should have a nice smooth flight into the land of the rising sun."

"Excellent. What is our flight time?"

"Just under three hours from wheels up."

"Superb. I will now take my seat and strap in."

The master sergeant walked slowly through the plane, visually checking every paratrooper before operating the lever that closed the wide ramp and turned it into the rear bulkhead of the aircraft. He spoke into his headset and the first engine began to turn over. Twelve minutes later they lifted off the ground accompanied by two Messerschmitt 322 fighters.

CHAPTER 56

"Bush warbler:

shits on the rice cakes

on the porch rail."

— Matsuo Basho

YUKON FAIRBANKS RAILROAD

STEVE SMITH KEYED THE WALKIE-TALKIE AND WAITED FOR BARNES OR Ferranti to answer. During the war he had been a nervous private in Ft. Lewis, Washington waiting for orders to Europe or the Pacific. Before that could happen the Krauts dropped the bomb on Washington and he followed the orders the colonel gave them.

"Hide your equipment, take care of your weapons, and wait – this isn't over."

This morning, for the very first time, he had used his Garand to kill an enemy. The act hadn't bothered him at all. He looked forward to killing more Japs. He had grown to loathe them.

"Whattya need, Steve?"

"Shorty, how am I supposed to know where to go?"

Just follow the tracks, Steve!" Ferranti's laughter cut off with a click.

"Cute, asshole. I mean where are they supposed to—"

A man stood in the middle of the tracks waving his arms.

"Never mind, I see the answer to my question, Shorty. Thanks for your help." He broke the contact before the man could laugh even more. He slowed the engine down to walking speed and stopped next to the man.

"You must be Smith," the man said. "I'm Jim Spreter. There's a switch up ahead, we want you to pull your load through it and stop.

When we give you the high sign back it into the spur we built."

"You got it, Jim."

Within minutes he was backing the load toward a hill. Since he didn't know where he was going, he kept the speed down. The hill loomed closer and closer and he wondered what the people in charge planned to do.

The track curved to his right and the caboose disappeared into a large tunnel.

"I'll be damned," he muttered. "These fellows have been working their tails off!"

Spreter climbed up on the step of the engine.

"Slow a bit more. In a minute I'll have you drop the caboose and then you'll pull forward again. Okay, stop."

Spreter disappeared briefly and reappeared on the step.

"Okay, pull forward, a little more, good. Stop."

The train was in a tunnel barely large enough to clear the roof of the locomotive but seemed to increase in size toward the back.

Spreter popped back onto the step. "Okay, Smitty, back it up again. You're doing great. Okay, stop!"

Steve checked his cab mirror and saw light on the tunnel wall to the right but nothing to the left. Usually he loathed the nickname, Smitty. However, Spreter was so amiable he didn't mind it this time.

"Okay, pull forward again until we pass the switch. There you go, stop. Okay, they threw it, now back up again."

Steve backed again and they hooked the caboose up. Moments later he was backing the caboose onto the same spur where they had dropped the flatcar. They stopped him again and unhooked the caboose. Once more he moved past the switch, stopped and backed into the second spur.

What the hell do they have back there? He wondered.

"Okay, now we're going to collect the caboose and we're out of here," Spreter said with a wide grin.

Ten minutes later Steve was pulling his load into the sunlight again. As the engine chugged along at a slow speed he crawled up on the coal car and looked back. He still had a flatcar with a big metal box secured to it along with the armored caboose.

Spreter swung up into the cab.

"Hope you don't mind some company. Since you're the only Smith on the roster your first name is Steve, right?"

"That's right, Jim. What the hell did we just do? I'm still pulling a bomb down the tracks."

Spreter's grin grew wider.

"Yeah, but not the one the Japs think is in there. We have Little Guy stored away for the future. Our people are tearing out the switch and the spur we built. In a few hours all evidence of it will be gone."

"Little Guy?"

"That's what we named the bomb, I don't know what the Japs called it."

"Why all this hullabaloo over one bomb? Don't they have more?"

"You didn't know your cargo was an *atomic* bomb?"

If he hadn't been sitting on the engineer's seat he would have collapsed on the spot. As it was he felt faint. Nobody had told him what this was about until now.

"Like the one the Krauts dropped on Washington?" he whispered.

"Yeah. Hey, you okay, man? Don't worry. It's in a nice safe place now, but we aren't. Watch for Jap aircraft."

CHAPTER 57

YUKON STATION,
ALASKA PREFECTURE

MAJOR GENERAL TSUJI HEARD THE EXPLOSIONS AND FROWNED, THE telephone rang and he put the receiver to his ear.

"Yes?"

The voice on the other end carried more panic than information. A word came through, abruptly but clearly.

"Sabotage! Where? Talk more slowly so I can understand you, sergeant!"

He quickly heard about a hijacked train carrying an atomic bomb and also about destroyed tracks and a destroyed vehicle bridge. For a moment he found it difficult to breathe.

"Did they attack or damage the Annex?"

As soon as he heard the answer he cut the connection and dialed the aerodrome duty desk. "This is Major General Tsuji. Launch all of our fighters immediately!"

"We have reports of liquid on the runway, general. We need to first check out the source."

"It's probably water. Aren't you aware that there are flood conditions all over the Interior?' How deep is it?"

"It does not appear to be deep, General Tsuji, but–"

"Then launch our aircraft! Rebels have seized our train; it is carrying an atomic bomb. They must be stopped!"

"I understand, General Tsuji. We will launch at once."

"Instruct the pilots not to target the train itself! Have them destroy the track in front of it. If the train itself is hit we are all dead!"

"I will tell them personally, general."

✪

The klaxon brayed through the hangar and crews immediately prepared the four Fuji F-1 fighters for flight. Armorers fitted the jets with rocket pods to enhance the firepower of the 20mm wing cannons. The pilots were in their aircraft before the ground crews were finished.

Finally the ground crew scattered and the sergeant in charge had each jet start as one of his privates manned a huge fire extinguisher on wheels. One by one all four jets roared into life and the ground crew pulled the chocks as the sergeant gave the pilots the *go* sign.

Two by two the jets taxied out of the large hangar and onto the runway. All could see what they thought was water coursing over the runway but barely deep enough to matter in the slightest. They all ignored the soldier waving his arms running across the tarmac toward the hangar from the fueling station – it was obviously a ground crew problem.

Engines whining at maximum, the first two pilots released their brakes and shot down the runway. The second pair followed within seconds. The landing gear on the leading aircraft hit the "water" on the runway and a split second later all of the mixed aviation fuel and petrol erupted into flame.

All four jets exploded, creating huge tumbling fireballs still hurtling down the runway. Rockets ignited and roared into the south perimeter fence, blowing it to pieces. Pieces of flaming jets rained all over the compound, igniting fires in the air force barracks and two of the three aviation maintenance buildings.

Major General Tsuji watched the events through his office window, his mind fought with total disbelief. That nothing hit the administration building was a miracle of the first order. The emergency fire vehicles couldn't approach the fiercely burning jets until they put out the fires from the spewing fuel pipelines.

General Tsuji, aware that time had ceased to be his ally, grabbed his phone and dialed again.

CHAPTER 58

"Bitter–tasting ice —
Just enough to wet the throat
Of a sewer rat."
— Matsuo Basho

PRINCE AKIHITO AERODROME, ALASKA PREFECTURE

"No, WE DON'T HAVE ANY MORE SANDBAGS," MAJOR AKAGI SAID INTO THE microphone. "We are now cut off from Fairbanks to the north and Anchorage to the south. All of the land between here and the Tanana River is under water. Make do with what you have."

His telephone shrilled; headquarters was calling yet again.

"Tower, this is Major Akagi," he said into the receiver.

"You are ordered to launch fighters immediately!" an authoritative voice said.

"Launch aircraft, are you insane? Half of the runway is under water and the water is rising fast!"

The voice on the phone went flat and sharp, reminding Akagi of a sword blade. "This is Major General Tsuji at Yukon Station. I *order* you to launch as many fighters as you can and send them north. Have the pilots contact us for further instructions. Do you understand, Major Akagi?"

"Yes, General, I understand. We will do the best we can under the circumstances."

The general hung up. Sweat saturated Akagi's uniform shirt. He dialed the number for the flight line.

"This is Major Akagi, who is the senior officer there? Put him on."

In moments another man spoke, "This is Captain Honda. Do you have the sandbags we requested?"

"Forget the sandbags." He related the conversation with General Tsuji.

"He wants us to launch aircraft on a flooded runway? Is he crazy?"

"Captain, he gave me a direct order, which I now I now pass on to you. Launch as many fighters as you can and send them toward the Yukon River."

"How many have to crash before you rescind this murderous insanity?"

"I'll let you know." Akagi snapped and hung up, sick in his heart.

The Fuji F-1 was a nimble craft and could do many things. What it couldn't do, what any small jet could not do, was lift off of a flooded runway without sucking water into the engine if the air scoop was part of the lower fuselage. These thoughts ran through Akagi's mind as he lifted the binoculars to his eyes and glassed the flight line.

A Fuji F-1 taxied onto the runway. A quick sweep showed the plane had less than five hundred feet of runway before hitting water of unknown depth. The pilot throttled up to full power before releasing the brakes and rushing down the runway.

When the wheels hit the water it sprayed out like an opened fan and Akagi thought it might make it into the air. Unfortunately the water deepened and the belly disappeared in a new spray of icy floodwater.

When the cold water was sucked into the rapidly heating engines the fans shattered, sending shards through the assembly–then it exploded.

Akagi screamed in agony and pounded his fist on the desk. He called the flight line.

"Who was in that aircraft? Do not try to launch any more aircraft. General Tsuji will have to deal with his problems himself."

Captain Honda had followed orders as well as proving himself right. He had died for the Emperor. Major Akagi had ordered him to die and had just countermanded an order from General Tsuji.

The guilt of the situation overwhelmed the major. His *giri* had been savaged in both directions. The only honorable way out this was *seppuku* or its equivalent. Alone in the tower, Major Akagi pulled out his service pistol, made a first-degree bow to the east, and shot himself in the head.

CHAPTER 59

YUKON STATION

LEVI SLOWED HIS UTILITY AND STOPPED TO ASSESS THE REMAINS OF THE anti-aircraft gun emplacement. Farther into the area scores of soldiers milled about. He realized the curtain had gone up while he was returning from Livengood. He turned the utility around, drove back to the Old Wolf River Village Road and headed for the village.

He turned onto the gravel toward the village and a car sitting off the edge of the road flashed its headlights. It was Tomiko Watanabe's green Toyota coupe. He pulled up beside the driver's window and rolled his down.

"Tomiko?"

"There is no time to waste, Levi. They are waiting for you around the next bend: two lorries and a command car. You need to abandon your vehicle, now!"

"And go where?"

"Get behind the seat in my car, cover yourself with the blanket."

He drove his utility into the trees and switched off the engine. He slogged back through the still overflowing ditch and crawled behind the passenger seat of her car. The vehicle began to move.

"Why are you doing this?"

"Be quiet. We are coming to a checkpoint. Try to be less than you are."

He settled into the floor, trying to sink on either side of the hump created for the driveshaft. The car slowed and stopped. A genial conversation in Japanese ensued then ceased. The car moved forward.

"You may sit up if you wish, Levi."

"What is going on?"

"Captain Atsumi has put out an arrest order for Gunther Charles, Timothy Keegan, and you."

"So she finally realized she had a problem on her hands. Tomiko. I think perhaps we have come to a turn in the road of our lives, for better or for worse."

"Isn't that part of Christian wedding vows?"

"It could be. I don't know since I'm a Jew."

"And I am of the Shinto faith, yet I know that piece of information. What others label us in no way defines us."

"Are you part of the Yukon Station Underground?"

"Yes, I have been for years."

"Why? You are native born Japanese."

"Not true, even though the Imperial Army believes it to be true. I am actually Nisei. I was born in Seattle, Washington in 1938. My father was in the 442nd Infantry and fought the Germans."

"'Go for Broke,' huh? Sounds like you're just like him."

She laughed. "Okay, be quiet now, we are approaching another check point."

He dropped back to the floor again and went rigid.

He listened intensely to the conversation.

"You may not pass this point, woman," the sentry said with an air of dismissal.

"Do you know who I am?" Tomiko demanded.

"No." The tone had shifted to neutral.

"I am the assistant to the Chief of Operations, and I was told to proceed to Wolf River Lodge."

"You were?" His voice stiffened. "Do you have a written order to that effect?"

"No. The situation is fluid. If you are going to detain me, I need your name and rank so I may explain to *my* superior *who* it was that detained me."

"Pass," he said, defeat evident in his voice.

They were under way again.

"What the hell is going on?" Levi asked.

"Something has them stirred up. He did not want to let me through. Ah, there are four Imperial Army lorries around the roadhouse. We dare not stop."

"Do you have any weapons with you?"

"That is an interesting thing to ask. What on Earth do you have in mind?"

"You didn't answer the question, Tomiko."

"Yes, I have some weapons. Why?"

"If the Army has the drop on everyone in the roadhouse, we might make a big difference."

"As much as I don't wish to, I must agree."

"Where are the weapons?"

"Under the driver's seat on the floor, probably next to your head."

Levi reached under the seat and found three bundles of varying sizes wrapped in rags. The first one turned out to be a 1911 model .45 Colt automatic with three clips of ammunition. The second was a MP-40 German assault machine-gun with five full clips and a carrying strap. The third and last proved to be a scoped .223 Winchester with a bag of rounds tied to it.

"This is an arsenal! Where did you get all of these?"

"I have incurred a few favors over time, many were not strictly official."

Levi elected not to press the question. "Are you proficient with all of these?"

"Yes," she said. "Are you?"

"No. I never have fired a machine-gun of any sort. But I am a good shot with a rifle as well as a pistol, so I could handle the Colt and the Winchester."

"Very well. I will park as far from the sentries as possible and walk into the building, if they will allow it. I will carry the machine-gun under my raincoat. Should they block my entrance I will kill them and you need to get out here as fast as you can."

"Raincoat? It's not raining."

"They will not question an older woman about a thing like that."

"And if you get into the building?"

"Wait for the sound of gunfire; then kill the sentries. So far I only see two. These are arrogant people."

"Be careful, okay?"

"Thank you, Levi. The Liberty Underground has trained me well.

I want *you* to be careful."

"No argument."

"Give me the machine-gun and clips."

He passed them up to her through the space between the seats. He heard zippers. She stopped the car.

"Like them, we must show no mercy. Besides, they wouldn't understand the concept," she said in a firm voice before getting out of the car and shutting the door behind her.

Levi waited for a few moments then poked his head up to watch her progress. She stood chatting with one of the sentries as the other watched from a dozen yards away. Neither of the soldiers seemed tense or ill at ease with her.

The parking area resembled a used car lot. Eight civilian vehicles sat blocked by four mustard-colored Imperial Army lorries. Fading light, reflecting off the wide Yukon River, leached out of the sky as the late summer evening waned into a fragrant, pastel landscape.

It's a beautiful place to die, he thought,

Levi pushed the passenger seat forward and quietly exited the coupe keeping the vehicle between him and the sentries. He made sure the firing chamber held a round and took careful aim at the far sentry.

Tomiko laughed and said something in Japanese before walking on up the steps. Everything felt surreal, from watching the transformation of his secretary into a warrior woman with nerves of steel, to aiming a weapon at a Japanese soldier while waiting for the right moment to pull the trigger.

Tomiko Watanabe carried the machine-gun dangling down her front with the strap around her neck. The clips lay hidden in separate pockets so they didn't clank together. She walked through the door, lifted her gaze and shook her head to focus herself.

About twenty Japanese soldiers faced away from her, holding weapons on the Americans at the back of the room. A large white man lay on the floor with blood pooling around his head. She decided he was dead. The tang of fresh cordite stung her nostrils, and tension filled the air.

Major Summatsu broke off from speaking when she came through the door. He turned to see who had entered and his eyes widened when he recognized her.

"Miss Watanabe. What are you doing here?"

"I came to visit my good friend, Audrey Louise," she said loudly.

As soon as Tomiko said the last word, Audrey yelled, "Hit the deck!" All of the Americans fell to the floor in front of the startled Japanese. Summatsu's attention abruptly snapped back to the Americans, and Tomiko whipped out the machine-gun and commenced firing short bursts. Major Hakari Summatsu died before he hit the floor.

As she continued to fire, the other Americans scrambled for their weapons and the room filled with gunfire.

When the first shot echoed through the parking lot, Levi put a bullet through the far sentry's heart and shifted his aim to the second. The second man had not heard the sharp report of the .223 over the war raging in the roadhouse.

Levi dropped him with a bullet to the back of his head.

The driver's door on one lorry flew open and a Japanese soldier jumped out holding a pistol. He looked around wildly, fear writ large on his face. Levi's bullet gave him a third eye and the man dropped into the muddy parking lot.

Levi carefully looked around and, finding no other targets, sprinted for the roadhouse door. At the exact moment he got to the first step the front door opened and a Japanese lieutenant reeled out, holding one blood soaked hand to his side as he fired back into the room with a pistol in the other.

Levi shot him twice in the head and the soldier fell like a sack of rice. Gunfire inside the building ceased. Levi ran up to the door and edged in.

Three weapons pointed at him from different parts of the room.

"It's okay, it's Levi!" Tomiko shouted. She lay propped against the wall, blood running out of wounds in her right leg and left arm.

Levi ripped off his belt, ran to her and used the belt as a tourniquet on her thigh above the leg wound.

"I knew you were a leg man the minute I saw you," she said with a chuckle and then passed out.

Levi took a second and looked around at the carnage in the room. Japanese bodies lay in heaps and blood was everywhere. Two Americans looked dead and a number were dressing wounds on themselves or others.

"Is there a medic here? I think she's going to need surgery."

Mike Christenson hurried over.

"Let me see, hmm, yeah, I think you're right. I don't know if we're going to have time to do it now, there may be more Japanese on the way."

"She'll lose the leg if we have to wait, maybe her life," Levi said.

"You seem to know a lot about wounds, Levi."

"I was trained as a medic's helper in the Rockies right after the war. We didn't have too many hospitals to choose from in those days."

The man held out his hand, "Good to see you."

"Same here," Levi said as they quickly shook.

"Help me carry her into one of the bedrooms."

"What happened here before the shooting started?"

"We were having a meeting when our look-out said there were Jap trucks coming down the road. Before anyone could grab a gun, this fellow I had never seen before stood up with an automatic in his hand and told us all to relax and nobody would get hurt. Everybody started shouting at him, calling him names and cursing him.

"We got him so rattled that he couldn't watch all of us, and Glen Bassett dropped him with a shot from a revolver. Then the Kempeitai stormed through the door and they lined us up in the back. I thought we were all going to die on the spot.

"Then in walks Tomiko as if it's ladies night and they're serving free drinks. She saved our collective ass. I had no idea she could shoot like that."

"Once we get through all of this," Levi said, "I'm putting her up for a medal of some kind. She saved my ass, too."

Audrey hurried up and looked into Tomiko's face. "Is she gonna be okay, Dr. Pinky?"

"Yeah," Mike said. "She's lost some blood but Levi got a tourniquet on her fast enough that she'll get through this just fine."

"Okay, just wanted to remind you guys to get out of here as soon as you can."

Levi looked up at her. "I didn't see many Japanese troops back there."

"That's not why we have to get out of here. A lot of Germans are on their way!"

CHAPTER 60

"When the winter chrysanthemums go,
there's nothing to write about
but radishes."
— Matsuo Basho

YUKON STATION ANNEX

WITH A FINAL OKAY FROM THE TOP SCAFFOLD AROUND THE Chrysanthemum Rocket, the tap of a switch began the prelaunch sequence. Doctor Hiro Tommatsu wiped his brow and stood. The office door opened and two Japanese entered.

Not recognizing either of them, Tommatsu performed a third-degree bow and waited politely for them to speak.

The largest one smashed a fist into his solar plexus, knocking him backward to drop into his chair, gasping for breath and stunned with pain.

"Doctor Tommatsu," the shorter man said, "we need to know the location of your two colleagues. If you do not give us the information willingly we will extract it from you in a most unpleasant manner. Before that, however, we require you to stop the launch sequence. Now."

He frowned through his pain and focused on the speaker. "Wh-who *are* you?"

"Our names do not matter, we act for the vast number of people in the Home Islands who do not wish another war."

"Don't, understand. Stop, stop the sequence, why?"

"We wish to assure that the Chrysanthemum Project has not been subverted. A few days' delay will not matter in the greater scheme of things."

"You're wrong about that, but I will do as you say."

He turned to his control board and fingered a switch. He looked back at the two men and said, "This is my *giri*, and it seems that it is yours as well." He flipped the switch.

The shaped charge explosion vaporized everyone and everything in the office while blowing the debris away from the rocket. During the ensuing panic as military and civilians erupted from the building like maddened ants from a hill, the rocket launch clicked down through its web of micro switches toward ignition. Only pulling the power and negating the past three months of work by hundreds of people could stop the launch, and their only rocket scientist now walked with his ancestors.

The pilots were told there had been an explosion but there was nothing for them to worry about. The Emperor's Great Plan would not be halted. Engineers swiftly assessed the damage to the launch chamber and found it to be negligible.

The remaining two agents waiting outside the building had no idea the rocket launch had not been stopped. They only knew that the remaining two architects of the plan were not present. They therefore retreated carefully.

Emergency sirens blared all over Yukon Station. The anti-aircraft crews didn't know whether to watch the sky or the Project complex, so they had to watch both.

CHAPTER 61

"On the white poppy,
a butterfly's torn wing
is a keepsake."
— Matsuo Basho

WOLF RIVER VILLAGE DOCK

THE *RAMONA*, A FIFTEEN-METER BOAT WITH TWO DECKS AND PILOTHOUSE atop, sat behind the barge she pushed up and down the Yukon. Every village on the river from St. Mary's to Fort Yukon knew Claude Demientieff, Sr., his wife Martha, and their personable fifteen-year-old son, Claude, Jr., who was in constant motion while working the boat. Village kids called it the "store boat" and knew there would always be some free candy upon its arrival.

Now people filed onto a barge newly rigged with a sturdy framework to support the tarps covering the passengers. The tarps were for camouflage if the Japanese put up observation planes. Nobody at the dock had any idea what was coming next.

Levi and Dr. Christenson tended Tomiko and three other wounded as they roared up in a liberated lorry. Some of the people at the dock brought out weapons at first then put them away when they recognized the vehicle's occupants.

"This is the last of the Wolf River people," Christenson said. "There's a lot of cargo in there, more tied up dogs in one place than I could have imagined. They all know they might be leaving their home for the last time. I hope their sacrifice is worth it."

"I do, too," Levi said. "Coming back here before all of this is over might not be a good idea."

"I'm totally in the dark about what is supposed to happen—"

An amplified shout cut Christenson off.

"You will all exit the barge, now!"

Levi recognized the voice of Sergeant Major Fukita.

"Continue loading and keep your head down," Levi said as he grabbed the machine-gun and remaining two clips.

"Where are you going?" Christenson asked.

"To settle a score."

❂

Sergeant Major Fukita motioned for his men to spread to out farther than they already had, but in the heavy brush not many saw or understood his hand signals. He only had thirty-five men, but all carried Type 100 machine-guns or trusty Ariska Type 99 rifles complete with sixteen-inch bayonets. Fukita wanted his men to be ready for anything.

What he hadn't anticipated was the automatic gunfire that erupted from a variety of locations along the river and from the south end of the village. A man less than a meter from Fukita cried out and dropped with a bullet through the chest.

"They're armed! Take cover!" he screamed. "Aim for the flashes, fire at will!"

He felt despair wash over him. None of his men had ever seen combat. They were all in their late teens or twenties and were used to being obeyed simply because they were Japanese.

Peacetime is a waste of good soldiers!

The people he had hoped to subdue with fear were all older and many, he suspected, were veterans of the war. Their fire proved more effective than that of his men. His mind flashed back to the Aleutians and he found an answer to his immediate problem.

"Prepare to charge!" he shouted.

One of his men said, "Are you crazy, Sergeant Major? They'll cut us down like wheat!"

"They will be surprised, overwhelmed, fraught with fear! For the Emperor, now with me, *Banzai!*"

He whipped out his samurai sword and rushed forward. After a split second his men screamed in defiance and charged after him.

❂

Levi slid behind a crate where another man fired toward the dim figures now rushing at them. Levi waited, realizing that his machine-gun was far more effective at close quarters. The man glanced over at him.

"Levi Fischer! What a surprise."

"Gunther! Where the hell have you been?"

"Setting up elements and combat teams along the railroad, around Fairbanks, and positioning for an assault on Akihito Aerodrome; we're ready for these bastards!"

"I knew you were on the War Council, but didn't know you were part of the combat phase."

"Christ on a crutch, Levi. *Everyone* is part of this!"

A Japanese soldier ran past and Gunther cut him down.

Levi sensed motion and looked up.

"Look out!" he screamed.

Sergeant Major Fukita stood atop the crate and swung his sword down, cutting off Gunther Charles' left arm at the elbow. He whipped the sword up again and swung down at Levi.

Without conscious thought, Levi snapped the machine-gun up in both hands and blocked the swing. The sword bit deep into the weapon, but not through it.

Fukita's eyes widened and Levi abruptly twisted the machine-gun to the right, snapping off part of the blade.

Fukita shrieked as if he had been wounded, pulled the broken sword up in front of his eyes and stared at it for a split second before swinging the twenty-inch stub at Levi.

"You ignorant barbarian! You have insulted my *kami*, my *giri*, and my *on* to the Emperor! You must die!"

Levi threw himself to the side, grabbed Gunther's dropped rifle and parried Fukita's second swing. The sergeant major knocked the rifle out of Levi's hands with the hilt of his weapon and jumped off the crate while swinging yet again. Levi stumbled backward and remembered Tomiko's .45 on his hip.

He frantically snapped open the holster flap and pulled the automatic free while dodging yet another swing from the frenzied sergeant major. Levi shot him twice in the chest. By the time the sergeant major hit the ground the charge had been stopped.

Many Japanese soldiers sprawled moaning in pain, most lay in dead silence. The twin odors of cordite and blood rode the breeze off the river.

He rolled Fukita over. The sergeant major's life was quickly ebbing.

Blood bubbled out of his mouth and his eyes were wide, flashing back and forth between here and there. Levi knew where *here* was, but where was *there*?

"You… may have, won," Fukita gasped, "…this battle. But we will win, the war."

"Not this time," Levi said with a vicious smile. "Not this time. We are going to kick you butchering bastards out of our country."

"I wish to, to be cremated."

"We'll take care of that, too. Now go burn in hell."

Sergeant Major Isu Fukita died.

He tore Fukita's belt off and used it as a tourniquet on Gunther's arm. The man had grabbed his arm above the cut and clenched as hard as he could to keep from bleeding out. Yet he had still lost a lot of blood and, coupled with the shock of his injury, was slipping into unconsciousness.

Levi yelled for help and two villagers he didn't know trotted over.

"We need to get him on the boat with the doctor!"

Before he could get off his knees, the two men had grabbed Gunther and were moving toward the *Ramona* at a high rate of speed. He checked through the area for more wounded and found only dead Japanese soldiers.

Levi looked up. The *Ramona* had started down river with her precious cargo. Levi wondered where Thelma was; it had been such a long time since he had seen her.

With a last glance at the body of Sergeant Major Fukita he grabbed a machine-gun and ammo pouch off a dead Japanese soldier and trotted toward the Yukon.

CHAPTER 62

"How wild the sea is,
and over Sado Island,
the River of Heaven."
— Matsuo Basho

TANANA,
ALASKA PREFECTURE

"SPUD, THE HELIOGRAPH GUY SAYS THERE'S A BUNCH OF BOATS COMING down river like a bat out of hell!"

Spud Williams looked at Jimmy Demoski standing in the cabin door with a wide grin spreading over his face.

"Ya think this is *it?*"

"I sure hope so. I'm ready to kick Jap ass, y'know?

Spud went over to a cupboard and pushed on what appeared to be a knot in the wood. A panel swung open, he pulled out an assault rifle and a bag of ammunition.

"Okay, Jimmy, let's get our people to the boats."

They ran down to the river. Under normal circumstances the water would be at the bottom of a twenty-foot bank. With all the rain the Yukon had risen nearly to the top of the bank. All of the villagers had moved their possessions to higher ground and only those men and women in the Tanana Warriors of the Liberty Underground remained in the village.

The village was strung out along the north bank of the Yukon River a few miles downstream from where the Tanana River joins the larger river. Far above flood stage and still rising, both rivers surged along. The huge lake forming in Alaska's Interior grew steadily by the hour.

While the majority of the flotilla of riverboats turned to go up the Tanana River, two came down to where the Tanana Unit was busily launching their boats. One of the boats stayed out on the river while the other came into shore.

An Asian wearing a uniform jumped to the bank.

"I am Captain Vu Doan, Who is in charge here?

"That would be me," Spud said. "Is this the big attack?"

"Yes. We talked with the pilot of the mail plane and he said we should actually be able go all the way to Akihito Aerodrome by boat to make an amphibious assault. Our people watching the aerodrome have reported that the Japs are in complete turmoil trying to keep the runway open. Only a small part of the Richardson Highway is still open, most of it is under water."

"So the garrison outside Fairbanks can't reinforce the airfield?" Spud asked.

"No. They are completely cut off by water. I think we can take the airfield and hold it."

"For how long?" Jimmy asked. "Until they send a squadron of fighters up from the states and blow us to hell?"

"Attacks like this are happening everywhere, not just here," Captain Doan said.

"Are you a deserter, or what?" Jimmy asked.

"I'm not Japanese. I am Vietnamese. The Japs took over our country, too."

Doan turned to look at the river and Jimmy caught Spud's attention, rolled his eyes and shrugged. Spud grinned and shook his head.

"So where do you want us in this thing?" Spud asked.

"There are four lead boats. You people follow the one flying the blue pennant. You'll be hitting the aerodrome at its south end. Good luck!"

Captain Doan returned to his boat and motored back up river.

Spud grinned and stepped onto a boat with four other men and a woman. "We need to pass the word–follow the blue pennant. It's time to go kill Japs!"

One of the men bent to the line-of-sight radio to relay the orders to the other task force participants.

Their riverboat roared after the assault force.

CHAPTER 63

"Behind this door now buried in deep grass
A different generation will celebrate
The Festival of Dolls."
— Matsuo Basho

KEMPEITAI HEADQUARTERS
YUKON STATION

"I WANT EVERY ROUND EYE ON THIS BASE ARRESTED IMMEDIATELY!" Captain Hirako Atsumi screamed at her subordinates. "We are surrounded by traitors! Now go, bring them to me!"

The assembly room cleared in under a minute.

Captain Atsumi hurried toward the stairs and encountered General Yamashita and General Tsuji descending toward her. She snapped to attention and bowed.

"There is no time for formality, Captain," Yamashita said with a slight wheeze. "What is the situation with the weapons?"

"The train with the railcar weapon was hijacked. We are rushing repairs to the bridge so we may pursue the fools. There really is nowhere for them to go. The Chrysanthemum Rocket is in the final stages of launching. Doctor Tommatsu was killed in an explosion that we are still investigating."

"What about his assistants?" General Tsuji snapped.

"Doctor Rose and Dr. Hyakawa have disappeared. I have ordered the detention of all non-Japanese on the base."

"Where are Major Summatsu and Sergeant Major Fukita?" Yamashita said in his gravel voice.

"I, I don't know, general," Captain Atsumi said, wishing she could stop sweating. "Both left with detachments of troops some hours ago. I have heard nothing since."

"Is it possible they were overwhelmed by insurgents?" Tsuji asked.

"I do not think that could happen, General. Our people were fully armed with modern weapons. The Americans possess only hunting rifles and—"

"Then from where did all the automatic weapons fire originate an hour ago?" Tsuji demanded. "Why have you not sent someone to investigate?"

"I did not hear the weapons fire, General. I was in my office fielding reports and orders."

"That can wait," Yamashita said. "I wish to observe the launch of our rocket presentation to the Greater German Reich."

Captain Atsumi followed them and wondered what she was missing. So many pieces of this strange puzzle had become elusive, and the pieces she had didn't seem to fit. The two generals waved her into their command car and as soon as she shut the door the driver drove quickly toward the Project Building.

The Army firefighters had finally stopped the flow of fuel through the shattered lines and cooled the eight huge fuel tanks before they had collected sufficient heat to explode.

At least something went right, Captain Atsumi thought.

Lieutenant General Yamashita stepped out of the car and moved as fast as he could toward the Project Building entrance. This moment was the capstone of a long and illustrious career. He knew he had served the Emperor well and would be rewarded in kind.

The explosion that had killed Doctor Tommatsu puzzled him. There was nothing in that part of the building that could have malfunctioned in such a deadly manner. Once inside the building he could see the Chrysanthemum Rocket through the heavy glass of the observation window and all else flew from his mind like swallows leaving a barn.

Lights winked out on a board visible to anyone within sight and a section of the roof began to move to one side. Horns went off inside the launch chamber and red warning lights rhythmically strobed over every door. Yamashita could feel his heart pounding in his chest and his breath came in gasps.

The roof moved past the three-quarter mark and he looked up at the blue sky through the opening in time to see a huge aircraft bearing a swastika on its tail fly over. Men poured from it, parachutes blossomed.

"No! This cannot be!" he shrieked. His chest erupted in crushing pain and he crumpled to the floor.

"General Yamashita!" Captain Atsumi yelled.

He wanted to answer her. He wanted to tell her so many things, but the spots before his eyes confused him and he could not form the words before everything faded away.

"What's wrong with him?" General Tsuji shouted.

"I, I don't know," Captain Atsumi lied. She jerked her head upward. "But I do know that you're in command and we're being attacked!"

At that moment the Chrysanthemum Rocket engines ignited with a roar and the craft slowly climbed up and out of the building. The glass in the window rippled with the pressure and she thought it was going to explode inward at them. As the tail of fire passed out of sight her new fear was that the Germans would shoot the thing down on top of them.

"We must get out of here," Tsuji bellowed, spittle flying from his twisted mouth.

Gunfire from outside cut the guards down at the door. Atsumi sprinted over and scooped up the machine-gun one of them had dropped. When the first three German paratroopers rushed through the door she shot them down.

Where the hell are Fukita and his men? She wondered. *They were supposed to be back by now!*

A grenade hit the floor and rolled to a sputtering stop. She scuttled over and put a pillar between her and it. Major General Masanobu Tsuji took the full brunt of the explosion and his mangled body slammed to the floor, lifeless.

A trio of German paratroopers rushed through the door and she gave them time to get into the room before she stepped out and emptied her clip into the three. Nobody followed them. She hurried over to the nearest casualty and scooped up his weapon.

A glance down at his bloody form gave her the location of his ammo belt. She tensely watched the door while she opened the buckle and ripped the belt from him. Throwing it over her shoulder she ran to the doorway and peered out.

The Germans were engaged in a firefight with the ground troops guarding the anti-aircraft positions. As far as she could tell, she was the senior officer on Yukon Station. She ran back through the building and carefully opened the door leading to the worker's barracks.

The conscripts should be easy to manage, she thought.

CHAPTER 64

"Flower

under harvest sun —stranger

To bird, butterfly."

— Matsuo Basho

YUKON STATION,
ALASKA PREFECTURE

OBERSTLEUTNANTS DIETER HOFFMAN AND GEORG HOYT WATCHED THE drop pattern of their troops. The attack had been far from textbook. Three sticks of *Fallshirmjäger* had landed in the wide Yukon River and immediately disappeared forever. Anti-aircraft fire poured upward from at least three positions. Two of the huge German aircraft had already been hit and crashed into the forest.

The two Messerschmitt jet fighters had strafed the burning runway and aerodrome until all buildings were engulfed in flames.

Even though the Luftwaffe maintained numerical superiority here, the waste sickened both men. Dieter stuck his head in the cockpit.

"If you don't mind going around again," he shouted. "We would like to jump over the compound itself."

"As you wish!" the pilot shouted back and put the aircraft into a wide turn.

They could see firefights on the ground. The cannon fire from the ground continued unabated and Hoffmann wondered if he was tempting fate to go over a second time. Many *Fallshirmjäger* floated down to Earth already dead from gunfire, but most landed safely and immediately went into action.

"Are you ready, Dieter?" Georg shouted to his friend.

"Yes! For Fatherland and Fuhrer!"

They ran down the ramp and leaped from the aircraft.

Dieter wondered why this was so much more complicated then he thought it would be.

CHAPTER 65

WORKER HOUSING, YUKON STATION

As soon as Bao Li heard the air raid siren go off he shouted at everyone in the room.

"Run! Go through the garden and follow the instructions of the people you find there!"

Used to following orders immediately and explicitly, all of the workers did as they were told. Bao followed them out into the large garden. As he stepped through the door the fence at the back of the garden erupted in great gouts of earth along the left side and the whole thing fell over.

He grabbed a pry bar and raced for the promise of freedom. A Japanese soldier rushed around the corner of the building, eyes wide in fear. He jerked to a stop, stared at the tide of humanity rushing toward the absent fence, and looked around in time to catch Bao's pry bar full in the face.

Bao kept running. Men and women in olive drab uniforms directed the fleeing Chinese across the perimeter road and down the hill toward the river. They asked as many escapees as they could, "Do you know how to use this?" and held up rifles. Many happily grabbed weapons. The escape progressed with no shouting or yelling; all of the Chinese knew this was the only way they would live.

Down the road them the anti-aircraft guns fired incessantly and the roar of heavy aircraft seemed to be everywhere. Bao stopped short of the fence and looked back. Only a few Chinese were behind him and he waited for them to run across the wide boards someone had thrown on the razor-sharp wire formerly atop the fence.

As he exited the enclosure Sergeant Da Chen, whom he had spoken to a week ago, hurried over to him and handed him a machine-gun.

"You know how to use this, yes?"

Bao glanced down at the reassuring weight in his hands, energized and happy at the power sweeping through him.

"I will make it work!" he said with a nod and a grin.

"Follow the others. That was good work. You had them ready to—" a bullet hit him the arm and he stumbled from the impact.

Gunfire came from above. Bao jerked his head up and saw three German paratroopers falling toward them shooting as they descended. He took aim and killed two of them immediately. Someone else shot the third man and they hit the ground like sacks, the light green chutes settling over them like shrouds.

Bao helped Sergeant Chen to his feet.

"Thank you. I guess you do know how to make it work. Do you know how to reload?"

"You're bleeding, Sergeant!"

"Yes, so I am." He pulled a packet from one of his pockets. "Please tie this around my arm above the wound."

Bao quickly tied the arm off, kicked a branch off one of the stunted spruce surrounding them, and tied it on the bandage.

"There, twist that until the bleeding stops and I'll tie it down."

"Keep moving," Sergeant Chen said. His breathing was becoming labored and Bao stayed next to him as the made their way down the riverbank. People in uniform grasped ropes to hold fast a small flotilla of riverboats while Chinese laborers boarded.

"Where did you get all the boats?"

Sergeant Chen made a small laugh. "The Japanese didn't seem to need them today. So we borrowed all we could find."

Close to the boats now, Bao shouted, "This man needs medical attention!"

Two women in uniform hurried over. "Thank you, we have him now. Get in a boat, quickly!"

Bao hurried to the end of the group where the boats weren't as full. He stepped on board and sat down.

A woman sitting next to him looked up and said, "Even if we die now, we will die free."

"We aren't going to die!" he said. "Not until we have killed many Japanese."

The boats pushed away from the bank and motored to the middle of the channel before turning down river and picking up speed. Gunfire sounded from all directions around them but didn't seem to be directed at them.

Bao saw firefights on the shore near the west end of the Project; it was impossible to know who was winning. A German aircraft flew low over the river trailing smoke from one feathered engine. As Bao watched the plane flew directly into one of the anti-aircraft mounts firing at other planes.

The plane exploded when it hit and the concussion rocked their boat.

Bao turned to the man steering the boat. "Where are we going?"

"To safety. For now you are out of this war. You will be needed later."

The Annex exploded and a split second later the fuel tanks behind the building went up in an even bigger detonation. It flattened all of the fencing and spruce around the area, as well as leveling the offices and barracks.

Bao wondered how anyone could have lived through that. He saw the burning woman run from the debris only to fall unmoving before reaching the river.

Her charred uniform hung in tatters and agonizing flash burns covered her body. Captain Hirako Atsumi lay on the scorched ground, her destroyed lungs strained fruitlessly for breath, and she wondered what she could have done to change these circumstances.

Unenlightened, she died.

CHAPTER 66

WOLF RIVER VILLAGE,
ALASKA PREFECTURE

DIETER AND GEORG FELL TOWARDS THE GROUND MUCH FASTER THAN Dieter remembered from previous jumps. The ground teemed with figures running, falling, hiding, and some boarding boats. He decided they would both land safely on uncontested land.

One of the Heinkel transports, shot to pieces and engines smoking, flew into the anti-aircraft position next to the buildings housing the bomb project. The resulting explosion set off something in the main building that also exploded.

The concussion of the two explosions blew the oberstleutnants closer to the river. Dieter quickly reconsidered their probable landing sites and deduced they had meters to spare. He grinned in relief.

The fuel tanks behind the bomb project structure exploded, throwing fuel into the burning project building. The heat wave didn't incinerate their parachutes only because the initial shock wave blew them farther north and east. Now he realized they would land in the Yukon River.

Dieter saw that he would come down less than a meter off the riverbank. A quick glance told him that Georg would land well out into the river. Seconds later he hit the water with his legs straight and toes pointed downward for entry.

He screamed at the agonizing impact and pain of his feet smashing into the sloping bank a few hundred centimeters under the swiftly moving surface of the river. He heard his left ankle snap and the abrupt shockwave of additional agony lifted his scream into the higher octaves. He floundered in the water, falling away from the steep bank into deeper water.

Trying to ignore the renewed shock of pain every time his damaged foot touched something solid, he continued to scramble for the shore; he knew he was a dead man if he didn't reach the bank immediately. His chute settled into the river and the current caught the silk canopy. Dieter frantically paddled with his hands toward the shore before being pulled over backward and under the water.

✪

Oberstleutnant Georg Hoyt concluded he was going to land in the river. A parachute would drag him to the bottom no matter what else happened. He grabbed his emergency release, ripped it open, and dropped free of the harness and parachute.

A riverboat materialized under him and he landed on people. He distinctly heard a neck break. One man jumped over the side, his eyes wide and face filled with fear.

Georg decided these were Japanese civilians fleeing the attack. The man at the tiller wore a pistol on his side and a machine-gun rested at his feet. Time slowed for him, and he realized that their attack had gone wrong for a lot of people—including him—and there was no good way out of this.

He made a show of throwing his machine-gun into the river and raised his arms.

"I surrender!" he shouted.

The armed man driving the riverboat frowned at him and asked, "Where the hell did you come from?"

English, the Japanese spoke to him in English!

"I am a German paratrooper! I will not resist."

"They told me that Krauts were smart," the driver said, holding a pistol in one hand and working the tiller with the other, "but you're also very quick. I like that in a person."

"Are you in the Japanese Army?" Georg asked.

"Righteous Fists of the Liberty Underground," the man said with a smile. "I'm not Japanese, I'm Chinese, which is one reason why you're still alive."

"The Liberty Underground has units up here, too?"

"Yes. That's the other reason you're still alive."

The *Ramona* rounded the first bend in the river when six German paratroopers floated down between Levi and the boat landing. All of the Germans fired at everything that moved. Levi dove behind a pile of wood rounds and scrambled around the pile on his elbows. He heard two people behind him get hit and wondered who they were.

He edged around and saw the paratroopers fanning out, seeking protection and still laying down an incredible amount of fire.

How many rounds do those things hold? Levi wondered.

At that moment two of the Germans ran out of ammo and had to shift focus long enough to replace their clips. One of them was the closest to Levi. As the paratrooper glanced down to put in the new clip, Levi rolled over once and put two rounds into him.

Two of the other Germans fell lifeless from heavy fire behind them. The remaining three turned to their new threat and Levi jumped up and fired a long burst. His weapon ceased firing and the breech snapped open. All three of the Germans were dead.

He was out of ammo and he dropped the clip. Gunfire, explosions, and screams sounded from every direction. A lot of Germans were on the ground and regrouping. The Japanese soldiers kept up a withering defense.

What the hell am I going to do? He thought as he wiped his eyes.

"Levi! Levi! Over here!"

He looked toward the river and saw Thelma waving frantically. As soon as she knew he saw her, she dropped from sight. Levi reached into his pouch, pulled out a new clip, and snapped it into the machine-gun.

Renewed fire came from his left and he twisted around to see a number of Germans falling back toward the river away from a Japanese attack. For a moment he nearly fired at them before realizing if he took them out the Japanese would then shoot at him. He scrambled to his feet and sprinted toward Thelma's location.

He jumped over the bank feet-first and caught himself before he tumbled into the water. Doubtful Thomas and Thelma stared up at him from where they held the riverboat against the bank. Levi felt like weeping in relief but knew there wasn't time to waste on tears.

Doubtful laid down the machine-gun he had been holding under his right elbow.

"Good to see you, Levi," he said with a wide smile. "Now maybe she'll let us leave."

Thelma laughed and said, "Get in, Dad, I'll push us off."

Levi slid down the bank and stepped onto the riverboat. He hesitated and looked down at her lovingly.

"Over there," She said through a quick smile as she pushed him toward a bench seat. As soon as he moved she pushed the boat out into the river and dropped down next to him.

"I am so happy to see you," she said, staring up into his eyes. "Now kiss me."

CHAPTER 67

"A cold rain starting
And no hat —
So?"
— Matsuo Basho

CHENA RIDGE NEAR FAIRBANKS, ALASKA PREFECTURE

Paul Stoddard ambled into the living room he shared with his longtime friend and team leader.

"Sam, fresh off the shortwave. The curtain just went up."

Skagway Sam Kalin looked up from the old novel he was reading.

"Really, we're finally going to shoot Japs?"

"LU says go for it. Who's got the duty in Fairbanks?"

"Hell, the place is flooded. Even the Kempeitai building has water on the first floor."

"Do we know for sure if the cells flooded?"

"Yeah, but some major put the prisoners in box cars and sent them down to Anchorage before the flood hit."

"That's good. I hope he had the brains to get in that box car with them."

"Last I heard Mark hadn't said anything about that." Sam stood up and started for the door. "Yeah, I hope this is the real thing because if it is, we're finally going to get to use Beulah."

"But we still need a forward observer," Paul said as he followed Sam out the door.

They walked over to a large garage and Sam put a key into the massive padlock holding the ends of a steel chain together. He turned the key and levered the lock up so the chain thudded to the ground.

After pulling the chains aside each man grabbed a door and pulled it open. Inside, the rusty body of a 1939 Packard sat under layers of dust. Sam walked over to the wall, put his finger in a knothole and pulled down. The wood slid smoothly, the front of the Packard emitted a metallic click, and the nose of the hood bobbed up.

Paul was already positioned and Sam grabbed the other fender and they lifted the entire body up until they heard the second click when the brace engaged. They carefully rolled back the exposed tarp and hung the ends on pegs set into the posts.

"We haven't had her out in daylight since we put her in there back in '45," Paul said. "That's damn near twenty-two years!"

"Christ, but you're getting sappy in your old age! Go get the truck."

"We've both been in on this from the start, and I know you realize this is a pivotal occasion, so stop being such an asshole!" Paul stomped off toward the pickup parked on the other side of the sturdily built house.

To the casual observer, once they got past the security on Chena Ridge Road, left the road and made it past the trees, would see was a sturdy house with a high-pitched roof designed for low snow accumulation and an equally sturdy, similarly roofed garage. At the far side of the parking lot sat a twenty-foot by twenty-foot area covered in gravel and free of trees and brush.

Paul backed the pickup over to the open garage and expertly stopped in the preordained spot. Leaving the engine running, he got out and went back to the winch on the rear steel bumper. He flipped off the brake and handed the large hook to Sam who walked it down onto the ramp below the Packard.

"Did they say we were still going with Plan A?" Sam asked.

He ran the hook through the lunette and snagged it back on the cable. He trudged back up to the truck. "Okay, reel her in."

"There's been a change in the plan for Yukon Station, but for us it's still Plan A."

"Good," Sam said as he watched the wire cable go taut. The winch's whine grew louder by the second. "We already have the coordinates for our targets so we don't really need a forward observer."

"Mark is in there somewhere. Which bar has a second floor?"

"Um, let's see, the Sun Goddess Haven has a second floor. He can see the Kempeitai headquarters from there, too."

"That's where Mark is. Give you three to one odds," Paul said through a grin.

"I agree. No bet. However, I will bet you that he's drunk."

Stoddard rolled his eyes.

The gathered steel of the trail emerged into the sunlight. Paul turned off the winch and ran a safety chain welded to the bumper through the lunette and secured it.

"Okay, Lieutenant Kalin," Paul said as he came to a semblance of attention and tossed off a loose salute. "Where do you want Beulah positioned?"

"Fire Step B, Staff Sergeant Stoddard, if you please."

As Paul walked back to the truck, he spoke over his shoulder, "Y'know, after twenty-four years in the army I should be more than a staff sergeant."

"Okay, I hereby award you a battlefield promotion to master sergeant. That work for you?"

"Really, master sergeant? Thanks!"

"Now position the field piece, if you would, Master Sergeant Stoddard."

Paul laughed and slid behind the wheel. He shifted into first gear and let the clutch out. He swung wide and expertly backed the cannon over to the graveled area.

"This is sure as hell a lot easier in the daylight!"

"It has to be," Sam said, nodding. "But I still bet you could do it with your eyes closed."

Within five minutes they had unhooked the cable and spread the trail out to its widest angle of support. After uncovering the ends, they dropped the handspikes into pipes built into the ground. The weapon's dull green metal shone with a thin coating of oil and glistened in the summer sun.

"Which shell you want to use first?" Paul asked.

"High explosive, just like they used on Pearl Harbor. This is war."

Paul stepped over to a set of shelves holding various pots of plants and pulled it open to reveal a steel door. The door opened smoothly on well-oiled hinges to reveal stacks of 105mm shells. Paul picked one up and staggered back to the breech assembly that

Sam had already opened.

"These things are heavier than I remember," Paul said.

"You're older than you remember," Sam said. "Here let me help you with that, old timer."

"Fuck you," Paul said amiably. "Thanks."

They slid the shell in and Sam closed the breech.

Paul adjusted the elevation, cranked the barrel over to the exact direction, and then stood up.

"You're the officer. Would you like to pull the first shot?"

"Thanks, yes I would."

The cannon fired and rocked back against the handspikes from the recoil. The breech snapped open and the spent casing flew out and rolled across the ground.

"Damn, that was fun!" Sam said. "Let's do it again!"

"What kind of round this time?"

"We're still at war. Make it high explosive again."

"You're the lieutenant," Paul said and ambled toward the ammunition locker.

CHAPTER 68

KEMPEITAI HEADQUARTERS, FAIRBANKS, ALASKA PREFECTURE

THE SENIOR SERGEANT RADIO OPERATOR SNAPPED ERECT IN HIS CHAIR and his eyes went wide. He tore off his headset.

"Colonel, Yukon Station is under attack by German paratroopers!"

Okakura turned from the window where he had been watching the floodwater rise slowly up the sides of the buildings across the street. His anger had dissipated to despair, and the bottle of sake in his office weighed heavily on his mind.

"Is that the secure channel?"

"It's on *all* the channels, Colonel!"

"Put it on the speaker!" He turned to a corporal. "Go get the engineering colonel, now!"

The speaker crackled and a shaking voice said, "–dozens of German transport planes. We estimate over a thousand paratroopers are attacking us. The Chrysanthemum moon rocket launched just before they hit us."

"Moon rocket!" Colonel Okakura exclaimed as Colonel Hideki hurried into the room. "Is that what that damned project has been all about?"

"Colonel," Hideki said, "...is there any way we can render aid?"

"We can't even leave this damned building, Colonel! The only good thing in all of this is that we aren't threatened here."

"I'm getting a message from Akihito Aerodrome," the radio operator said loudly. "The runway is completely submerged by flood water."

"We are completely cut off from the Empire," Colonel Okakura said. "I don't think this can get any worse."

"With all due respect, Colonel," Colonel Hideki said in a sharp tone. "You should never say something like–"

They all heard the shrill scream of the shell as it arced down toward them.

"Take cover!" Hideki screamed and threw himself under a desk.

The high explosive shell penetrated the roof and third floor before exploding in the large room, blowing out the walls and collapsing the ceiling and roof above it. Moments later the second shell hit the base of the first floor, throwing up a geyser of water and destroying what remained of the building. The debris fell into the rising floodwater.

Anyone not killed by the shelling drowned in the floodwater.

CHAPTER 69

BERLIN, GERMANY

REICHSFUHRER HERMANN GÔRING PUSHED HIS LUNCH DISH ASIDE AND examined the latest dispatches. The Alaska strike was well under way and their surprise attack on Tokyo seemed to be succeeding beyond his wildest dreams. He smiled.

An aide ran into the room. "Mein Fuhrer!"

"What is it, Klein?"

"The Japanese moon rocket!"

"What about it?" He loved the irony of the situation; there would be no way to retrieve the crew.

In the distance air raid sirens sounded, something the city had not heard in over twenty years. Hubristically, the anti-aircraft batteries had been removed or preserved as monuments years ago. The Greater German Reich dominated the world, who could challenge it?

"It's heading toward Berlin!"

"Vas? When will it arrive?"

"Any moment n—"

The ancient city of Berlin vanished in an atomic blast unprecedented on Earth. The Japanese had created the largest bomb they could devise and it obliterated the German capitol in the wink of an eye.

Yet even though the heart of the Third Reich had now ceased to exist, it left a large part of the monster still alive, for the moment.

CHAPTER 70

"Stillness—

the cicada's cry

drills into the rocks."

— Matsuo Basho

IMPERIAL PALACE, TOKYO, EMPIRE OF JAPAN

EMPEROR HIROHITO SIPPED JASMINE TEA AND CONTEMPLATED HIS PLACE IN history. There had never been a warrior emperor in all of history who ruled as much of the world as he did at this moment. The imminent destruction of Berlin seemed the harbinger of further conquests to the west.

Events seemed to be moving swiftly and surely to an age of Japanese domination of the world. This pleased him. He set aside his cup of tea at the gentle knock on the door.

"Enter."

His oldest, and therefore the most senior, retainer soundlessly stepped inside the huge door and bowed deeply.

"What is it?"

"Your Majesty, there has been an incident in Alaska Prefecture."

"What has the Imperial Army done now?"

"It seems the Germans are overrunning the Imperial Army weapons project."

"I thought we just eliminated Berlin."

"Yes, Majesty, we have. The attack took place at the same time as the rocket launch."

"I see. Then this is just a temporary situation?"

"That is our hope. The flood around Fairbanks does not help–"

Outside the palace an air raid alarm shrilled, a sound not heard in Tokyo since early 1945. Both men looked up, questioning the sky they could not see.

An eye-searing light, brighter than the sun, washed through the palace a split second ahead of the cleansing blast. The mushroom cloud climbed into the sky where the ancient city of Tokyo once stood. Three million humans, a government, and a social system vanished beneath its lethal spread.

CHAPTER 71

PRINCE AKIHITO AERODROME,
ALASKA PREFECTURE

"WE NEED MORE SANDBAGS AT THE SOUTH END OF THE RUNWAY!" Sergeant Takeshi bellowed at his men. "We are going to lose the runway completely if you don't work harder!"

The sergeant stood on a narrow neck of land leading up to the runway. The perimeter fence had washed away two days earlier, most of the base lay under a minimum of a meter of water and some locations lay three meters below the surface. Water already covered the runway, but not deeply. If they could only divert the flow they might reclaim it for emergency use.

Corporal Toyoda ran up to him, pointing at the horizon. "Sergeant, we are being attacked!"

"Attacked, by who? Have you broken into the sake this early in the day?"

Toyoda thrust binoculars at him. "Look for yourself! They are coming across the floodwaters!"

Takeshi could not smell alcohol on his subordinate's breath. Toyoda was a well-grounded man, easily in line for another stripe. He accepted the binoculars and trained them where Toyoda pointed.

Scores of riverboats loaded with people wove through the tops of submerged spruce and alder toward them at a high rate of speed.

The boats spread out as soon as they cleared the trees and widened into a three-mile-wide wave of people bearing weapons.

"We do not need this!" Takeshi screamed. Close to dumbfounded, he reached for the traditional. "Where are our security troops?"

"They are sandbagging south of here, on the Richardson Highway, Sergeant."

"Get weapons. Prepare for an assault!"

"Get them where? The armory is surrounded by floodwater."

Neither man moved. Both knew they had run out of time and options to face this new threat.

Deep in his heart, Sergeant Takeshi mentally congratulated the attackers for their timing and audacity. At that point a scout car skidded to a stop behind them. A private jumped out and hurried over to him.

"Sergeant Takeshi, there has been a German invasion at Yukon Station. The entire project is under siege. We are on high alert!"

"Where are the perimeter guards?" Takeshi screamed, wondering how this new information would affect the situation unfolding in front of him.

"They are fighting the flood, dammit!" Corporal Toyoda screamed back.

Takeshi could remember when, and not all that long ago, corporals did not scream at sergeants, no matter what the situation.

"Man the .50 caliber machine-guns," he ordered. "Mow them down!"

"The weapons are not mounted, Sergeant Takeshi. You anticipated that the positions would be flooded and..."

The buzz of the boat motors carried easily over the water, growing louder by the moment.

All armament had been locked away safely in the sandbagged confines of the base armory. The Japanese Army had been fighting a losing battle with the flood and now faced an even greater loss.

"Contact headquarters, now!" Takeshi snapped.

The private turned toward the scout car. Something hit him in the middle of his back, blood sprayed out of his chest and he fell soundlessly to the ground. The firecracker reports of weapons fire rolled over them and bullets snapped past their heads.

"Take cover!" Takeshi screamed. He pulled his pistol from its holster and crouched behind the command car next to Corporal

Toyoda.

The riverboats roared toward them. Muzzle flashes winked from the boats in the leading edge of the wave. The rate of fire grew and Sergeant Takeshi realized they had automatic weapons.

Who are these people? Germans?

The scout car shook with the high rate of hits. A round hit Corporal Toyoda in the face and he fell backward silently.

Sergeant Takeshi absently wiped wetness off his cheek and aimed at the boat racing directly at him. He considered the range, the speed of the advance, the limits of his pistol, raised the muzzle a few millimeters higher, and fired.

One of the figures in the boat dropped. It wasn't the one the sergeant had aimed at, but he felt a rush of elation nonetheless.

The muzzle flash of his shot gave the attackers in the boats something to aim at. Four rounds hit Sergeant Takeshi at the same time. He was dead seconds after he hit the ground. Floodwater continued to creep across the narrowing spit toward his staring eyes.

CHAPTER 72

ON THE YUKON RIVER

The 26-foot riverboat tore through the water at amazing speed, throwing up a six-foot rooster tail of water. Levi thought the boat that he, Doubtful, Bill Fredson, and Boston Titus had taken to visit the training camp had been fast. This one seemed to move at least half again faster.

Thelma, sitting beside him and wrapped in a rain slicker like the other six people aboard, tightly held his hand.

The bouncing bow would slap the water every few dozen feet and throw spray back over them like hard rain. An insulated box muted the inboard engine. The ancient Johnson outboard that was ostensibly the power source was lashed to the back of the stern with the prop out of the water.

Glen Bassett, who had manned the helm for the past two hours, shouted something. The boat slowed and the bow dropped so they could all see the *Ramona* pushing a barge. People came out from under the tarps covering the cargo and motioned to Glen who expertly pulled the riverboat along side the barge as the *Ramona* continued to make way.

Many others, especially children, peeked out from beneath the tarps. While Doubtful Thomas and another man handed mooring ropes up to men on the barge.

Levi looked at Thelma. "I was amazed to see you in the last batch of people to leave. Why were you so late?"

"I was helping Jake and Jerry pass the word to other units here and down in the states."

Levi was at a loss for words for longer than he liked. "You what? I mean, when did you learn to work with radios?"

She grinned at him. "Once again, you thought I was just a simple little village girl, huh?"

"I already told you the other day, not *simple*, but certainly not technical. I admit to being surprised."

"Almost everyone in the Liberty Underground is trained for two jobs. I am a communications technician as well as head of security."

"Security? I thought you were head of intelligence."

"Think about it, one works hand-in-hand with the other. I liked you the first time I saw you, Levi. That's why I used all of our resources to make sure you were truly not an enemy agent."

"So when they said, when *you* said, 'an honest, good man,' you were making an official report to the Underground."

"Yes. And they knew I wouldn't say that if I didn't know it for a fact."

"Please tell me if you thought you would find anything damning."

"No, but I had to prove it others."

He swallowed and felt so lucky it frightened him. "Did you have to make more than one transmission?"

"We contacted, or tried to contact, fourteen different communications centers. Some of them were skeptical and we had our hands full trying to convince them this really was the day they had trained and planned for."

"Where did you hide the antennas?"

"A lot of the really tall trees have antennas in the tops. We tried to put them where the Japanese rarely went and we worked hard on camouflaging them. We did it, though, we have started a revolution."

"I know," Levi said. "However, I am not happy with the odds against winning."

"With Berlin and Tokyo both out of the picture there will be enough chaos for anything to happen."

"Tokyo? How are we going to take out Tokyo?"

"We aren't, the Germans are. They knew about the Yukon Station Project and planned to seize it. At the same time, they were going to drop an atom bomb on Tokyo."

"I, I thought this was just a local thing, just Yukon Station. How do you know what the Germans are planning?"

"There are people in Germany who are as rabidly anti-Nazi as we are. They have all evacuated Berlin by now. They know what's coming."

"I hope this works as well as you think it will."

The riverboat engine rumbled into life and ropes were cast off.

"We're not going to travel with them?" Levi asked, nodding at the *Ramona*.

"No. We anticipate Japanese aircraft and don't want to put all of our eggs in one basket. Besides, this is a faster moving target if it comes to that. We just needed more fuel."

"Still in the bullseye, huh?"

"What?"

"Nothing worth talking about. When this is over will you marry me?"

She stared at him and a grin blossomed on her face. "You, I..." She shook her head and smiled at him. "I would have married you any time you asked. Since the night we talked I have been hoping you would take the final step."

"I told you I really liked you."

"I was beginning to think that was as far as it went for you. Why did you wait on this?"

"Like I said then, we live in an uncertain world, Thelma–"

"Ha, when haven't we? Yes."

"Yes, what?"

"I answered your question. I'll marry you if you want, or just live with you if you'd rather have it that way."

He grinned. "I like the commitment aspect of marriage."

"Me, too," she said, and pulled his head down to kiss him. The boat picked up speed.

CHAPTER 73

PRINCE AKIHITO AERODROME, ALASKA PREFECTURE

CORDITE EDDIED THROUGH SMASHED WINDOWS AS THE INCESSANT DIN OF machine-gun and rifle fire filled the air. Colonel Yoshio Markino, wearing the helmet he had worn as a lieutenant during the war, directed fire from the second floor of the headquarters building.

"Put another machine-gun in that window!" he shouted as he pointed. "Keep them from encircling the building at all costs."

A string of rounds cut across the back wall shattering more windows and two hanging lights. A piece of glass cut a streak in the colonel's cheek. If he even felt the wound, it didn't slow him for a moment.

"Is there any way we can get weapons from the armory?" Lieutenant Colonel Nakura, his adjutant, asked.

"We've already lost six soldiers who tried." He glanced around and lowered his voice. "We don't have many left. Most of the troops were sandbagging the highway to Anchorage when all of this began."

"Who are these people and from where did they come?"

"All I know is this started after the Yukon Station Project came under attack by the Germans."

"Those are not German soldiers. Many aren't wearing any

uniforms at all."

The radioman cried out in anguish.

"Quick, see to that man's wound!" Colonel Markino ordered.

"Nothing can help! The wound is in my heart!" The radioman screamed. "We all are lost!"

In three strides the colonel closed on the man and slapped him across the face. "Your defeatist attitude will earn you a firing squad!"

"I am sorry, Colonel. I could not help myself. I just received word that Tokyo has been destroyed by an atomic bomb. The Emperor and all of the Imperial Palace are gone."

The man collapsed to the floor, sobbing.

Colonel Markino blinked as an intense, bereft, emptiness surged through him even as his heart seemed to slow. He staggered to a chair and dropped into it.

"How will I repay my *giri*, or carry out my *on* to the Emperor if He is not really here? How will *any* of us be able to carry on without His guidance?" Markino muttered loud enough to be heard over the intensifying gunfire from outside the building. "We no longer have worth or direction!"

'Prime Minister Tojo?" Lieutenant Colonel Nakura screamed into the radioman's face.

"Gone, the Imperial Army Staff, the ministers, everything–" a ricochet hit him between the eyes and the radioman fell over backward onto the floor.

Colonel Markino whipped out his samurai sword.

"I choose to accompany the Emperor as a warrior!" He rushed down the stairs. Every man in the room grabbed weapons and rushed after him.

On the first floor quickly shouted conversations turned the defenders into screaming maniacs. They all followed Colonel Markino through the door in a *banzai* charge against the attackers.

✪

Spud Williams tried to ignore the pain as the medic cleaned his arm wound and dressed it. Major Doan came over and stared down at him, his face streaked with cordite and heavy with weariness.

"How are you doing, Captain Williams?"

"The name is 'Spud,' Major. I'm just a village kid."

"As we all once were, Captain. How is the arm?"

"Doc here says the bullet messed up my bicep but missed the bone. He said I was lucky, but I think that might be a matter of perspective."

Major Doan laughed. "Keep your sense of humor. We won here, somehow, but they still hold everything south of the Alaska Range and they won't give this up without a fight."

"They quit fighting here." Spud jerked his head toward the administration building. "They made a good defense and then just gave it all up and charged us like idiots! Why?"

I don't know. I have studied the Japanese for my entire life, and nothing I know about them would explain what just happened. This was an act that went far beyond mere desperation."

Spud's brain swirled as his eyelids fluttered. "Whoa, I think that stuff he gave me—" He fell sleep.

CHAPTER 74

ISOROKU YAMAMOTO AERODROME, ANCHORAGE, ALASKA PREFECTURE

MAJOR GENERAL KIYOMIZU SCREAMED AT HIS SUBORDINATE, "WHY haven't you launched fighters to aid Yukon Station?

Colonel Tennoji made a first-degree bow. "I was not sure the report was credible, General. I thought I should confer with you first."

"It's official, the damn Nazis are attacking us! This means war! Launch every fighter you can get in the air!"

✪

A siren sounded over the airfield and telephones pealed in all hangars. Japan was once again at war. Fuel trucks were ordered to immediately replenish all aircraft. American fuel handlers rushed to do the jobs for which they had trained long and hard.

This day had been anticipated and the Americans were prepared. Small bags of sand, or sugar, were surreptitiously added to wing tanks, into fuel trucks, and also into the main fuel storage tanks. Once finished fueling the aircraft they left the base as quickly and unobtrusively as possible.

The gate guards had not been told to limit people leaving the base, only to carefully check people coming on to the aerodrome. The preparations on the field reached fever pitch and pilots eagerly climbed into cockpits and started their engines.

✪

Major General Kiyomizu watched from the great window in his second floor office as the first two fighters raced down the runway and soared into the air. He wished he could be with them. The second pair of aircraft roared into the air.

One of the newly airborne jets seemed to falter. Kiyomizu snapped on the speaker that allowed him to listen in to the tower communications.

"…losing thrust! I will try to return to the field!"

"Yamamoto tower to 048, runway three is open for you."

Kiyomizu saw the plane veer off to the right in a wide turn and come back toward the base.

"It's getting worse, tower. I, oh, my ancestors! The engine just stopped!"

"Attempt a restart!" the man in the tower screamed. "You're losing altitude and heading for us!"

"It won't start! Something is wrong with the fuel."

"If you hit the tower or runway you will destroy our effectiveness! Veer off!"

Kiyomizu knew the pilot only had one direction he could turn in time to not put a crater in the runway or destroy the tower –toward the administration building– where the general stood watching from the second floor.

The pilot muscled the jet over and cleared both tower and runway. Rapidly losing altitude, the plane curved around and crashed into the ground in front of the administration building. The resulting explosion blew out the windows and rocked the building but only the pilot died.

The next pair of jets had been accelerating down the runway when their engines failed and they both smashed into the fence at the end of the runway. The three aircraft already airborne faltered and fell into the foothills of the Alaska Range. The engines of the waiting aircraft abruptly stopped. The air-worthiness of the entire wing had been nullified.

Major General Kiyomizu had long been of the opinion that the Americans did not believe themselves to have been beaten in the War. He protested when Lieutenant General Yamashita decreed that American civilians would be used for labor on military bases due to lack of Imperial Army manpower. Over the years of exemplary service on their part, Kiyomizu had relaxed his stance in his hope the Americans had finally accepted their place in the world.

As he stood wiping blood from glass shards off his face he knew he had been right all along. The Empire had been duped. Pearl Harbor flashed through his mind before he suppressed the thought.

Were they in league with the Germans? He wondered. *How could they have received Nazi help without us knowing about it?*

"General, I just received a message from Hiroshima..." the radio operator's mouth moved but he suddenly couldn't speak.

"Well, what did they say?" the general demanded.

"Th, that Tokyo, and the Imperial Palace, have been bombed."

"Bombed? Is the Emperor safe?"

"*Atomic* bombed, general," the man said as tears coursed down his face. "The Emperor is dead!"

Every man in the room sucked in his breath in horror. The basis of civilization as they knew it was gone.

"In our history," the general thundered, thinking fast, "there have been times when Emperors were defeated and the Sun Goddess gave us a new one even stronger than the one before!"

All eyes fixed on the general as his words gave them a glimmer of hope.

"That plane out there," he pointed at the burning wreck in front of the building, "was pushed by the Emperor's hand to crash there instead of hitting this building. What you see before you is a divinely protected warrior and the next Imperial Emperor of Japan!"

In moments all of the personnel in the room were on their knees, bowing to Major General Kiyomizu.

CHAPTER 75

SOUTH CENTRAL, ALASKA PREFECTURE

FROM THE QUIET, RURAL AREAS AROUND ANCHORAGE, AND UP INTO THE Matanuska and Susitna Valleys, the various elements that comprised the Liberty Underground rushed into action. Tarps were pulled off war machines. Equipment emerged into daylight from beneath the ground, from under garage floors, and out of old mines and caves.

Military weapons and machines lovingly preserved and maintained since 1945 roared to life in the light of day and moved toward preordained collection points where heavily armed units formed in the open and commanders finalized plans. Many of the younger people bearing arms grinned and joked to push away fear of the unknown. The veterans all shared the grim intensity of finally seeing the day they were able to strike back.

The Japanese had flown light observer aircraft over these areas once, sometimes twice, a year, but did few or no ground patrol investigations. Their attitude was that the Americans had been defeated and accepted their subordinate place in history, which was exactly what the Americans wanted them to think. The Japanese understood the Americans about as much as the Americans understood the Japanese.

Infantry units comprising young men and women who had

received their training through Scout troops formed up under the watchful eyes of NCOs and officers who were veterans of the US Army and US Marine Corps. Drivers using smooth-running Jeeps deployed men and women around the perimeter of the Isoroku Yamamoto Aerodrome where they penetrated right up to the sparsely patrolled fence.

Imperial Army firefighting equipment had been rushed from Tojo Army Base a few miles away and, combined with the equipment from the air base, were busily fighting fires ignited by crashing jets. The Underground Liberation scouts could not detect patrols, guards, or security of any kind.

Gunnery Sergeant Keith Busch touched one of the privates on his shoulder and bent close to his ear. The private listened, nodded, and slipped away through the brush back to the Jeep. Busch pulled out his binoculars, made sure the sun wouldn't reflect off the lenses, and glassed the area.

The airfield hummed with activity. In addition to the two burning aircraft at the end of the base, another crash site sent up a smoke column on the far side of the runway in front of a three-story building. The saboteurs had done their job perfectly. Not one aircraft in sight moved.

✪

As Gunnery Sergeant Busch watched, a truck roaring across the field toward the fires suddenly shuddered to a stop. The Japanese driver jumped out, popped the hood, and stared inside. The gunnery sergeant grinned and checked his map.

He identified the headquarters building and realized one of the jets had nearly taken it out.

"I guess that would have been too easy for us," he muttered. He located the armory and carefully glassed the area around it but detected no additional security from what was usually present.

Private Ambrose edged up beside him.

"Gunny," the private whispered, "the artillery and armored elements are in place. Lieutenant Wright said we should pull back for our own safety."

"Who has our radio?"

"Corporal Bannister, Gunny."

"Send him forward. The rest of you report back to Lieutenant

Wright. Tell the lieutenant that Bannister and I will correct any inaccurate fire or notify him of unforeseen activity. We'll keep our heads down while we're at it."

"Aye, aye, Gunny. Good luck."

Ambrose was gone before Busch could thank her. He and the other vets had trained these young folks well. Knowing that this day would come, they had all shared their combat experiences, no matter how many of the bad dreams took on new dimension or increased in occurrence.

Their stories displaced any notions of glory the young people may have entertained. Add that to the fact that they grew up in a world where the Empire of Japan ruled them, and could kill them on a whim, gave them all the determination needed to see this through. Busch didn't envy the Japs what they were about to receive.

Bannister slid up next to him and slapped him on the shoulder. *Let's do it!*

He glanced at Bannister and nodded. Bannister clicked his send key twice. Thunder sounded in the distance and shells whistled in from three directions.

The administration building absorbed four of them and exploded into flinders. Four rounds hit the armory and it erupted like a volcano, throwing fire in all directions. A larger secondary explosion blew a crater where the armory once sat.

The firefighters stared at the destruction in stunned perplexity. Busch watched them through the glasses as they gestured and pointed in all directions. When they heard the second volley, all flattened on the ground.

The whole spread hit the three barracks housing the enlisted men. After the explosions ceased the buildings were engulfed in flame, as was the administration building. The armory was gone; it had ceased to exist.

Busch sensed movement all around him as the machine-gun squads took position and fed ammo belts in the guns. Lieutenant Wright scooted up next to him.

"Did you really think the artillery would miss?"

"Of course not, Ja—uh, Lieutenant Wright," Busch said through a grin. "I just didn't want to miss any of it."

"Wish I'd thought of that. Give 'em the high sign, Gunnery

Sergeant Busch."

Busch blew two short blasts on his whistle.

Squads along the entire fence line poured .30-caliber machine-gun fire into the firefighters and anyone else that moved. He blew his whistle again, three times before all the fire stopped. The entire air base blazed including the firefighting equipment, which had been set off from bullets igniting fuel tanks.

He leaned over to Corporal Bannister. "Bud, tell them to move in!"

"Yes, Gunny." He pressed down the send key and said, "Armor up!"

Busch shouted, "Watch your ass, our tanks are coming! Pass it on, now!"

The Shermans slowly clanked up to the fence and pushed it over it like it was made of paper. The nine tanks were spread out enough that most of the fence went down and the infantry poured in right behind them. No sirens or other alerts shrilled through the bright afternoon.

Smoke rolled across the runway and Gunnery Sergeant Busch hoped the attack on Fort Tojo had gone as smoothly.

CHAPTER 76

REICH CHANCERY,
NEW YORK CITY

REICHSFÜHRER WILHELM RAPKE WALKED INTO THE OPERATIONS ROOM as quickly as his arthritic hips could move. The room buzzed with activity. All four of the radio talkers carried on conversations as they transcribed their notes on keyboards that fed into the main logic machine.

Situation maps covered every wall. Officers and NCOs stood in small groups talking and marking up each of them. A row of female clerks typed messages and orders, putting them in a variety of baskets depending on their next destination. Male and female clerks scurried back and forth ferrying papers.

Two lieutenant generals discussed the lines on a map of Alaska when Rapke walked up behind them.

"Have you made sense of this chaos yet, gentlemen?"

Both men snapped to attention before he could stop them.

"No time for that. Tell me." He waved at the map.

"Our Anchorage office has been destroyed by partisans," General Major Lanz said. "We have heard nothing from either of our agents and assume they have both been killed. Our Japanese traffic intercepts verify that Tokyo has been annihilated and the Empire is now a headless, thrashing body."

"The same might be said of the Third Reich," Rapke said dryly.

"With Berlin and the Führer gone, it is our opinion that you are now the head of the Greater German Reich, mein Führer," Lieutenant General Blücher said, snapping to attention and clicking the heels on his perfectly shined jackboots.

"As Reichsführer of the Greater German Reich of North America, I *do* seem to be senior, and in command," he said in a genial tone. "However, I keep expecting to hear from one of our far-flung posts that someone more senior than myself survived."

Major General Lanz cleared his throat. "We took it upon ourselves to ascertain that very question, mein Führer. Having contacted all of the Armee Oberkommandos where anyone senior would have reasonably been in residence, we found no rank higher than major general."

Blücher, still at attention, said, "God has ordained that you are the most powerful man in the world. Heil Rapke!" He gave him a perfect, classic Nazi salute.

"Very well," Rapke said. "Please continue with your situation report."

"Both of the bases near Fairbanks have not only been overrun by partisans, but they are also flooded," Lanz said.

"Flooded? With water?" Raapke asked.

"Yes, mein Führer. The interior portions of the Alaska Territory have had record rains, actually four more days than the biblical forty days and forty nights. There is permafrost, as we found in Scandinavia, which does not allow the water to sink into the ground. At the present time there is a huge lake, the size of the American State of New Jersey, in the middle of Alaska."

"Incredible!" Rapke said in a whisper. "And this is when the partisans chose to attack?"

"We believe it had more to do with the launch of the Japanese *moon* rocket than anything else. It seems there was another atomic weapon that was shipped to Akihito Aerodrome to be dropped on us here in New York. The partisans hijacked the train and the whereabouts of the weapon is unknown."

"The partisans have the atomic bomb?" Rapke gasped.

"Unfortunately, yes."

"What about Anchorage? Didn't the Japs have a huge military presence there?"

"Indeed," Blücher said. "The partisan forces there overran the

Yamamoto Air Base with the aid of saboteurs. Fort Tojo is under attack as we speak and the outcome is unclear. Our only sources of information are from radio intercepts of Japanese traffic. That traffic has noticeably lessened over the past few hours."

"What about the rest of the Japanese territory in the American west?"

"Allow me to preface my reports with the fact that the Japanese made the fatal assumption that once they conquered a nation, the subject nation would willing accept its place under their heel. They made no attempt, as we have here, to assimilate the conquered into their empire."

"Noted," Rapke said with a hint of asperity.

"Sorry, mein Führer," Blücher said quickly. "The Americans were able to hide a number of warships in the Puget Sound area as well as in the southeastern portion of the Alaska Territory."

"*Warships?* What kind of warships?"

"Our reconnaissance aircraft have identified three destroyer escorts, a Fletcher class destroyer, and numerous torpedo patrol boats."

"The Japanese Navy is doing nothing about this situation?"

"Even before the war deep hostility existed between the Japanese Army and the Japanese Navy. Since the Pacific War was fought over, and on, the ocean, the Japanese Navy lost all their aircraft and nearly every capital fighting ship before the capitulation of the United States. The Japanese had no way of truly knowing how many American warships actually existed."

"There were no records?"

"No, mein Führer. The Pacific Fleet Headquarters at Pearl Harbor was destroyed by fire prior to the capitulation. All records were destroyed. The Americans scuttled their aircraft carriers, battleships, cruisers, destroyers, well, their entire fleet. They made movies of the ships going down and gave them to the Japanese when they arrived."

"They faked some of the movies?" Rapke said in a puzzled tone.

"Our intelligence people think they just hid what ships they could. The Japanese Navy was in no condition to search for vessels along the coast of North America with a fleet they no longer possessed. It is our opinion that the Japs merely accepted what the Americans told them."

"The fools! They deserved to lose their empire! What is the situation in our portion of North America?"

"We have apprehended a large number of Liberation Underground personnel over the years. Our Hitler Youth have turned in their parents and relatives who were suspect. The accuracy rate is quite high." Blücher preened as if he had done it all by himself.

"However," Lanz said, frowning at Blücher, "...we still suffered some unexpected sabotage. The bomber base near Omaha lost its fuel depot last night to a suspicious explosion. Suspects and hostages have been shot."

"Were they interrogated first?"

"No, mein Führer, they were killed resisting our troops. We lost forty-five men quelling the insurgency."

"Anywhere else?"

"Yes, Führer, Lenz said. "The bases at, ah," he pulled a sheet of paper from his pocket, and glanced at it, "...yes, Minot, Olathe, Chicago, Pensacola–"

"Stop!" Rapke snapped. "The Liberty Underground is attacking us all over the map?"

"Yes, Führer," Lenz said. "Some of our bases have been overrun."

"Where are our armored units?"

"The ones that still possess mobility..."

"Why do some *not* have mobility?"

"Sabotage." Lenz seemed to quiver with indignation. "The dammed Americans have infiltrated nearly all of our bases to destroy petrol lines, storage tanks, and even delivery vehicles. Our base in Ontario was destroyed by arsonists."

"This is much worse than I was led to believe," Rapke said. "I am not Adolph Hitler or Hermann Göring, you do not have to hide hard facts behind gauzy curtains of bullshit! What is our real situation?"

"Grim," Lenz said. "Not as grim as what the Japs have on their plate, but dire enough."

"In what portion of North America are we *not* threatened?"

"In the large cities, Führer. We have fortified all cities with populations of 200,000 or more. Everywhere else we have a revolt on our hands."

Rapke went silent for a long moment and then looked at Blücher. "How would you handle this situation if you were in charge,

General?"

"Immediately heighten security around our bases, especially armor and Luftwaffe. *Closely* question every American working on any of our installations. Harden the perimeter of the cities and push out with combat forces into the countryside until they link up with troops from other power points."

"You are advocating fighting a war with a defeated country, General?"

"Yes, Führer. But this time we must truly win it, no matter how many Americans have to die."

"The Waffen-US troops might find it difficult to fight their own people, General." Raapke thought he might have found his first *Generalfeldmarschall.*

"That's why we back them up with Waffen SS troops."

Reichsführer Rapke thought this an auspicious moment. If the Americans wanted another war, they would have it! "I couldn't agree more. As my *Generalfeldmarschall,* you are in command."

Stoney Compton

(Leonard Wayne Compton)

Stoney Compton lives north of Farmington, New Mexico with his wife, Colette, one dog, and an ever-changing number of cats. He is a Navy veteran, and a past Writers of the Future Contest winner. He still holds Alaska and Alaskans near and dear.

www.ingramcontent.com/pod-product-compliance
Lightning Source LLC
Chambersburg PA
CBHW021038310726
48969CB00006B/1710